MARY HIGGINS CLARK

SIMON & SCHUSTER

The Lottery Winner

ALVIRAH AND WILLY STORIES

NEW YORK • LONDON • TORONTO • SYDNEY • TOKYO • SINGAPORE

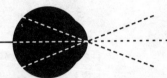

This Large Print Book carries the
Seal of Approval of N.A.V.H.

SIMON & SCHUSTER
ROCKEFELLER CENTER
1230 AVENUE OF THE AMERICAS
NEW YORK, NY 10020

DESIGNED BY EVE METZ
MANUFACTURED IN THE UNITED STATES OF AMERICA

1 3 5 7 9 10 8 6 4 2

LIBRARY OF CONGRESS CATALOGING-IN-PUBLICATION DATA
IS AVAILABLE.
ISBN 0-684-80222-8

"Death on the Cape" appeared in *Woman's Day*, July 18, 1989.
"Body in the Closet" appeared in *Woman's Day*, August 7, 1990.
"Plumbing for Willy" appeared in *Family Circle*, August 1992.
"A Clean Sweep" appeared in *Justice in Manhattan* published by
Longmeadow Press (Bill Adler Books). Copyright © October 1994 by
Mary Higgins Clark.

ACKNOWLEDGMENTS

ALVIRAH MEEHAN made her debut—if you can call it that—as a character in my novel *Weep No More, My Lady*. A cleaning woman in her late fifties, she and her plumber husband, Willy, had won forty million dollars in the New York State Lottery. Alvirah immediately decided to satisfy her long held dream of going to the Cypress Point Spa and mingling with the celebrities who frequented it.

Unfortunately for Alvirah, she was too smart, got on the track of a killer and became a victim herself. In the early drafts of *Weep No More, My Lady*, poor Alvirah did not survive to the last page.

Then my daughter Carol Higgins Clark read the manuscript and protested, "You can't do that. Alvirah is much too funny. Besides, haven't you knocked off enough people in this book?"

"She has to die," I said firmly.

But Carol was so persuasive that I brought Alvirah back from death's door.

I'm certainly glad I did. I count her and Willy as dear friends. They are my only continuing characters, and now I hope you enjoy reading about their adventures as much as I enjoy writing about them.

Thanks, Carol.

FOR MY SIBLINGS-IN-LAW AND FRIENDS,

JUNE M. CLARK AND IN MEMORY OF ALLAN CLARK
KEN AND IRENE CLARK
AGNES PARTEL AND IN MEMORY OF GEORGE PARTEL

DEAR COMPANIONS OF MY SALAD DAYS,
AREN'T WE ALL STILL TWENTY-TWO?

Contents

The Body in the Closet

If Alvirah had known on that July evening what was waiting for her at her fancy new apartment on Central Park South, she would never have gotten off the plane. As it was, there was absolutely no hint of foreboding in her usually keen psyche as the plane circled for a landing.

Even though she and Willy had been bitten by the travel bug after they won forty million dollars in the lottery, and had by now taken a number of exciting trips, Alvirah was always glad to get back to New York. There was something heartwarming about the view from the airplane: the skyscrapers silhouetted against the clouds, the lights of the bridges that spanned the East River.

Willy patted her hand, and Alvirah turned to him with an affectionate smile. He looked grand, she thought, in his new blue linen jacket that matched the color of his eyes. With those eyes and his thick head of white hair, Willy was a double for Tip O'Neill, no mistake about it.

Alvirah smoothed her russet-brown hair, recently tinted and styled by Dale of London. Dale had marveled to hear that Alvirah was pushing sixty. "You're funning me," he had gasped. She knew such compliments were probably hollow, but she liked to hear them anyway.

Yes, Alvirah reflected as she watched the city below, life had been grand to her and Willy. In addition to allowing them to travel at will and to buy all the creature comforts one could desire, their newfound wealth had also opened new doors of opportunity in unexpected ways, such as her involvement with one of the city's major newspapers, the *New York Globe.* It all began when a *Globe* editor talked to her and Willy after they won the lottery. Alvirah had told him that she was re-alizing her longtime ambition to be a guest at the elegant Cypress Point Spa, and it wasn't just the makeover she was looking forward to—it was also the chance to be min-gling with all the celebrities she loved to read about.

The newspaper editor, obviously spotting in Alvirah some special talent for sniffing out news, plus the perseverance to pursue it to the end, persuaded her to take on an assign-ment for him. He asked her to keep her eyes open and her ears alert, with the idea in mind of writing an article about her experiences at the exclusive spa. And to further aid her in the process of gathering news and impres-sions, he gave her a lapel pin in the shape of a sunburst that actually contained a tiny recording device. That way she could record her impressions while they were fresh, and she might even pick up a few bits of conver-sation from those very people she was so anxious to meet.

The results had proved even more dra-matic than either she or the editor had hoped, for at the spa she recorded someone who was in the act of trying to kill her, an attack brought on by her sleuthing into a murder that had occurred there. With the help of her detection—and the handy recording device—Alvirah had not only helped to solve a crime but had embarked on a whole new and unexpected career as occasional columnist and amateur sleuth.

Now, as she sat buckled into her seat, thinking back over her most recent trip, she fingered the sunburst pin—a more-or-less permanent fixture on any outfit she wore—and reflected on how disappointed her editor was going to be. "This trip was wonderful," she said to Willy, "but there wasn't a single adventure I could write about. The most exciting thing during the whole trip was when the Queen stopped in for tea at the Stafford Hotel, and the manager's cat attacked her corgis."

"Well I for one am glad we had a nice, calm vacation," Willy said. "I can't take much more of you almost getting killed solving crimes."

The British Airways flight attendant was walking down the aisle of the first-class cabin, checking that seat belts were fastened. ''I certainly enjoyed talking with you,'' she told them. Willy had explained to her, as he would to almost any willing ear, that he'd been a plumber and Alvirah a cleaning woman until they won the forty-million-dollar lottery two years ago. ''My goodness,'' the flight attendant said now to Alvirah, ''I just can't *believe* you were ever a char.''

In a mercifully short time after landing they were in the waiting limousine, their matching Vuitton luggage stacked in the trunk. As usual, New York in August was hot, sticky and sultry. The air-conditioning in the limo had just gone on the fritz, and Alvirah thought longingly ahead to their new apartment on Central Park South, which would be wonderfully cool. They still kept their old three-room flat in Flushing where they'd lived for forty years before the lottery changed their lives. As Willy pointed out, you never knew if someday New York would go broke and tell the lottery winners to take a flying leap for the rest of their winnings.

When the limo pulled up to the apartment building, the doorman opened the door for them. ''You must be melting,'' Alvirah said.

"You'd think they wouldn't bother dressing you up until they finished the renovations."

The building was undergoing a total overhaul. When they had bought the apartment in the spring, the real estate agent had assured them that the refurbishing would be completed in a matter of weeks. It was clear from the scaffolding still in the lobby that he had been wildly optimistic.

At the bank of elevators they were joined by another couple, a tall, fiftyish man and a slender woman wearing a white silk evening suit and an expression that reminded Alvirah of someone who has opened a refrigerator and encountered the odor of eggs gone bad. I know them, Alvirah thought and began ruffling through her prodigious memory. He was Carlton Rumson, the legendary Broadway producer, and she was his wife, Victoria, a sometime actress who had been a Miss America runner-up some thirty years ago.

"Mr. Rumson!" With a warm smile, Alvirah reached out her hand. "I'm Alvirah Meehan. We met at the Cypress Point Spa in Pebble Beach. What a nice surprise! This is my husband, Willy. Do you live here?"

Rumson's smile came and went. "We keep an apartment here for convenience." He nodded to Willy, then grudgingly introduced his wife. The elevator door opened as Victoria Rumson acknowledged them with the flicker of an eyelid. What a cold fish, Alvirah thought, taking in the perfect but haughty profile, the pale-blond hair pulled back in a chignon. Long years of reading *People*, *US*, the *National Enquirer* and gossip columns had resulted in Alvirah's brain becoming the repository of an awesome amount of information about the rich and famous.

They had just stopped at the thirty-fourth floor as Alvirah remembered her Rumson tidbits. He was famous for his wandering eye, while his wife's ability to overlook his indiscretions had earned her the nickname "See-No-Evil Vicky." Obviously a perfect match, Alvirah thought.

"Mr. Rumson," Alvirah said, "Willy's nephew, Brian McCormack, is a wonderful playwright. He's just finished his second play. I'd love to have you read it."

Rumson looked annoyed. "My office is listed in the phone book," he said.

"Brian's first play is running off Broadway right now," Alvirah persisted. "One of the critics said he's a young Neil Simon."

"Come on, honey," Willy urged. "You're holding up these folks."

Unexpectedly the glacier look melted from

Victoria Rumson's face. "Darling," she said, "I've heard about Brian McCormack. Why don't you read the play here? It will only get buried in your office. Mrs. Meehan, send it by our apartment."

"That's real nice of you, Victoria," Alvirah said heartily. "You'll have it tomorrow."

As they walked from the elevator to their apartment, Willy asked, "Honey, don't you think you were being a little pushy?"

"Absolutely not," Alvirah said. "Nothing ventured, nothing gained. Anything I can do to help Brian's career is A-OK with me."

Their apartment commanded a sweeping view of Central Park. Alvirah never stepped into it without thinking that not so long ago she had considered her Thursday cleaning job, Mrs. Chester Lollop's house in Little Neck, a miniature palace. Boy, had her eyes been opened these last few years!

They'd bought the apartment completely furnished from a stockbroker who'd been indicted for insider trading. He had just had it done by an interior designer who, he assured them, was the absolute rage of Manhattan. Secretly Alvirah now had serious doubts about just what kind of rage he'd been talk-ing about. The living room, dining room and kitchen were stark white. There were low white sofas that she had to hoist herself out of, thick white carpeting that showed every speck of dirt, white counters and cabinets and marble and appliances that reminded her of all the tubs and sinks and toilets she'd ever tried to scrub free of rust.

And tonight there was something new, a large printed sign taped to the door leading to the terrace. Alivrah crossed to the door to read it.

A building inspection has revealed that this is one of a small number of apartments in which a serious structural weakness has been found in the guardrailing and the pan-els of the terrace. Your terrace is safe for normal use, but do not lean on the guardrail or permit others to do so. Repairs will be completed as rapidly as possible.

After reading the notice silently, she read it aloud to Willy, then shrugged. "Well, I cer-tainly have brains enough not to lean on any guardrail, safe or not."

Willy smiled sheepishly. He was scared

silly of heights and never set foot on the terrace. As he'd said when they bought the apartment, "You love a terrace, I love terra firma."

Willy went into the kitchen to put the kettle on. Alvirah opened the terrace door and stepped outside. The sultry air was a hot wave against her face, but she didn't care. There was something she loved about standing out here, looking across the park at the festive glow from the decorated trees around the Tavern on the Green, the ribbons of headlights of the cars and the glimpses of horse-drawn carriages in the distance.

Oh, it's good to be back! she thought again as she went inside and surveyed the living room, her expert eye observing the degree of efficiency of the weekly cleaning service that should have been in yesterday. She was surprised to see fingerprints smeared across the glass cocktail table. Automatically she reached for a handkerchief and vigorously rubbed them away. Then she noticed that the tieback on the drapery next to the terrace door was missing. Hope it didn't end up in the vacuum, she thought. At least I was a good cleaning woman. Then she remembered what the British Airways attendant had said—or a good char, whatever that is.

"Hey, Alvirah," Willy called. "Did Brian leave a note? Looks like he may have been expecting someone."

Brian, Willy's nephew, was the only child of his oldest sister, Madaline. Six of Willy's seven sisters had gone into the convent. Madaline had married in her forties and produced a change-of-life baby, Brian, who was now twenty-six years old. He had been raised in Nebraska, written plays for a repertory company out there and came to New York after Madaline's death two years ago. All of Alvirah's untapped maternal instincts were released by Brian, with his thin, intense face, unruly sandy hair and shy smile. As she often told Willy, "If I'd carried him inside me for nine months, I couldn't love him more."

When they'd left for England in June, Brian was finishing the first draft of his new play and had been glad to accept their offer of a key to the Central Park South apartment. "It's a heck of a lot easier to write there than in my place," was his grateful comment. He lived in a walk-up in the East Village, surrounded by large noisy families.

Alvirah went into the kitchen. She raised her eyebrows. A bottle of champagne, standing in a wine cooler which was now half full of water, and two champagne glasses were on a silver tray. The champagne was a gift from the broker who'd handled the apartment sale. The broker had several times informed them that that particular champagne cost a hundred dollars a bottle and was the brand the Queen of England herself enjoyed sipping.

Willy looked troubled. "That's the stuff that's so crazy expensive, isn't it? No way Brian would help himself to that without asking. There's something funny going on." Alvirah opened her mouth to reassure him, then closed it. Willy was right. There *was* something funny going on, and her antenna told her trouble was brewing.

The chimes rang. An apologetic porter was at the door with their bags. "Sorry to be so long, Mr. Meehan. Since the remodeling began, so many residents are using the service elevator that the staff has to stand in line for it." At Willy's request, he deposited the bags in the bedroom, then departed smiling, his palm closing over a five-dollar bill.

Willy and Alvirah shared a pot of tea in the kitchen. Willy kept staring at the champagne bottle. "I'm gonna call Brian," he said.

"He'll still be at the theater," Alvirah said, closed her eyes, concentrated and gave him the telephone number of the box office.

Willy dialed, listened, then hung up. "There's a recorder on," he said flatly. "Brian's play closed. They talk about how to get refunds."

"The poor kid," Alvirah said. "Try his apartment."

"Only the answering machine," he told her a moment later. "I'll leave a message for him."

Alvirah suddenly realized how weary she was. As she collected teacups she reminded herself that it was 5:00 A.M., English time, so she had a right to feel as though all her bones were aching. She put the teacups in the dishwasher, hesitated, then rinsed out the unused champagne glasses and put them in the dishwasher too. Her friend Baroness Min von Schreiber—who owned the Cypress Point Spa where Alvirah had gone to be made over after she won the lottery—had told her that expensive wines should never be left standing. With a damp sponge, she gave a vigorous rub to the unopened bottle, the silver tray and bucket and put them away. Turning the lights out behind her, she went into the bedroom.

Willy had begun to unpack. Alvirah liked the bedroom. It had been furnished for the bachelor stockbroker with a king-sized bed, a triple dresser, comfortable easy chairs, and night tables large enough to hold at the same time a stack of books, reading glasses and mineral ice for Alvirah's rheumatic knees. The decor, however, convinced her that the trendy interior designer must have been weaned on bleach. White spread. White drapes. White carpet.

The porter had left Alvirah's garment bag laid out across the bed. She unlocked it and began to remove the suits and dresses. Baroness von Schreiber was always pleading with her not to go shopping on her own. "Alvirah," Min would argue, "you are natural prey for saleswomen who have been ordered to unload the buyers' mistakes. They sense your approach even while you're still in the elevator. I'm in New York enough. You come to the spa several times a year. Wait till we're together; I will shop with you."

Alvirah wondered if Min would approve of the orange-and-pink plaid suit that the saleswoman in Harrods had raved over. Looking at it now, she was sure Min wouldn't.

Her arms filled with clothing, she opened the door of the closet, glanced down and let out a shriek. Lying on the carpeted floor between rows of Alvirah's size-10 extra-wide designer shoes, with green eyes staring up, crinkly blond hair flowing around her face, tongue slightly protruding and the missing drapery tieback around her neck, was the body of a slender young woman.

"Blessed Mother," Alvirah moaned as the clothes fell from her arms.

"What's the matter, honey?" Willy demanded, rushing to her side. "Oh my God," he breathed. "Who the hell is that?"

"It's . . . it's . . . you know. The actress. The one who had the lead in Brian's play. The one Brian is so crazy about." Alvirah squeezed her eyes shut, glad to free herself from the glazed expression on the face of the body at her feet. "Fiona Winters."

Willy's arm firmly around her, Alvirah walked to one of the low couches in the living room that made her knees feel as though they were going to meet her chin. As he dialed 911, she forced her head to clear. It doesn't take a lot of brains to know that this could look very bad for Brian, she told herself. I've got to get my thinking cap on and remember everything I can about that girl. She was so nasty to Brian. Had they had a fight?

Willy crossed the room, sat beside her and

reached for her hand. "It's going to be all right, honey," he said. "The police will be here in a few minutes."

"Call Brian again," Alvirah told him.

"Good idea." Willy dialed quickly. "Still that darn machine. I'll leave another message. Try to rest."

Alvirah nodded, closed her eyes and immediately turned her thoughts to the night last April when Brian's play had opened.

The theater had been crowded. Brian had arranged for them to have front-row-center seats, and Alvirah wore her new silver-and-black sequin dress. The play, *Falling Bridges*, was set in Nebraska and was about a family reunion. Fiona Winters played the socialite who is bored with her unsophisticated in-laws, and Alvirah had to admit she was very believable, though she liked the girl who played the second lead much better—Emmy Laker had bright-red hair, blue eyes and portrayed a funny but wistful character to perfection.

The performances brought a standing ovation, and Alvirah's heart swelled with pride when the cries of "Author! Author!" brought Brian to the stage. When he was handed a bouquet and leaned over the footlights to give it to Alvirah, she started to cry.

The opening-night party was in the upstairs room of Gallagher's Steak House.
Brian kept the seats on either side of him for
Alvirah and Fiona Winters. Willy and Emmy
Laker sat opposite. It didn't take Alvirah long
to get the lay of the land. Brian hovered over
Fiona Winters like a lovesick calf, but she
kept putting him down and letting them
know about her high-class background, saying things like, ''The family was appalled
when after Foxcroft I decided to go into the
theater.'' She then proceeded to tell Willy
and Brian, who were thoroughly enjoying
sliced-steak sandwiches with Gallagher's
special fries, that they were likely candidates
for heart attacks. Personally, she never ate
meat, she said.

She took potshots at all of us, Alvirah re-
called. She asked me if I missed cleaning
houses. She told me Brian should learn how
to dress, and with our income she was surprised we didn't help him out. And she had
really jumped on that sweet Emmy Laker
when Emmy said Brian had better things to
think about than his wardrobe.

On the way home Alvirah and Willy had sol-
emnly agreed that though Brian might show

a lot of maturity as a playwright, he had a lot of growing up to do if he didn't see what a shrew Fiona was. "I'd like to see him together with Emmy Laker," Willy had announced. "If he had the brains he was born with he'd know that she's crazy about him. And that Fiona has been around a lot. She must have eight years on Brian."

Alvirah was drawn back to the reality of the moment by the vigorous ringing of the front doorbell. Mother-in-heaven, she thought, that must be the police. I wish I'd had a chance to talk to Brian.

The next hours passed in a blur. As her head cleared a bit, Alvirah was able to separate the different kinds of law enforcement people who invaded the apartment. The first were the policemen in uniform. They were followed by detectives, photographers, the medical examiner. She and Willy sat together silently observing them all.

Officials from the Central Park South Towers office came too. "We hope there will be no unfortunate publicity," the resident manager said. "This is not the Trump Organization."

Their original statements had been taken by the first two cops. At 3:00 A.M., the door from the bedroom opened. "Don't look, honey," Willy said. But Alvirah could not keep her eyes away from the stretcher that two somber-faced attendants wheeled out. At least the body of Fiona Winters was covered. God rest her, Alvirah prayed, picturing again the tousled blond hair and the pouty lips. She was not a nice person, Alvirah thought, but she certainly didn't deserve to be murdered.

Someone sat down opposite them, a long-legged fortyish man who introduced himself as Detective Rooney. "I've read your articles in the Globe, Mrs. Meehan," he told Alvirah, "and thoroughly enjoyed them."

Willy smiled appreciatively, but Alvirah wasn't fooled. She knew Detective Rooney was buttering her up to make her confide in him. Her mind was racing, trying to figure out ways to protect Brian. Automatically she reached up and switched on the recorder in her sunburst pin. She wanted to be able to go over everything that was said later.

Detective Rooney consulted his notes. "According to your earlier statement, you've just returned from a vacation abroad and arrived here around 10:00 P.M.? You found the victim, Fiona Winters, a short time later? You recognized Miss Winters because she played the lead in your nephew Brian McCormack's play?"

Alvirah nodded. She noticed that Willy was about to speak and laid a warning hand on his arm. "That's right."

"From what I understand, you only met Miss Winters once," Detective Rooney said. "How do you suppose she ended up in your closet?"

"I have no idea," Alvirah said.

"Who had a key to this apartment?"

Again Willy's lips pursed. This time Alvirah pinched his arm. "Keys to this apartment," she said thoughtfully. "Now let me see. The One-Two-Three Cleaning service has a key. Well, they don't really *have* a key. They pick one up at the desk and leave it there when they finish. My friend Maude has a key. She came in Mother's Day weekend to go out with her son and his wife to Radio City. They have a cat and she's allergic to cats so she slept on our couch. Then Willy's sister, Sister Cordelia, has a key. Then—"

"Does your nephew, Brian McCormack, have a key, Mrs. Meehan?" Detective Rooney interrupted.

Alvirah bit her lip. "Yes, and Brian has a key."

This time Detective Rooney raised his voice slightly. "According to the concierge, Brian's been using this apartment frequently in your absence. Incidentally, although it's impossible to be totally accurate before an autopsy, the medical examiner estimates the time of death to be between 11:00 A.M. and 3:00 P.M. yesterday." Detective Rooney's tone became speculative. "It will be interest- ing to know where Brian was during that time frame."

They were told that before they could use the apartment, the investigating team would have to dust it for fingerprints and vacuum it for clues. "The apartment is as you found it?" Detective Rooney asked.

"Except—" Willy began.

"Except that we made a pot of tea," Alvirah interrupted. I can always tell them about the glasses and the champagne, but I can't until them, she thought. That detective is going to find out that Brian was crazy about Fiona Winters and decide it was a crime of passion. Then he'll make everything fit that theory.

Detective Rooney closed his notebook. "I understand the management has a furnished apartment you can use tonight," he said.

Fifteen minutes later, Alvirah was in bed, gratefully hunched against an already dozing Willy. Tired as she was, it was hard to relax in a strange bed, plus her mind was reviewing all that had transpired tonight. She knew that all this could look very bad for Brian. But she also knew there had to be an explanation. Brian wouldn't help himself to that hundred-dollar bottle of champagne, and he *certainly* wouldn't kill Fiona Winters. But how did she end up in the closet?

Despite the late bedtime, Alvirah and Willy were up the next morning at 7:00 A.M. As their mutual shock over finding the body in the closet wore off, they began to worry. "No use fretting about Brian," Alvirah said with a heartiness she did not feel. "When we talk to him, I'm sure everything will be cleared up. Let's see if we can get back into our place."

They dressed quickly and hurried out. Once again Carlton Rumson was standing at the elevator. His pink complexion was sallow. Dark pouches under his eyes added ten years to his appearance. Automatically, Alvirah reached up and switched on the microphone in her pin.

36

"Mr. Rumson," she asked, "did you hear the terrible news about the murder in our apartment?"

Rumson pressed vigorously for the elevator. "As a matter of fact, yes. Friends in the building phoned us. Terrible for the young lady, terrible for you."

The elevator arrived. After they got in, Rumson said, "Mrs. Meehan, my wife reminded me about your nephew's play. We're leaving for Mexico tomorrow morning. I'd very much like to read it today if I may."

Alvirah's jaw dropped. "Oh, that's wonderful of your wife to keep after you about it. We'll make sure to get it up to you."

When she and Willy got out at their floor, she said, "This could be Brian's big break. Provided that—" she said, stopping in mid-sentence.

A policeman was on guard at the door of their apartment. Inside, every surface was smeared because the investigators had dusted for fingerprints. And seated across from Detective Rooney, looking bewildered and forlorn, was Brian. He jumped up. "Aunt Alvirah, I'm sorry. This is awful for you."

To Alvirah he looked about ten years old. His T-shirt and khaki slacks were rumpled;

had he dressed to escape a burning building he could not have looked more disheveled.

Alvirah brushed back the sandy hair that fell over Brian's forehead as Willy grasped his hand. "You OK?" Willy asked.

Brian managed a troubled smile. "I guess so."

Detective Rooney interrupted. "Brian just arrived, and I was about to inform him that he is a suspect in the death of Fiona Winters and has a right to counsel."

"Are you kidding?" Brian asked, his tone incredulous.

"I assure you, I'm not kidding." Detective Rooney pulled a paper from his breast pocket. He read Brian his Miranda rights, then handed the paper to Brian. "Please let me know if you understand its meaning."

Rooney looked at Alvirah and Willy. "Our people are through. You can stay in the apartment now. I'll take Brian's statement at headquarters."

"Brian, don't you say one word until we get you a lawyer," Willy ordered.

Brian shook his head. "Uncle Willy, I have nothing to hide. I don't need a lawyer."

Alvirah kissed Brian. "Come right back here when you're finished," she told him.

The messy condition of the apartment gave her something to do. She dispatched Willy with a long shopping list, warning him to take the service elevator to avoid reporters.

As she vacuumed and scrubbed and mopped and dusted, Alvirah realized with increasing dread that cops don't give a Miranda warning unless they have a pretty good reason for suspecting someone's guilt. The most difficult part of her task was to vacuum the closet. It was as though she could see again the wide-open eyes of Fiona Winters staring up at her. That thought led her to another one: Obviously the poor girl hadn't been killed while she was standing in the closet, but where had she been when she was strangled?

Alvirah dropped the handle of the vacuum. She thought about those fingerprints on the cocktail table. If Fiona Winters had been sitting on the couch, maybe leaning forward a little, and her killer walked behind it, slipped the tieback around her neck and twisted it, wouldn't her hand have pulled back like that? "Saints and angels," Alvirah whispered, "I bet I destroyed evidence."

The phone rang just as she was fastening

the sunburst pin to her lapel. It was Baroness Min von Schreiber calling from the Cypress Point Spa in Pebble Beach, California. Min had just heard the news. "Whatever was that dreadful girl thinking about getting herself killed in your closet?" Min demanded.

"Buh-lieve me, Min," Alvirah said. "I don't know what she was doing here. I only met her once, the opening night of Brian's play. The cops are questioning Brian right now. I'm worried sick. They think he killed her."

"You're wrong, Alvirah," Min said. "You met Fiona Winters before then; you met her out here at the spa."

"Never," Alvirah said positively. "She was the kind who got on your nerves so much you'd never forget her."

There was a pause. "I am thinking," Min announced. "You're right. She came here another week, with someone, and they spent the weekend in the cottage. They even had their meals served there. I remember now. It was that hotshot producer she was trying to snare. Carlton Rumson. You remember him, Alvirah. You met him another time when he was here alone."

• • •

Alvirah went into the living room and out onto the terrace. Willy gets so nervous if I even step out here, she thought, and that's crazy. The only thing to be careful about is leaning on the railing.

The humidity was near saturation point. Not a leaf in the park stirred. Even so, Alivirah sighed with pleasure. How can anyone who was born in New York stay away from it for long? she wondered.

Willy brought in the newspapers with the groceries. One headline screeched MURDER ON CENTRAL PARK SOUTH; another, LOTTERY WINNER FINDS BODY. Alvirah carefully read the lurid accounts. "I didn't scream and faint," she scoffed. "Where'd they get that idea?"

"According to the *Post*, you were hanging up the fabulous new wardrobe you bought in London," Willy told her.

"Fabulous new wardrobe! The only expensive thing I bought was that orange-and-pink plaid suit—and I know Min is going to make me give it away."

There were columns of background material on Fiona Winters: The break with her socialite family when she went into acting. Her uneven career. (She'd won a Tony but was notoriously difficult to work with, which had cost her a number of plum roles.) Her break with playwright Brian McCormack when she accepted a film role and abruptly walked out of his play *Falling Bridges,* forcing it to close.

"Motive," Alvirah said flatly. "By tomorrow they'll be trying this case in the media, and Brian will be found guilty."

At 12:30 P.M. Brian returned. Alvirah took one look at his ashen face and ordered him to sit down. "I'll make a pot of tea and fix you a hamburger," she said. "You look like you're going to keel over."

"I think a shot of scotch would do a lot more good than tea," Willy observed.

Brian managed a wan smile. "I think you're right, Uncle Willy." Over the hamburgers and french fries he told them what had happened. "I swear I didn't think they'd let me go. You can tell they're sure I killed her."

"Is it OK if I turn on my recorder?" Alvirah asked. She fiddled with the sunburst pin, touching the microphone switch. "Now, tell us exactly what you told them."

Brian frowned. "Mostly about my personal relationship with Fiona. I was sick of her lousy disposition and I was falling in love with Emmy. I told them that when Fiona quit the play it was the last straw.''

''But how did she get in my closet?'' Alvirah asked. ''You must have been the one who let her into the apartment.''

''I did. I've been working here a lot. I knew you were coming back yesterday, so I cleared my stuff out the day before. Then yesterday morning Fiona phoned and said she was back in New York and would be right over to see me. By mistake I'd left my notes for the final draft of my new play here with my backup copy. I told her not to waste her time, that I was heading here to get my notes and then was going to be at the typewriter all day and wouldn't answer my door. When I arrived, I found her parked downstairs in the lobby, and rather than make a scene I let her come up.''

''What did she want?'' Alvirah and Willy both asked.

''Nothing much. Just the lead in *Nebraska Nights*.''

''After walking out on the other one!''

''She put on the performance of her life. Begged me to forgive her. Said she'd been a fool to leave *Falling Bridges*. Her role in the film was ending up on the cutting-room floor, and the bad publicity about dumping the play had hurt her. Wanted to know if *Nebraska Nights* was finished yet. I'm human. I bragged about it. Told her it might take time to find the right producer, but when I did it was going to be a big hit."

"Had she ever read it?" Alvirah asked.

Brian studied the tea leaves in his cup. "These don't make for much of a fortune," he commented. "She knew the story line and that there's a fantastic lead role for an actress."

"You certainly didn't promise it to her?" Alvirah exclaimed.

Brian shook his head. "Aunt Alvirah, I know she played me for a fool, but I couldn't believe she thought I was that much of a fool. She asked me to make a deal. She said she had access to one of the biggest producers on Broadway. If she could get it to him and he took it, she wanted to play Diane—I mean Beth."

"Who's that?" Willy asked.

"The name of the leading character. I changed it on the final draft last night. I told Fiona she had to be kidding, but if she could pull that off I might consider it. Then I got my notes and tried to get her out of here. She refused to budge, though, saying she had an audition at Lincoln Center early in the afternoon, and since it's close by, she wanted to stay here until it was time to be there. I finally decided there probably wasn't any harm in leaving her so I could get work done. The last time I saw her was just about noon, and she was sitting on that couch."

"Did she know you had a copy of the new play here?" Alvirah asked.

"Sure. I took it out of the drawer of the table when I was getting the notes." He pointed toward the foyer. "It's in that drawer now."

Alvirah got up, walked quickly to the foyer and pulled open the drawer. As she suspected, it was empty.

Emmy Laker sat motionless in the oversized club chair in her West Side studio apartment. Ever since she had heard about Fiona's death on the seven o'clock news she'd been trying to reach Brian. Had he been arrested? Oh God, not Brian, she thought. What should I do? Despairingly she looked at the luggage in the corner of the room. Fiona's luggage.

Her bell had rung yesterday morning at

8:30. When she opened the door, Fiona had swept in. "How can you stand living in a walk-up?" she'd demanded. "Thank God some kid was making a delivery and carried these up." She'd dropped her suitcases and reached for a cigarette. "I came in on the red-eye. What a mistake to take that film job. I told the director off and he fired me. I've been trying to reach Brian. Do you know where he is?"

At the memory, rage swelled in Emmy. As though she were still across the room she could see Fiona, her blond hair tousled, her body-hugging jumpsuit showing off every inch of that perfect figure, her cat's eyes insolent and confident.

Fiona was so sure that even after the way she treated Brian she could still walk back into his life, Emmy thought, remembering all the months when she had agonized at the sight of Brian with her. Would that have happened again? Yesterday she had thought it possible.

Fiona had kept phoning Brian until she finally reached him. When she hung up, she said, "Mind if I leave my bags here? Brian's on his way to the cleaning woman's fancy pad. I'll head him off." Then she shrugged.

"He's so damn provincial, but it's amazing how many people on the West Coast know about him. I must say from what I heard about *Nebraska Nights* it has all the earmarks of a hit—and I intend to play the lead."

Emmy got up. Her body felt stiff and achy. The old window-unit air conditioner was rattling and wheezing, but the room was still hot and humid. A cool shower and a cup of coffee, she decided. Maybe that would clear her head. She wanted to see Brian. She wanted to put her arms around him. I'm not sorry Fiona's dead, she admitted, but oh, Brian, how did you expect to get away with it?

She had just dressed in a T-shirt and cotton skirt and twisted her long bright-red hair in a chignon when the buzzer downstairs rang.

When she answered, it was to hear Detective Rooney announce that he was on the way up.

"This is starting to make sense," Alvirah said. "Brian, is there anything you left out? For instance, did you put the bottle of that fit-for-a-queen champagne in the silver bucket yesterday?"

Brian looked bewildered. "Why would I do that?"

"I didn't think you would." Oh boy, what a story, Alvirah thought—Fiona didn't hang around here because she had an audition. It's my bet that the producer she mentioned to Brian was Carlton Rumson, and that she phoned him and invited him down here. That's why the glasses and champagne were out. She gave him the script and then, who knows why, they got into a fight. But how do I prove it? Alvirah paused for a moment, thinking. Then she turned to Brian. "I want you to go home and get your final version of the play. I talked to Carlton Rumson about it; he wants to see it today."

"Carlton Rumson!" Brian exclaimed. "He's just about the biggest man on Broadway, as well as one of the hardest to reach. You must be a magician!"

"I'll tell you about it later," Alvirah said. "I also happen to know that he and his wife are going away on a little trip, so let's strike while the iron is hot."

Brian glanced at the phone. "I should call Emmy. She certainly must have heard about

Fiona by now." He dialed the number, waited, then left a message: "Emmy, I need to talk to you. I'm just leaving Aunt Alvirah's and I'm on my way home." When he hung up, his tone reflected his obvious disappointment. "I guess she's out," he said.

Even when she heard Brian's voice, Emmy made no move to pick up the receiver. Detective Rooney was sitting across from her and had just asked her to describe in detail what she had done the previous day. Now he raised his eyebrows. "You could have answered the phone. I don't mind waiting."

"I'll talk to Brian later," Emmy said. Then she paused for a moment, choosing her words carefully. "Yesterday I left here about 11:00 A.M. and went jogging. I got back about 1:30 P.M. and then just stayed in the rest of the day."

"Alone?"

"Yes."

"Did you see Fiona Winters yesterday?" Emmy's eyes slid over to the corner where the luggage was piled. "I . . ." She stopped.

"Emmy, I think I should warn you that it will be in your best interest to be completely truthful." Detective Rooney consulted his notes. "Fiona Winters came in on a flight from Los Angeles, arriving at approximately 7:30 A.M. We know she took a cab to this building, and that a delivery boy who recognized her assisted her with her luggage. She told him that you would not be glad to see her because you're after her boyfriend. When Miss Winters left, you followed her. A doorman on Central Park South recognized you. You sat on a park bench across the street, watching the building, for nearly two hours, then entered it by the delivery door, which had been propped open by the painters." Detective Rooney leaned forward. His tone became confidential. "You went up to the Meehans' apartment, didn't you? Was Miss Winters already dead?"

Emmy stared at her hands. Brian always teased her about how small they were. "But strong," he'd laugh when they'd arm-wrestle. Brian. No matter what she said she would hurt him. She looked up at Detective Rooney. "I want to talk to a lawyer."

Rooney got up. "That is, of course, your privilege. I would like to remind you that if Brian murdered his ex-lover, you can become an accessory after the fact by concealing evidence. And I assure you, Emmy, you won't do him any good. We're going to get an indictment from the grand jury, no doubt about it."

When Brian reached his apartment, there was a message on the recorder from Emmy. "Call me, Brian. Please." Brian's fingers worked with frantic haste as he dialed her number.

She whispered, "Hello."

"Emmy, what's the matter? I tried you before but you were out."

"I was here. A detective came. Brian, I have to see you."

"Take a cab to my aunt's place. I'm on my way back there."

"I want to talk to you alone. It's about Fiona. She was here yesterday. I followed her over to the apartment."

Brian felt his mouth go dry. "Don't say anything else on the phone."

At 4:00 P.M., the bell rang insistently. Alvirah jumped up. "Brian forgot his key," she told Willy. "I noticed it on the foyer table."

But it was Carlton Rumson rather than Brian she found standing at the door. "Mrs. Meehan, please forgive the intrusion." With that he stepped inside.

"I mentioned to one of my assistants that I was going to look at your nephew's play. Apparently he saw a performance of his first one and thought it was very good. In fact he had urged me to see it, but it closed suddenly and I never got the chance." Rumson had walked into the living room and sat down. Nervously he drummed his fingers on the cocktail table.

"Can I get you a drink?" Willy asked. "Or maybe a beer?"

"Oh, Willy," Alvirah said. "I'm sure that Mr. Rumson only drinks fine champagne. Maybe I read that in *People.*"

"As a matter of fact, it's true, but not right now, thank you." Rumson's expression was affable enough, but Alvirah noticed that a pulse was jumping in his throat. "Where can I reach your nephew?"

"He should be here any minute. You're welcome to wait, or I'll call you the minute he gets in."

Obviously opting for the latter choice, Rumson stood and headed for the door. "I'm a fast reader. If you would send the script up, he and I could get together an hour or so later."

When Rumson left, Alvirah asked Willy, "What are you thinking?"

"That for a hotshot producer, he's some nervous wreck. I hate people tapping their fingers on tabletops. Gives me the jitters."

"Well he certainly had the jitters, and I'm not surprised." Alvirah smiled at Willy mysteriously.

Less than a minute later the bell rang again. Alvirah hurried to the door. Emmy Laker was there, wisps of red hair slipping from the chignon, sunglasses covering half her face, the T-shirt clinging to her slender body, the cotton skirt a colorful whirl. Alvirah thought that Emmy looked about sixteen.

"That man who just left," Emmy stammered. "Who was he?"

"Carlton Rumson, the producer," Alvirah said quickly. "Why?"

"Because . . ." Emmy pulled off her glasses, revealing swollen eyes.

Alvirah put firm hands on the girl's shoulders. "Emmy, what is it?"

"I don't know what to do," Emmy wailed. "I don't know what to do."

• • •

Carlton Rumson returned to his apartment. Beads of perspiration stood on his forehead. Alvirah Meehan was no dope, he warned himself. That crack about champagne hadn't been social chitchat. How much did she suspect?

Victoria was standing on the terrace, her hands lightly touching the railing. Reluctantly he joined her. "For Pete's sake, haven't you read those signs all over the place?" he demanded. "One good shove and that railing would be gone."

Victoria was wearing white slacks and a white knit sweater. Sourly, Rumson thought it was a damn shame some fashion columnist had once written that with her pale-blond beauty, Victoria Rumson should never wear anything but white. Victoria had taken that advice to heart. Her dry cleaning bills alone would have broken most men.

She turned to him calmly. "I've noticed that you always get ugly with me when you're upset. Did you happen to know that Fiona Winters was staying in this building? Or was she here perhaps at your request?"

"Vic, I haven't seen Fiona in nearly two years. If you don't believe me, too bad."

54

"As long as you didn't see her yesterday, darling. I understand the police are asking lots of questions. It's bound to come out that you and she were—as the columnists say—an *item*." She paused. "Oh well, I'm sure you'll deal with it with your usual aplomb. In the meantime, have you followed up on Brian McCormack's play? I have one of my famous hunches about that, you know."

Rumson cleared his throat. "That Alvirah Meehan is going to have McCormack send me a copy this afternoon. After I've read it I'll go down and meet him."

"Let me read it too. Then I might just tag along. I'd love to see how a cleaning woman decorates." Victoria Rumson linked her arm in her husband's. "Poor darling. Why are you so nervous?"

When Brian rushed past Alvirah into the apartment, his play under his arm, he found Emmy lying on his aunt's couch, covered by a light blanket. Alvirah closed the door behind him and watched as he knelt beside Emmy and put his arms around her. "I'm going inside and let you two talk," she announced.

Willy was in the bedroom laying out

clothes. "Which jacket, honey?" He held up two sports coats.

Alvirah's forehead puckered. "You want to look nice for Pete's retirement party, but not like you're trying to show off. Wear the blue jacket and the white sports shirt."

"I still don't like to leave you tonight," Willy protested.

"You can't miss Pete's dinner," Alvirah said firmly. "And Willy, I wish you'd let me order a car and driver for you."

"Honey, we pay big bucks to garage our car here. No use wasting money."

"Well then, if you have too good a time, I want you to promise me not to drive home. Stay at the old apartment. You know how you can get when you're with the boys."

Willy smiled sheepishly. "You mean if I sing 'Danny Boy' more than twice, that's my signal."

"Exactly," Alvirah said firmly.

"Honey, I'm so bushed after the trip and with what happened last night, I'd just as soon have a few beers with Pete and come back."

"That wouldn't be nice. Pete stayed at our lottery-winning party till the morning rush started on the expressway. Now we've got to talk to those kids."

In the living room Brian and Emmy were sitting side by side, their hands clasped. "Have you two straightened things out yet?" Alvirah demanded.

"Not exactly," Brian said. "Apparently Emmy was given a rough time by Rooney when she refused to answer his questions."

Alvirah sat down. "I have to know everything he asked you."

Hesitantly Emmy told her. Her voice became calmer and her poise returned as she said, "Brian, you're going to be indicted. He's trying to make me say things that will hurt you."

"You mean you're protecting me." Brian looked astonished. "There's no need. I haven't done anything. I thought . . ."

"You thought that Emmy was in trouble," Alvirah told them. She settled with Willy on the couch opposite them. She realized that Brian and Emmy were sitting directly in front of the place on the cocktail table where the fingerprints had been smeared. The drapery was slightly to the right. To someone sitting on this couch, the tieback would have been in full view. "I'm going to tell you two something," she announced. "You each think the other might have had something to do with

57

this—and you're both wrong. Just tell me what you know or think you know. Brian, is there anything you've held back about seeing Fiona yesterday?"

"Absolutely nothing," Brian said.

"All right. Emmy, your turn."

Emmy walked over to the window. "I love this view." She turned to Alvirah and Willy and told them about Fiona's sudden and unwelcome appearance at her apartment. "Yesterday when Fiona left my apartment to meet Brian I think I went a little crazy. He had been so involved with her, and I just couldn't stand to see that happen all over. Fiona is—was the kind of woman who can just beckon to men. I was so afraid Brian would take up with her again."

"I'd never—" Brian protested.

"Keep quiet, Brian," Alvirah ordered.

"I sat on the park bench a long time," Emmy said. "I saw Brian leave. When Fiona didn't come down I started to think maybe Brian had told her to wait. Finally I decided to have it out with her. I followed a maid through the delivery entrance and came up in the service elevator because I didn't want anyone to know I'd been here. I rang the doorbell and waited and rang it again, and then I left."

"That's all?" Brian asked. "Why were you afraid to tell that to Rooney?"

"Because when she heard Fiona was dead she thought maybe the reason she didn't answer was because you'd already killed her." Alvirah leaned forward. "Emmy, why did you ask about Carlton Rumson before? You saw him yesterday, didn't you?"

"As I came down the corridor from the rear service elevator, he was ahead of me, going to the passenger elevator. I knew he looked familiar but didn't recognize him until I saw him again just now."

Alvirah stood up. "I think we should call Mr. Rumson and ask him to come down, and I think we should call Rooney and ask him to be here too. But first, Brian, give Willy your play. He'll run it up to the Rumsons' apartment. Let's see. It's nearly 5:00 P.M. Willy, you ask Mr. Rumson to phone when he's ready to bring it back."

The intercom buzzer sounded. Willy answered it. "Rooney's here," he said. "He's looking for you, Brian."

There was no trace of warmth in the detective's manner when he entered the apartment a few minutes later. "Brian," he said without preface, "I have to ask you to come down to the station house for further questioning. You have received the Miranda warning. I remind you again that anything you say can be used against you."

"He's not going anywhere," Alvirah said firmly. "And before you leave, Detective, I've got an earful for you."

It was nearly 7:00 P.M., two hours later, when Carlton Rumson phoned. Alvirah and Willy had told Rooney about the champagne and the glasses and the fingerprints on the cocktail table and about Emmy seeing Carlton Rumson, but Alvirah could tell none of it cut much ice with the detective. He's closing his mind to everything that doesn't fit his theory about Brian, she thought.

A few minutes later, Alvirah was astonished to see both Rumsons enter her apartment. Victoria Rumson was smiling warmly. When introduced to Brian, she took both his hands and said, "You really *are* a young Neil Simon. I just read your play. Congratulations."

When Detective Rooney was introduced, Carlton Rumson's face went ashen. He stammered as he said to Brian, "I'm terribly sorry to interrupt you just now. I'll make this very brief. Your play is wonderful. I want to option it. Please have your agent contact my office tomorrow."

Victoria Rumson was standing at the terrace door. "You were so wise not to obscure this view," she told Alvirah. "My decorator put in vertical blinds, and I might as well be facing an alley."

She sure took her gracious pills this morning, Alvirah thought.

"I think we'd all better sit down," Detective Rooney suggested.

The Rumsons sat down reluctantly.

"Mr. Rumson, you knew Fiona Winters?" Rooney asked.

Alvirah began to think she had underestimated Rooney. His expression became intense as he leaned forward.

"Miss Winters appeared in several of my productions some years ago," Rumson said. He was sitting on one of the couches, next to his wife. Alvirah noticed that he glanced at her nervously.

"I'm not interested in years ago," Rooney told him. "I'm interested in yesterday. Did you see her then?"

"I did not." To Alvirah, Rumson's voice sounded strained and defensive.

"Did she phone you from this apartment?" Alvirah asked.

"Mrs. Meehan, if you don't mind, I'll conduct this questioning," the detective said.

"Show respect when you talk to my wife," Willy bristled.

Victoria Rumson patted her husband's arm. "Darling, I think you might be trying to spare my feelings. If that impossible Winters woman was badgering you again, please don't be afraid to tell exactly what she wanted."

Rumson seemed to age visibly before their eyes. When he spoke his voice was weary. "As I just told you, Fiona Winters acted in several of my productions. She—"

"She also had a private relationship with you," Alvirah interjected. "You used to take her to the Cypress Point Spa."

Rumson glared at her. "I haven't had anything to do with Fiona Winters for several years," he said. "Yes, she phoned yesterday just after noon. She told me she was here in the building and that she had a play she wanted me to read, assured me it had the earmarks of a hit and said she wanted to play the lead. I was waiting for a call from Europe and agreed to come down and see her in about an hour."

"That means she called after Brian left," Alvirah said triumphantly. "That's why the glasses and champagne were out. They were for you."

"Did you come to this apartment, Mr. Rumson?" Rooney asked.

Again Rumson hesitated.

"Darling, it's all right," Victoria Rumson said softly.

Not daring to look at Detective Rooney, Alvirah announced: "Emmy saw you in this corridor a few minutes after 1:00 P.M."

Rumson sprang to his feet. "Mrs. Meehan, I won't tolerate any more insinuations! I was afraid Fiona would keep contacting me if I didn't set her straight once and for all. I came down here and rang the bell. There was no answer. The door wasn't completely shut, so I pushed it open and called her. As long as I'd come this far I wanted to be finished with it."

"Did you enter the apartment?" Rooney asked.

"Yes. I walked through this room, poked my head in the kitchen and glanced in the bedroom. She wasn't anywhere. I assumed she'd changed her mind about seeing me, and I can assure you I was relieved. Then when I heard the news this morning all I could think of was that maybe her body was in that closet when I was here and I'd be in the middle of this." He turned to his wife. "I guess I am in the middle of it, but I swear what I've told you is true."

Victoria touched his hand. "There is no way they're going to drag you into this. What a nerve that woman had to think she should have the leading role in *Nebraska Nights*." Victoria turned to Emmy. "Someone your age should play the role of Diane."

"She's going to," Brian said. "I just hadn't told her yet."

Rumson turned to his wife, impatiently. "Don't you mean—?"

Rooney interrupted him as he folded his notebook. "Mr. Rumson, I'll ask you to accompany me down to headquarters. Emmy, I'd like you to give a complete statement as well. Brian, we need to talk to you again, and I do strongly urge you to engage counsel."

"Now just one minute," Alvirah said indignantly. "I can tell you believe Mr. Rumson over Brian." There goes the option on the play, but this is more important, she thought. "You're going to say that Brian maybe started to leave, decided to come back and tell Fiona to clear out and then ended up killing her. I'll tell you how I think it happened. Rumson came down here and got into a fight with Fiona. He strangled her but was smart enough to take the script she was showing him."

"That is absolutely untrue," Rumson snapped.

"I don't want another word discussed here," Rooney ordered. "Emmy, Mr. Rumson, Brian—I have a car downstairs. Let's go."

When the door closed behind them, Willy put his arms around Alvirah. "Honey, I'm going to skip Pete's party. I can't leave you. You look ready to collapse."

Alvirah hugged him back. "No, you're not. I've been recording everything. I need to listen to the playback and I do that better alone. You have a good time."

The apartment felt terribly quiet after Willy left. Alvirah decided that a warm soak in the bathtub Jacuzzi might take some of the stiffness out of her body and clear her brain.

Afterward, she dressed comfortably in her favorite nightgown and Willy's striped terrycloth robe. She set the expensive cassette player her editor at the *Globe* had bought for her on the dining-room table, then took the tiny cassette out of her sunburst pin, inserted it in the recorder and pushed the playback button. She put a new cassette in the back of the pin and fastened the pin to the robe just in case she wanted to think out loud. She sat listening to her conversations with Brian, with Detective Rooney, with Emmy, with the Rumsons.

What was it about Carlton Rumson that bothered her so much? Methodically, Alvirah reviewed that first meeting with the Rumsons. He was pretty cool that night, but when we bumped into him the next morning he sure had changed his tune, she told herself, even reminded me he wanted to read the new play right away. She remembered Brian saying that nobody could get to Carlton Rumson.

That's it, she thought. He *already* knew how good the play was. He couldn't admit that he'd already read it.

The phone rang. Startled, Alvirah hurried over to pick it up. It was Emmy. "Mrs. Meehan," she whispered, "they're still questioning Brian and Mr. Rumson, but I know they think Brian's guilty."

"I just figured everything out," Alvirah said triumphantly. "How good a look at Carlton Rumson did you get when you saw him in the hall?"

"Pretty good."

"Then you could see he was carrying the script, couldn't you? I mean if he was telling the truth that he only went down to tell Fiona off, he'd never have picked up that script. But if they talked about it and he read some of it before he killed her, he'd have taken it. Emmy, I think I've solved the case."

Emmy's voice was barely audible. "Mrs. Meehan, I'm sure Carlton Rumson wasn't carrying anything when I saw him. Suppose Detective Rooney thinks to ask me that question? It's going to hurt Brian, isn't it, if I tell them that?"

"You have to tell the truth," Alvirah said sadly. "Don't worry. I still have my thinking cap on." When she hung up, she turned the cassette player on again and began to replay her tapes. She replayed her conversations with Brian several times. There was something he had told her that she was missing.

Finally she stood up, deciding that a breath of fresh air wouldn't hurt. Not that New York air is fresh, she thought as she opened the terrace door and stepped out. This time she went right to the guardrail and let her fingers rest lightly on it. If Willy were here he'd have a fit, she thought, but I'm not going to lean on it. There's just something so restful about looking out over the park. The park. I think one of the happiest memories in Mama's life was the day she had a sleigh ride through the park. She was sixteen at the time and she talked about it the rest of her life. She'd taken the ride because her girlfriend Beth asked for that for her birthday.

Beth!

Beth!

That's it! Alvirah thought. Again she could hear Brian saying that Fiona Winters wanted to play the part of Diane. Then Brian corrected himself and said, "I mean Beth." Willy had asked who that was, and Brian said it was the name of the lead in his new play, that he'd changed it in the final draft. Alvirah switched on her microphone and cleared her throat. Better get this all down, she reminded herself. It would help to have her immediate impression when she wrote the story up for the *Globe.*

"It wasn't Carlton Rumson who killed Fiona Winters," she said aloud, her voice confident. "It has to have been his wife, See-No-Evil Vicky. *She* was the one who kept after Rumson to read the play. *She* was the one who said Emmy should play Diane—she didn't know Brian had changed the name. And Rumson started to correct her, because he had read only the revised version of the play. She must have listened in when Fiona phoned him. She came here while he was waiting for his call from Europe. She didn't want Fiona to get involved with Rumson again, so she killed her, then took the script. That was the copy she read, not the final draft."

"How very clever of you, Mrs. Meehan."

The voice came from directly behind her, but before she could even blink, Alvirah felt strong hands push at the small of her back. She tried to turn as she felt her body press against the guardrail and panel. How did Victoria Rumson get in here? she wondered. Then, in a flash, she remembered that Brian's key had been on the foyer table. Victoria must have taken it.

With all her strength she tried to throw herself against her attacker, but a blow on the side of her neck stunned her. She was able to spin around so that she was facing the other woman, but the blow had been an effective one, and she sagged against the railing. Only vaguely was she aware then of a creaking, tearing sound and the feeling of her body teetering over yawning space.

Pete's retirement party was a blast. The room at the K of C in Flushing was filled with Willy's old buddies. The aromas of sausage and peppers and corned beef and cabbage mingled together enticingly. The first keg of beer had been tapped, and a beaming Pete was going from friend to friend, insisting they drink up.

But Willy could not get in the spirit of the evening. Something was bugging him, gnawing at him, telling him he should be heading home. He sipped his beer, nibbled half-heartedly at a corned-beef sandwich, congratulated Pete on his retirement, and then, without waiting for even one chorus of "Danny Boy," he slipped away and got in his car.

When he reached the apartment, the door was slightly ajar; immediately his internal panic button began to shrill a warning. "Alvirah," he called nervously. Then he saw two figures poised at the terrace railing. "Oh my God!" he moaned, then raced across the room, shouting Alvirah's name.

"Come in, honey," he pleaded. "Get back. Get away from there." Then he suddenly realized what was happening. The other woman was trying to push Alvirah through the guardrail. He took one step out onto the terrace just as a section of the railing separated and fell away behind Alvirah.

Willy took a second step toward the struggling women and then passed out.

Emmy sat in the precinct station, waiting for her statement to be typed up, heartsick with worry about Brian. She knew that Detective Rooney believed Carlton Rumson's story that he'd gone into Alvirah's apartment, thought it was empty and had left. It was obvious that Rooney had made up his mind that Brian had killed Fiona.

Why can't he see that Brian had no reason to kill her? Emmy agonized. Brian had told her that Fiona had done him a favor when she walked out on the play. That it showed him just what kind of person she was. Oh, I shouldn't have been so upset when Fiona showed up at my apartment yesterday, she thought. Brian never would have gotten involved with Fiona again, Emmy was sure of that. But when she'd tried to convince Detective Rooney of it, he'd asked, "Then if you were so sure that Brian was finished with Fiona, why did you follow her over to his aunt's apartment?"

Emmy rubbed her forehead. She had such a headache! It was impossible to believe that only a few nights ago Brian had let her read the new play and asked her advice about changing the name of the lead from Diane to Beth.

"Diane is a pretty strong name," he'd said. "I see the character as someone who comes across as vulnerable, even wistful; then as the action unfolds, we get to know just how strong she is. What do you think of calling her Beth instead of Diane?"

"I like it," she'd replied.

"That's good," Brian had said, "because you were the model for her, and I want you to be happy with the name. I'll make the change in the final draft."

Emmy sat up straight and stared ahead, no longer aware of the harsh lights in the precinct room, or even of the bustle of activity and confusion around her. *Beth . . . Diane . . .*

That's it! she thought suddenly. Tonight Victoria Rumson told me I should play the part of Diane. But the final script, the one she's supposed to have read, has the name change in it. So she must have read the copy of the play that is missing from the apartment. That means she was there with Fiona. Of course, it all fits! Perhaps Victoria Rumson's ability to overlook her husband's indiscretions had been strained to the breaking point when she had almost lost him a couple of years ago—to Fiona Winters!

Emmy jumped up and ran from the station house. She had to talk to Alvirah right away. She heard a policeman call after her but didn't answer him as she hailed a cab.

When she reached the building, she charged past a stuttering doorman and raced to the elevator. She heard Willy shouting as she came down the corridor. The door to the apartment was open. She saw Willy stumble onto the terrace and fall. Then she saw the silhouettes of two women and realized what was happening.

In a burst of speed, Emmy rushed out to the terrace. Alvirah was facing her, swaying over empty space. Her right hand was grasping the part of the railing that was still in place, but she was quickly losing her grip because Victoria Rumson was pummeling that hand with her fists.

Emmy grabbed Victoria's arms and twisted them behind her. Victoria's howl of rage and pain rose above the crash as the rest of the railing collapsed and fell. Emmy shoved her aside and managed to grasp the cord of Alvirah's robe. Alvirah was teetering. Her bedroom slippers were sliding backward off the terrace. Her body swayed as she hovered thirty-four stories over the sidewalk below. With a burst of strength, Emmy pulled her forward and they fell together over the collapsed form of the unconscious Willy.

Alvirah and Willy slept until noon. When they finally woke up, Willy insisted Alvirah stay put. He went out to the kitchen, returning fifteen minutes later with a pitcher of orange juice, a pot of tea and a piece of toast. After her second cup of tea, Alvirah regained her customary optimism. "Boy, was it good that Detective Rooney came barging in here after Emmy and caught Victoria trying to escape. And do you know what I think, Willy?"

"I never know what you think, honey," Willy said with a sigh.

"Well, I bet you one thing—that Carlton Rumson will still want to produce Brian's play. You can be sure he won't be shedding any tears over seeing Victoria going to prison."

"You're probably right," Willy conceded. "Those two certainly weren't a pair of love-birds."

"And Willy," Alvirah concluded, "I want you to have a talk with Brian, to tell him he'd better marry that darling Emmy before somebody else snaps her up." She beamed. "I have the perfect wedding present for them, a load of white furniture."

Death
on the
Cape

*I*t was on an August afternoon shortly after they arrived at their rented cottage in the village of Dennis on Cape Cod that Alvirah Meehan noticed that there was something very odd about their next-door neighbor, a painfully thin young woman who appeared to be in her late twenties.

After Alvirah and Willy looked around their cottage a bit, remarking favorably about the four-poster maple bed, the hooked rugs, the cheery kitchen and the fresh, sea-scented breeze, they unpacked their expensive new clothes from their matching Vuitton luggage. Willy then poured an ice-cold beer for each to enjoy on the deck of the house, which overlooked Cape Cod Bay.

Willy, his rotund body eased onto a padded wicker chaise lounge, remarked that it was going to be one heck of a sunset, and thank God for a little peace. Ever since they had won forty million dollars in the New York State lottery, it seemed to Willy, Alvirah had been a walking lightning rod. First she went to the famous Cypress Point Spa in California and nearly got murdered. Then they had gone on a cruise together and—wouldn't you know—the man who sat next to them at the community table in the dining room ended up dead as a mackerel. Still, with the accumulated wisdom of his years, Willy was sure that in Cape Cod, at least, they'd have the quiet he'd been searching for. If Alvirah wrote an article for the *New York Globe* about this vacation, it would have to do with the weather and the fishing.

During his narration, Alvirah was sitting at the picnic table, a companionable few feet away from Willy's stretched-out form. She wished she'd remembered to put on a sun hat. The beautician at Sassoon's had warned her against getting sun on her hair. "It's such a lovely rust shade now, Mrs. Meehan. We don't want it to get those nasty yellow streaks, do we?"

Since recovering from the attempt on her life at the spa, Alvirah had regained all the weight she'd paid three thousand dollars to lose and was again a comfortable size somewhere between a 14 and a 16. But Willy constantly observed that when he put his arms around her, he knew he was holding a woman—not one of those half-starved zombies you see in the fashion ads Alvirah was so fond of studying.

Forty years of affectionately listening to Willy's observations had left Alvirah with the ability to hear him with one ear and close him out with the other. Now as she gazed at the tranquil cottages perched atop the grass-and-sand embankment that served as a seawall, then down below at the sparkling blue-green water and the stretch of rock-strewn beach, she had the troubled feeling that maybe Willy was right. Beautiful as the Cape was, and even though it was a place she had always longed to visit, she might not find a newsworthy story here for her editor, Charley Evans.

Two years ago Charley had sent a *New York Globe* reporter to interview the Meehans on how it felt to win forty million dollars. What would they do with it? Alvirah was a cleaning woman. Willy was a plumber. Would they continue in their jobs?

Alvirah had told the reporter in no uncertain terms that she wasn't that dumb, that the next time she picked up a broom it would be when she was dressed as a witch for a Knights of Columbus costume party. Then she had made a list of all the things she wanted to do, and first was the visit to the Cypress Point Spa—where she planned to hobnob with the celebrities she'd been reading about all her life.

That had led Charley Evans to ask her to write an article for the *Globe* about her stay at the spa. He gave her a sunburst pin that contained a microphone so that she could record her impressions of the people she spoke with and play the tape back when she wrote the article.

The thought of her pin brought an unconscious smile to Alvirah's face.

As Willy said, she'd gotten into hot water at Cypress Point. She'd picked up on what was really going on and was nearly murdered for her trouble. But it had been so exciting, and now she was great friends with everyone at the spa and could go there every year as a guest. And thanks to her help solving the murder on the ship last year, they had an invitation to take a free cruise to Alaska anytime they desired.

Cape Cod was beautiful, but Alvirah had a sneaking suspicion Willy might be right, that this might be an ordinary vacation that wouldn't make good copy for the *Globe*.

Precisely at that moment she glanced over the row of hedges on the right perimeter of their property and observed a young woman with a somber expression standing at the railing of her porch next door and staring at the bay.

It was the way her hands were gripping the railing: Tension, Alvirah thought. She's stuffed with it. It was the way the young woman turned her head, looked straight into Alvirah's eyes, then turned away again. She didn't even see me, Alvirah decided. The fifty- to sixty-foot distance between them did not prevent her from realizing that waves of pain and despair were radiating from the young woman.

Clearly it was time to see if she could help. "I think I'll just introduce myself to our neighbor," she said to Willy. "There's something up with her." She walked down the steps and strolled over to the hedge. "Hello," she said in her friendliest voice. "I saw you drive in. We've been here for two hours, so I guess that makes us the welcoming committee. I'm Alvirah Meehan."

The young woman turned, and Alvirah felt instant compassion. She looked as though she had been ill. That ghostly pallor, the soft, unused muscles of her arms and legs. "I don't mean to be rude, but I came here to be alone, not to be neighborly," she said quietly. "Excuse me, please." That probably would have been the end of it, as Alvirah later observed, except that as she spun on her heel the girl tripped over a footstool and fell heavily onto the porch. Alvirah rushed to help her up, refused to allow her to go into her cottage unaided and, feeling responsible for the accident, wrapped an ice pack around her rapidly swelling wrist. By the time she had satisfied herself that the wrist was only sprained and made her a cup of tea, Alvirah had learned that her name was Cynthia Rogers and that she was a schoolteacher from Illinois. That piece of information hit with a resounding thud on Alvirah's ears because, as she told Willy when she returned to their place an hour later, within ten minutes she'd recognized their neighbor. "The poor girl may call herself Cynthia Rogers," Alvirah confided to Willy, "but her real name is Cynthia Lathem. She was found guilty of murdering her stepfather twelve years ago. He had big bucks and was well known. All the papers carried the story. I remember it like it was yesterday."

"You remember everything like it was yesterday," Willy commented.

"That's the truth. And you know I always read about murders. Anyhow, this one happened here on Cape Cod. Cynthia swore she was innocent, and she always said there was a witness who could prove she'd been out of the house at the time of the murder, but the jury didn't believe her story. I wonder why she came back. I'll have to call the *Globe* and have Charley Evans send me the files on the case. She's probably just been released from prison. Her complexion is pure gray. Maybe"—and now Alvirah's eyes became thoughtful—"she's up here because she really is innocent and is still looking for that missing witness to prove her story!"

To Willy's dismay, Alvirah opened the top drawer of the dresser, took out her sunburst pin with the hidden microphone and began to dial her editor's direct line in New York.

That night, Willy and Alvirah ate at the Red Pheasant Inn. Alvirah wore a beige-and-blue print dress she had bought at Bergdorf Goodman but which, as she remarked to Willy, somehow didn't look much different on her than the print dress she'd bought in Alexander's just before they won the lottery. "It's my full figure," she lamented as she spread butter on a warm cranberry muffin. "My, these muffins are good. And, Willy, I'm glad that you bought that yellow linen jacket. It shows up your blue eyes, and you still have a fine head of hair."

"I feel like a two-hundred-pound canary," Willy commented, "but as long as you like it."

After dinner they went to the Cape Playhouse and thrilled to the performance of Debbie Reynolds in a new comedy being tried out for Broadway. At intermission, as they sipped ginger ale on the grass outside the theater, Alvirah told Willy how she'd always enjoyed Debbie Reynolds from the time Debbie was a kid doing musicals with Mickey Rooney, and that it was a terrible thing Eddie Fisher ditched her when they had those two small babies. "And what good did it do him?" Alvirah philosophized as the warning came to return to their seats for the second act. "He never had much luck after that. People who don't do the right thing usually don't win in the end." That comment led Alvirah to wonder whether Charley had sent the information on their neighbor by Express Mail. She was anxious to read it.

As Alvirah and Willy were enjoying Debbie Reynolds, Cynthia Lathem was at last beginning to realize that she was really free, that twelve years of prison were behind her. Twelve years ago . . . she'd been about to start her junior year at the Rhode Island School of Design when her stepfather, Stuart Richards, was found shot to death in the study of his mansion, a stately eighteenth-century captain's house in Dennis.

That afternoon Cynthia had driven past the house on her way to the cottage and pulled off the road to study it. Who was there now? she wondered. Had her stepsister Lillian sold it or had she kept it? It had been in the Richards family for three generations, but Lillian had never been sentimental. And then Cynthia had pressed her foot on the accelerator, chilled at the rush of memories of that awful night and the days that followed. The accusation. The arrest, arraignment, trial. Her early confidence. "I can absolutely prove that I left the house at eight o'clock and didn't get home till past midnight. I was on a date."

Now Cynthia shivered and wrapped the light-blue woolen robe more tightly around her slender body. She'd weighed 125 pounds when she went to prison. Her present weight, 110, was not enough for her five-foot eight-inch height. Her hair, once a dark blond, had changed in those years to a medium-brown. Drab, she thought as she brushed it. Her eyes, the same shade of hazel as her mother's, were listless and vacant. At lunch that last day, Stuart Richards had said, "You look more like your mother all the time. I should have had the brains to hang on to her."

Her mother had been married to Stuart from the time Cynthia was eight until she was twelve, the longer of his two marriages. Lillian, his only birth child, ten years older than Cynthia, had lived with her mother in New York and seldom visited the Cape.

Cynthia laid the brush on the dresser. Had it been a crazy impulse to come here? Two weeks out of prison, barely enough money to live on for six months, not knowing what she could do or would do with her life. Should she have spent so much to rent this cottage, to rent a car? Was there any point to it? What did she hope to accomplish?

A needle in a haystack, she thought. Walking into the small parlor, she reflected that compared to Stuart's mansion, this house was tiny, but after years of confinement it seemed palatial. Outside, the sea breeze was blowing the bay into churning waves. Cynthia walked out on the porch, only vaguely aware of her throbbing wrist, hugging her arms against the chill. But, oh God, to breathe fresh, clean air, to know that if she wanted to get up at dawn and walk the beach the way she had as a child, no one could stop her. The moon, three-quarters full, looking as though a wedge had been neatly sliced from it, made the bay glisten, a silvery midnight blue. But where the moon did not reach it, the water appeared dark and impenetrable.

Cynthia stared unseeingly as her mind wrenched her back to the terrible night when Stuart was murdered. Then she shook her head. No, she would not allow herself to think about that now. Not tonight. This was a time to let the peace of this place fill her soul. She would go to bed, and she'd leave the windows wide open so that the cool night wind would pour into her room, making her pull the covers closer around her, deepening her sleep.

Tomorrow morning she would wake up early and walk on the beach. She'd feel the wet sand under her feet, and she'd look for shells, just as she had when she was a child. Tomorrow. Yes, she'd give herself the morning to help bridge her reentry into the world, to regain her sense of equilibrium. And then she would begin the quest, probably hopeless, for the one person who would know that she had told the truth.

The next morning, as Alvirah prepared breakfast, Willy drove to get the morning papers.

When he returned he was also carrying a bag of still-hot blueberry muffins. "I asked around," he told a delighted Alvirah. "Everyone said to go to the Mercantile behind the post office for the best muffins on the Cape."

They ate at the picnic table on the deck. As she nibbled on her second blueberry muffin, Alvirah studied the early-morning joggers on the beach. "Look, there she is!"

"There *who* is?"

"Cynthia Lathem. She's been gone at least an hour and a half. I bet she's starving."

When Cynthia ascended the steps from the beach to her deck, she was met by a beaming Alvirah, who linked her arm in Cynthia's. "I make the best coffee and fresh-squeezed orange juice. And wait till you taste the blueberry muffins."

"I really don't want—" Cynthia tried to pull back but was propelled across the lawn. Willy jumped up to pull out a bench for her.

"How's your wrist?" he asked. "Alvirah's been real upset that you sprained it when she went over to visit."

Cynthia realized that her mounting irritation was being overcome by the genuine warmth she saw on both their faces. Willy —with his rounded cheeks, strong pleasant

expression and thick mane of white hair—
reminded her of Tip O'Neill. She told him
that.

Willy beamed. "Fellow just remarked on
that in the bakery. Only difference is that
while Tip was *speaker* of the house, I was
savior of the *out*house. I'm a retired
plumber."

As Cynthia sipped the fresh orange juice
and the coffee and picked at the muffin, she
listened with disbelief, then awe, as Alvirah
told her about winning the lottery, going to
Cypress Point Spa and helping to track down
a murderer, then going on an Alaskan cruise
and figuring out who killed the man who sat
next to her at the community table.

She accepted a second cup of coffee.
"You've told me all this for a reason, haven't
you?" Cynthia said. "You recognized me
yesterday, didn't you?"

Alvirah's expression became serious.
"Yes."

Cynthia pushed back her bench. "You've
been very kind, and I think you want to help
me, but the best way you can do that is to
leave me alone. I have a lot of things to work
out, but I have to do them myself. Thank you
for breakfast."

Alvirah watched the slender young woman walk between the two cottages. "She got a little sun this morning," she observed. "Very becoming. When she fills out a little, she'll be a beautiful girl."

"You may as well plan on getting the sun too," Willy observed. "You heard her."

"Oh, forget it. Once Charley sends the files on her case I'll figure out a way to help her."

"Oh my God," Willy moaned. "I might have known. Here we go again."

"I don't know how Charley does it," Alvirah sighed approvingly an hour later. The overnight Express Mail envelope had just arrived. "It looks as though he sent every word anyone ever wrote about the case." She made a tsk-tsking sound. "Look at this picture of Cynthia at the trial. She was just a scared kid."

Methodically, Alvirah began sorting the clippings on the table; then she got out her lined pad and pen and began to make notes.

Willy was reclining on the padded chaise he had claimed for his own, deeply immersed in the sports section of the *Cape Cod Times*. "I'm just about ready to give up on the Mets getting the pennant," he commented sadly, shaking his head.

He looked up for reassurance, but it was clear that Alvirah had not heard him.

At one o'clock Willy went out again, returning this time with a quart of lobster bisque. Over lunch Alvirah filled him in on what she had learned. "In a nutshell, here are the facts: Cynthia's mother was a widow when she married Stuart Richards. Cynthia was eight at the time. They divorced four years later. Richards had one child by his first marriage, a daughter named Lillian. She was ten years older than Cynthia and lived with her mother in New York."

"Why'd Cynthia's mother divorce Richards?" Willy asked between sips of the bisque.

"From what Cynthia said on the witness stand, Richards was one of those men who always belittled women. Her mother would be dressed to go out, and he'd reduce her to tears by ridiculing what she was wearing— that kind of thing. Sounds like he just about gave her a nervous breakdown. Apparently, though, he had always been fond of Cynthia, always taking her out around her birthday and giving her presents.

"Then Cynthia's mother died, and Richards invited the young girl to visit him here at Cape Cod. Actually she wasn't so young by then—she was about to start her junior year at the Rhode Island School of Design. Her mother had been sick for a while, and there apparently wasn't much money left; she said she was planning on dropping out of school and working for a year or two. She claimed that Stuart told her that he'd always planned to leave half his money to his daughter Lillian and the other half to Dartmouth College. But he stayed so angry after Dartmouth let women in as full-time students that he changed his will. She said he told her he was leaving her the Dartmouth portion of his estate, about ten million dollars. The prosecutor got Cynthia to admit that Richards also told her she'd have to wait for him to die to get it; that it was too bad about college, but that her mother should have provided for her education."

Willy put down his spoon. "So there's your motive, huh?"

"That's what the prosecutor said, that Cynthia had wanted the money right away. Anyhow, a guy named Ned Creighton happened to drop in to visit Richards and overheard their conversation. He was a friend of Lillian's, about her age. Cynthia apparently had known him slightly from when she and her mother had lived with Richards at the Cape. So Creighton invited Cynthia to have dinner with him, and Stuart urged her to go.

"According to her testimony, she and Creighton had dinner at the Captain's Table in Hyannis, and then he suggested they go for a ride in his boat, which was anchored at a private dock. She said they were out on the Nantucket Sound when the boat broke down; nothing was working, not even the radio. They were stranded until nearly eleven, when he was finally able to get the motor going again. She apparently had only had a salad at dinner, so once they made shore she asked him to stop for a hamburger.

"She testified that Creighton wasn't very happy about having to stop on the way home, although he did finally pull in at some hamburger joint around Cotuit. Cynthia said she hadn't been on the Cape since she was a child and didn't know the area all that well, so she wasn't sure exactly where they stopped. Anyway, he told her to wait in the car, that he would go in and get the burger. All she remembered about being there was a lot of rock music blaring and seeing teenagers all over the place. But then a woman drove up and parked next to their car, and when she opened her door, it slammed into the side of Creighton's car." Alvirah handed Willy a clipping. "That woman, then, is the witness no one could find."

As Alvirah absentmindedly sipped the bisque, Willy scanned the paper. The woman had apologized profusely and had examined Ned's car for scratches. When she found none, she'd headed into the hamburger joint. According to Cynthia, the woman had been in her mid- to late-forties, chunky, with blunt-cut hair dyed an orange-red shade, and she'd been wearing a shapeless blouse and elastic-waisted polyester slacks.

The clipping went on to recount Cynthia's testimony that Creighton had returned complaining about the line for food and about kids who couldn't make up their minds when they gave an order. She said he'd been obviously edgy, so she didn't tell him at the time about the woman banging the door into his car.

On the witness stand, Cynthia had testified

that during the forty-five-minute drive back to Dennis, all of it along unfamiliar roads, Ned Creighton had hardly said a word to her. Then, once they reached Stuart Richards' house, he'd just dropped her off and driven away. When Cynthia went into the house, she'd found Stuart in his study, sprawled on the floor next to his desk, blood drenching his forehead, blood caked on his face, blood matting the carpet beside him.

Willy read more of the account: "The defendant stated that she thought Richards had had a stroke and had fallen, but that when she brushed his hair back she saw the bullet wound in his forehead, then spotted the gun lying next to him, and she telephoned the police."

"She said she thought then that he had committed suicide," Alvirah recounted. "But then she picked up the gun, of course putting her fingerprints on it. The armoire in the study was open, and she admitted that she knew Richards kept a gun in it. Then Creighton contradicted just about everything she had told the police, saying that, yes, he had taken her out to dinner, but that he had gotten her home by eight o'clock, and that all through the meal she had gone on about how she blamed Stuart Richards for her mother's illness and death, and that she intended to have it out with him when she got home. The time of death was established at about nine o'clock, which of course looked bad for her, given Creighton's contrary testimony. And even though her lawyers advertised for the woman she'd met at the burger joint, nobody came forward to verify her story."

"So do you believe Cynthia?" Willy asked. "You know an awful lot of murderers can't face the reality of what they've done and actually end up believing their own lies, or at least go through the motions of trying to confirm them. She could just be looking for this missing witness in an effort to finally convince people of her innocence, even though she's already served her time. I mean, why on earth would Ned Creighton lie about the whole thing?"

"I don't know," Alvirah said, shaking her head. "But you can be sure that somebody is lying, and I'll bet my bottom dollar that it isn't Cynthia. If I were in her boots, I'd set off to try and find out what it was that made Creighton lie, what was in it for him."

With that, Alvirah turned her attention to

the bisque, not speaking again until she had finished it off. "My, that was good. What a great vacation we're going to have, Willy. And isn't it wonderful that we took this cottage right next to Cynthia so that I'm here to help her clear her name?"

Willy's only response was the clatter of a spoon and a deep sigh.

The long and peaceful night's sleep followed by the early-morning walk had begun to clear the emotional paralysis that Cynthia had experienced from that moment twelve years earlier when she'd heard the jury pronounce the verdict: *Guilty.* Now as she showered and dressed she reflected that these past years had been a nightmare in which she had managed to survive only by freezing her emotions. She had been a model prisoner. She had kept to herself, resisting friendships. She had taken whatever jailhouse college courses were offered. She had graduated from working in the laundry and the kitchen to desk assignments in the library and assistant teaching in the art class. And after a while, when the awful reality of what had happened finally set in, she had begun to draw. The face of the woman in the parking lot. The hamburger stand. Ned's boat. Every detail she could force from her memory. When she was finished she had pictures of a hamburger place that could be found anywhere in the United States, a boat that looked like any Chris Craft of that year. The woman was a little more clearly defined but not much. It had been dark. Their encounter had lasted only seconds. But the woman was her only hope.

The prosecutor's summation at the end of the trial: "Ladies and gentlemen of the jury, Cynthia Lathem returned to the home of Stuart Richards sometime between 8:00 and 8:30 P.M. on the night of August 2, 1981. She went into her stepfather's study. That very afternoon Stuart Richards had told Cynthia he had changed his will. Ned Creighton heard that conversation, overheard Cynthia and Stuart quarreling. She needed money immediately to pay for her education and demanded he help her. That evening Vera Smith, the waitress at the Captain's Table, overheard Cynthia tell Ned that she would have to drop out of school.

"Cynthia Lathem returned to the Richards mansion that night, angry and worried. She went into that study and confronted Stuart Richards. He was a man who enjoyed upsetting the people around him. He *had* changed his will to include her, but she knew it would be just like him to change it again. And the anger she'd harbored for the way he had treated her mother, the anger that rose in her at the thought of having to leave school, at being turned out into the world virtually penniless, made her go to the armoire where she knew he kept a gun, take out that gun and fire three shots point-blank into the forehead of the man who loved her enough to make her an heiress.

"It is ironic. It is tragic. It is also murder. Cynthia begged Ned Creighton to say that she had spent the evening with him on his boat. No one saw them out on the boat. She talks about stopping at a hamburger stand. But she doesn't know where it is. She admits she never entered it. She talks about a stranger with red-orange hair to whom she spoke in a parking lot. With all the publicity this case has engendered, why didn't that woman come forward? You know the reason. Because she doesn't exist. Because like the hamburger stand and the hours spent on a boat on Nantucket Sound, she is a figment of Cynthia Lathem's imagination."

Cynthia had read the transcript of the trial so often that she had the district attorney's summation committed to memory. "But the woman did exist," Cynthia said aloud. "She does exist." For the next six months, with the little insurance money left her by her mother, she was going to try to find that woman. She might be dead by now, or moved to California, Cynthia thought as she brushed her hair and twisted it into a chignon.

The bedroom of the cottage faced the sea. Cynthia walked to the sliding door and pulled it open. On the beach below she could see couples walking with children. If she was ever to have a normal life, a husband, a child of her own, she had to clear her name.

Jeff Knight. She had met him last year when he came to do a series of television interviews with women in prison. He'd invited her to participate, and she'd flatly refused. He'd persisted, his strong intelligent face filled with concern. "Don't you understand, Cynthia, this program is going to be watched by a couple of million people in New England. The woman who saw you that night could be one of those people."

That was why she finally had agreed to go on the program, had answered his questions, told about the night Stuart died, held up the shadowy sketch of the woman she had spoken with, the sketch of the hamburger stand. And no one had come forward. From New York, Lillian issued a statement saying that the truth had been told at the trial and she would have no further comment. Ned Creighton, now the owner of the Mooncusser, a popular restaurant in Barnstable, repeated how very, very sorry he was for Cynthia.

After the program, Jeff kept coming to see her on visiting days. Only those visits had kept her from total despair when the program produced no results. He would always arrive a little rumpled looking, his wide shoulders straining at his jacket, his unsettled dark-brown hair curling on his forehead, his brown eyes intense and kind, his long legs never able to find enough room in the cramped visiting area of the prison. When he asked her to marry him after her release, she told him to forget her. He was already getting bids from the networks. He didn't need a convicted murderer in his life.

But what if I weren't a convicted murderer? Cynthia thought as she turned away from the window. She went over to the maple dresser, reached for her pocketbook and went outside to her rented car.

It was early evening before she returned to Dennis. The frustration of the wasted hours had finally brought tears to her eyes. She let them run down her cheeks unchecked. She'd driven to Cotuit, walked around the main street, inquired of the bookstore owner —who seemed to be a longtime native— about a hamburger stand that was a teenage hangout. Where would she be likely to find one? The answer, with a shrug, was, "They come and go. A developer picks up property and builds a shopping center or condominiums, and the hamburger stand is out." She'd gone to the town hall to try to find records of food-service licenses issued or renewed around that time. Two hamburger joint–type places were still in business. A third had been converted or torn down. Nothing stirred her memory. And of course she couldn't even be sure they had been in Cotuit. Ned might have been lying about that too. And how do you ask strangers if they know a middle-aged woman with orange-red hair and a chunky build who had lived or summered on the Cape and hated rock-and-roll music?

As she drove through Dennis, Cynthia impulsively ignored the turn to the cottage and again drove past the Richards home. As she was passing, a slender blond woman came down the steps of the mansion. Even from this distance she knew it was Lillian. Cynthia slowed the car to a crawl, but when Lillian looked in her direction she quickly accelerated and returned to the cottage. As she was turning the key in the lock she heard the phone ring. It rang ten times before it stopped. It had to be Jeff, and she didn't want to talk to him. A few minutes later it rang again. It was obvious that if Jeff had the number he wouldn't give up trying to reach her.

Cynthia picked up the receiver. "Hello.

"My finger is getting very tired pushing buttons," Jeff said. "Nice trick of yours, just disappearing like that."

"How did you find me?"

"It wasn't hard. I knew you'd head for the Cape like a homing pigeon, and your parole officer confirmed it."

She could see him leaning back in his chair, twirling a pencil, the seriousness in his eyes belying the lightness of his tone. "Jeff, forget about me, please. Do us both a favor."

"Negative. Cindy, I understand. But unless you can find that woman you spoke to there's no hope of proving your innocence. And believe me, honey, I tried to find her. When I did the program, I sent out investigators I never told you about. If they couldn't find her, you won't be able to. Cindy, I love you. You know you're innocent. Ned Creighton lied, but we'll never be able to prove it."

Cindy closed her eyes, knowing that what Jeff said was true.

"Cindy, give it all up. Pack your bag. Drive back here. I'll pick you up at your place at eight o'clock tonight."

Her place. The furnished room the parole officer had helped her select. *Meet my girl-friend. She just got out of prison. What did your mother do before she got married? She was in jail.*

"Good-bye, Jeff," Cynthia said. She broke the connection, left the phone off the hook and turned her back to it.

Alvirah had observed Cynthia's return but did not attempt to contact her. In the afternoon, Willy had gone out on a half-day charter boat and returned triumphantly with two bluefish. During his absence, Alvirah again studied the newspaper clippings of the Stuart Richards murder case. At Cypress Point Spa she had learned the value of airing her opinions into a recorder. That afternoon she kept her recorder busy.

"The crux of this case is why did Ned Creighton lie? He hardly knew Cynthia. Why did he set her up to take the blame for Stuart Richards' death? Stuart Richards had a lot of enemies. Ned's father at one time had business dealings with Stuart, and they'd had a falling out. But Ned was only a kid at that time. Ned was a friend of Lillian Richards. Lillian swore that she didn't know that her father was going to change his will, that she'd always known she would get half his estate and that the other half was going to Dartmouth College. She said she knew he was upset after Dartmouth decided to accept women students but didn't know he was upset enough to finally change his will and leave the Dartmouth money to Cynthia."

Alvirah turned off the recorder. It certainly must have occurred to someone that when Cynthia was found guilty of murdering her stepfather, she would lose her inheritance, and Lillian would receive everything. Lillian had married somebody from New York shortly after the trial was over. She'd been divorced three times since then. So it didn't look as though Ned and she had ever had any romance going. That left only the restaurant. Who were Ned's backers? *Motive for Ned to lie,* she thought. Who gave him the money to open his restaurant?

Willy came in from the deck, carrying the bluefish fillets he'd prepared. "Still at it?" he asked.

"Uh-huh." Alvirah picked up one of the clippings. "Orange-red hair, chunky build, in her late forties. Would you say that description might have fit me twelve years ago?"

"Now you know I would never call you chunky," Willy protested.

"I didn't say you would. I'll be right back. I want to talk to Cynthia. I saw her coming in a few minutes ago."

The next afternoon, after having packed Willy off on another charter fishing boat, Alvirah attached her sunburst pin to her new purple print dress and drove with Cynthia to the Mooncusser restaurant in Barnstable. Along the way Alvirah coached her. "Now remember, if he's there, point him out to me right away. I'll keep staring at him. He'll recognize you. He's bound to come over. You know what to say, don't you?"

"I do." Was it possible? Cynthia wondered. Would Ned believe them?

The restaurant was an impressive white colonial-style building with a long, winding driveway. Alvirah took in the building, the exquisitely landscaped property that extended to the water. "Very, very expensive," she said to Cynthia. "He didn't start this place on a shoestring."

The interior was decorated in Wedgwood blue and white. The paintings on the wall were fine ones. For twenty years—until she and Willy hit the lottery—Alvirah had cleaned every Tuesday for Mrs. Rawlings, and her house was one big museum. Mrs. Rawlings enjoyed recounting the history of each painting, how much she paid for it then and, gleefully, how much it was worth right now. Alvirah often thought that with a little practice she could probably be a tour guide at an art museum. "Observe the use of lighting, the splendid details of sunrays brightening the dust on the table." She had the Rawlings spiel down pat.

Knowing Cynthia was nervous, Alvirah tried to distract her by telling her about Mrs. Rawlings after the maître d'hôtel escorted them to a window table.

Cynthia felt a reluctant smile come to her lips as Alvirah told her that, with all her money, Mrs. Rawlings never once gave her so much as a postcard for Christmas. "Meanest, cheapest old biddy in the world, but I felt kind of sorry for her," Alvirah said. "No one else would work for her. But when my time comes, I intend to point out to the Lord that I get a lot of Rawlings points in my plus column."

"If this idea works, you get a lot of Lathem points in your plus column," Cynthia said.

"You bet I do. Now don't lose that smile. You've got to look like the cat who ate the canary. Is he here?"

"I haven't seen him yet."

"Good. When that stuffed shirt comes back with the menu, ask for him."

The maître d' was approaching them, a professional smile on his bland face. "May I offer you a beverage?"

"Yes. Two glasses of white wine, and is Mr. Creighton here?" Cynthia asked.

"I believe he's in the kitchen speaking with the chef."

"I'm an old friend," Cynthia said. "Ask him to drop by when he's free."

"Certainly."

"You could be an actress," Alvirah whispered, holding the menu in front of her face. She always felt that you had to be so careful, because someone might be able to read lips. "And I'm glad I made you buy that outfit this morning. What you had in your closet was hopeless."

Cynthia was wearing a short lemon-colored linen jacket and a black linen skirt. A splashy yellow, black and white silk scarf was dramatically tied on one shoulder. Alvirah had also escorted her to the beauty parlor. Now Cynthia's collar-length hair was blown soft and loose around her face. A light-beige foundation covered her abnormal paleness and returned color to her wide hazel eyes. "You're gorgeous," Alvirah said.

Regretfully Alvirah had undergone a different metamorphosis. She'd had her Sassoon hair color changed back to its old orange-red and cut unevenly. She'd also had the tips removed from her nails and had left them unpolished. After helping Cynthia select the yellow-and-black outfit, she'd gone to the sale rack, where for very good reasons the purple print she was wearing had been reduced to ten dollars. The fact that it was a size too small for her accentuated the bulges

that Willy always explained were only na-
ture's way of padding us for the last big fall.

When Cynthia protested the desecration of
her nails and hairdo, Alvirah simply said,
"Every time you talked about that woman,
the missing witness, you said she was
chunky, had dyed red hair and was dressed
like someone who shopped from a pushcart.
I've got to be believable."

"I said her outfit looked inexpensive," Cynthia corrected.

"Same thing."

Now Alvirah watched as Cynthia's smile
faded. "He's coming?" she asked quickly.

Cynthia nodded

"Smile at me. Come on. Relax. Don't show
him you're nervous."

Cynthia rewarded her with a warm smile
and leaned her elbows lightly on the table.

A man was standing over them. Beads of
perspiration were forming on his forehead.
He moistened his lips. "Cynthia, how good to
see you." He reached for her hand.

Alvirah studied him intently. Not bad looking in a weak kind of way. Narrow eyes almost lost in puffy flesh. He was a good
twenty pounds heavier than in the pictures in
the files. One of the kind who are handsome

as kids and after that it's all downhill, Alvirah decided.

"Is it good to see me, Ned?" Cynthia asked, still smiling.

"That's him," Alvirah announced emphatically. "I'm absolutely sure. He was ahead of me on line in the hamburger joint. I noticed him 'cause he was sore as hell that the kids in front were hemming and hawing about what they wanted on their burgers."

"What are you talking about?" Ned Creighton demanded.

"Why don't you sit down, Ned?" Cynthia said. "I know this is your place, but I still feel as though I should entertain you. After all, you did buy me dinner one night years ago."

Good girl, Alvirah thought. "I'm absolutely sure it was you that night, even though you've put on weight," she snapped indignantly to Creighton. "It's a crying shame that because of your lies this girl had to spend twelve years of her life in prison."

The smile vanished from Cynthia's face. "Twelve years, six months and ten days," she corrected. "All my twenties, when I should have been finishing college, getting my first job, dating."

Ned Creighton's face hardened. "You're bluffing. This is a cheap trick."

The waiter arrived with two glasses of wine and placed them before Cynthia and Alvirah. "Mr. Creighton?"

Creighton glared at him. "Nothing."

"This is really a lovely place, Ned." Cynthia said quietly. "An awful lot of money must have gone into it. Where did you get it? From Lillian? My share of Stuart Richards' estate was nearly ten million dollars. How much did she give you?" She did not wait for an answer. "Ned, this woman is the witness I could never find. She remembers talking to me that night. Nobody believed me when I told them about a woman slamming her car door against the side of your car. But she remembers doing it. And she remembers seeing you very well. All her life she's kept a daily diary. That night she wrote about what happened in the parking lot."

As she kept nodding her head in agreement, Alvirah studied Ned's face. He's getting rattled, she thought, but he's not convinced. It was time for her to take over. "I left the Cape the very next day," she said. "I live in Arizona. My husband was sick, real sick. That's why we never did come back. I lost him last year." Sorry, Willy, she thought, but this is important. "Then last week I was watching television, and you know how boring television usually is in the summer. You could have knocked me over with a feather when I saw a rerun of that show about women in prison and then my own picture right there on the screen."

Cynthia reached for the envelope she had placed beside her chair. "This is the picture I drew of the woman I'd spoken to in the parking lot."

Ned Creighton reached for it.

"I'll hold it," Cynthia said.

The sketch showed a woman's face framed by an open car window. The features were shadowy and the background was dark, but the likeness to Alvirah was astonishing.

Cynthia pushed back her chair. Alvirah rose with her. "You can't give me back twelve years. I know what you're thinking. Even with this proof a jury might not believe me. They didn't believe me twelve years ago. But they might, just might, now. And I don't think you should take that chance, Ned. I think you'd better talk it over with whoever paid you to set me up that night and tell them that I want ten million dollars. That's my rightful share of Stuart's estate."

"You're crazy." Anger had driven the fear from Ned Creighton's face.

"Am I? I don't think so." Cynthia reached

into her pocket. "Here's my address and phone number. Alvirah is staying with me. Call me by seven tonight. If I don't hear from you, I'm hiring a lawyer and getting my case reopened." She threw a ten-dollar bill on the table. "That should pay for the wine. Now we're even for that dinner you bought me."

She walked rapidly from the restaurant, Alvirah a step behind her. Alvirah was aware of the buzz from diners at the other tables. They know something's up, she thought. Good.

She and Cynthia did not speak until they were in the car. Then Cynthia asked shakily, "How was I?"

"Great."

"Alvirah, it just won't work. If they check the sketch that Jeff showed on the program, they'll see all the details I added to make it look like you."

"They haven't got time to do that. Are you sure you saw your stepsister yesterday at the Richards house?"

"Absolutely."

"Then my guess is that Ned Creighton is talking to her right now."

Cynthia drove automatically, not seeing

the sunny brightness of the afternoon. "Stuart was despised by a lot of people. Why are you so sure Lillian is involved?"

Alvirah unfastened the zipper on the purple print. "This dress is so tight I swear I'm going to choke." Ruefully she ran her hand through her erratically chopped hair. "It'll take an army of Sassoons to put me back together after this. I guess I'll have to go back to Cypress Point Spa. What did you ask? Oh, Lillian. She has to be involved. Look at it this way. Your stepfather had a lot of people who hated his guts, but they wouldn't need a Ned Creighton to set you up. Lillian always knew her father was leaving half his money to Dartmouth College. Right?"

"Yes." Cynthia turned down the road that led to the cottages.

"I don't care how many people might have hated your stepfather, Lillian was the only one who *benefited* by you being set up to be found guilty of his murder. She knew Ned. Ned was trying to raise money to open a restaurant. Her father must have told her he was leaving half his fortune to you instead of Dartmouth. She always hated you. You told me that. So she makes a deal with Ned. He takes you out on his boat and pretends that it breaks down. Somebody kills Stuart Richards. Lillian had an alibi. She was in New York. She probably hired someone to kill her father. You almost spoiled everything that night by insisting on having a hamburger. And Ned didn't know you'd spoken to anyone. They must have been plenty scared that witness would show up."

"Suppose someone recognized him that night and said they'd seen him buying the burger?"

"In that case he'd have said that he went out on his boat and stopped afterward for a hamburger, and you were so desperate for an alibi you begged him to say you were with him. But no one came forward."

"It sounds so risky," Cynthia protested.

"Not risky. Simple," Alvirah corrected. "Buh-lieve me, I've studied up on this a lot. You'd be amazed in how many cases the one who commits the murder is the chief mourner at the funeral. It's a fact."

They had arrived back at the cottages. "What now?" Cynthia asked.

"Now we go to your place and wait for your stepsister to phone." Alvirah shook her head at Cynthia. "You still don't believe me. Wait and see. I'll make us a nice cup of tea. It's too bad Creighton showed up before we had lunch. That was a good menu."

They were eating tuna-salad sandwiches on the deck of Cynthia's cottage when the phone rang. "Lillian for you," Alvirah said. She followed Cynthia into the kitchen as Cynthia answered the call.

"Hello." Cynthia's voice was almost a whisper. Alvirah watched as the color drained from her face. "Hello, Lillian."

Alvirah squeezed Cynthia's arm and nodded her head vigorously.

"Yes, Lillian, I just saw Ned . . . No, I'm not joking. I don't see anything funny about this . . . Yes. I'll come over tonight. Don't bother about dinner. Your presence has a way of making my throat close. And, Lillian, I told Ned what I want. I won't change my mind."

Cynthia hung up and sank into a chair. "Alvirah, Lillian said that my accusation was ridiculous but that she knows her father could drive anyone to the point of losing control. She's smart."

"That doesn't help us clear your name. I'll give you my sunburst pin so you can record the conversation. You've got to get her to admit that you had absolutely nothing to do with the murder, that she set Ned up to trap

120

you. What time did you tell her you'd go over to her house?"

"Eight o'clock. Ned will be with her."

"Fine. Willy will go with you. He'll be on the floor in the backseat of the car. For a big man he sure can roll himself into a beach ball. He'll keep an eye on you. They certainly won't try anything in that house. It would be too risky. Next to Willy, my sunburst pin is my greatest treasure," she said. "I'll show you how to use it."

Throughout the afternoon, Alvirah coached Cynthia on what to say to her stepsister. "She's got to be the one who put up the money for the restaurant. Probably through some sham investment companies. Tell her unless she pays up, you're going to contact a top accountant you know who used to work for the government."

"She knows I don't have any money."

"She doesn't know who might have taken an interest in your case. That fellow who did the program on women in prison did, right?"

"Yes. Jeff took an interest."

Alvirah's eyes narrowed, then sparked. "Something between you and Jeff?"

"If I'm exonerated for Stuart Richards' death, yes. If I'm not, there'll never be anything between Jeff and me or anyone else and me."

At six o'clock the phone rang again. Alvirah said, "I'll answer. Let them know I'm here with you." Her booming "Hello" was followed by a warm greeting. "Jeff, we were just talking about you. Cynthia is right here. My, what a pretty girl. You should see her new outfit. She's been telling me all about you. Wait. I'll put her on."

Alvirah frankly listened in as Cynthia explained, "Alvirah rents the next cottage. She's helping me . . . No, I'm not coming back . . . Yes, there is a reason to stay here. Tonight just maybe I'll be able to get proof I wasn't guilty of Stuart's death . . . No, don't come down. I don't want to see you, Jeff, not now . . . Jeff, yes, yes, I love you . . . Yes, if I clear my name, I'll marry you."

When Cynthia hung up she was close to tears. "Alvirah, I want to have a life with him so much. You know what he just said? He quoted *The Highwayman.* He said, 'I'll come to thee by moonlight, though hell should bar the way.'"

"I like him," Alvirah said flatly. "I can read

a person from his voice on the phone. Is he coming tonight? I don't want you getting upset or being talked out of this."

"No. He's been made anchorman for the ten o'clock news. But I bet anything he drives down tomorrow."

"We'll see about that. The more people in this, the more chance of having Ned and Lillian smell a rat." Alvirah glanced out the window. "Oh, look, here comes Willy. Stars above, he caught more of those darn bluefish. They gave me heartburn, but I'd never tell him. Whenever he goes fishing I keep a package of Tums in my pocket. Oh, well."

She opened the door and waved over a beaming Willy, who was proudly holding a line from which two limp bluefish dangled forlornly. Willy's smile vanished as he took in Alvirah's bright-red mop of unruly hair and the purple print dress that squeezed her body into rolls of flesh. "Aw, nuts," he said. "How come they took back the lottery money?"

At seven-thirty, after having dined on Willy's latest catch, Alvirah placed a cup of tea in front of Cynthia. "You haven't eaten a thing," she said. "You've got to eat to keep your brain clear. Now, have you got it all straight?"

Cynthia fingered the sunburst pin. "I think so. It seems clear."

"Remember, money had to have changed hands between those two—and I don't care how clever they were, it can be traced. If they agree to pay you, offer to come down in price if they'll give you the satisfaction of admitting the truth. Got it?"

"Got it."

At seven-fifty Cynthia drove down the winding lane with Willy on the floor of the backseat.

The brilliantly sunny day had turned into a cloudy evening. Alvirah walked through the cottage to the back deck. Wind was whipping the bay into a frenzy of waves that slammed onto the beach. The rumbling of thunder could be heard in the distance. The temperature had plummeted, and suddenly it felt more like October than August. Shivering, she debated about going next door to her own cottage and getting a sweater, then decided against it. In case anyone phoned, she wanted to be right here.

She made a second cup of tea for herself

and settled at the dinette table, her back to the door leading from the deck. Then she began writing a first draft of the article she was sure she would be sending to the *New York Globe.* "Cynthia Latham, who was 19 years old when she was sentenced to a term of twelve years in prison for a murder she did not commit, can now prove her innocence. . . ."

From behind her a voice said, "Oh, I don't think that's going to happen."

Alvirah swiveled around and stared up into the angry face of Ned Creighton.

Cynthia waited on the porch steps of the Richards mansion. Through the handsome mahogany door she could hear the faint sound of chimes. She had the incongruous thought that she still had her own key to this place, and she wondered if Lillian had changed the locks.

The door swung open. Lillian was standing in the wide hallway, light from the overhead Tiffany lamp accentuating her high cheekbones, wide blue eyes, silvery blond hair. Cynthia felt a chill race through her body. In these twelve years, Lillian had become a clone of Stuart Richards. Smaller of course. Younger, but still a feminine version of his outstanding looks. And with that same hint of cruelty around the eyes.

"Come in, Cynthia." Lillian's voice hadn't changed. Clear, well bred, but with that familiar sharp, angry undertone that had always characterized Stuart Richards' speech.

Silently, Cynthia followed Lillian down the hallway. The living room was dimly lighted. It looked very much as she remembered it. The placement of the furniture, the Oriental carpets, the painting over the fireplace—all were the same. The baronial dining room on the left still had the same unused appearance. They'd usually eaten in the small dining room off the library.

She had expected that Lillian would take her to the library. Instead, Lillian went directly back to the study where Stuart had died. Cynthia narrowed her lips, felt for the sunburst pin. Was this an attempt to intimidate her? she wondered.

Lillian sat behind the massive desk.

Cynthia thought again of the night she'd come into this room and found Stuart sprawled on the carpet beside that desk. She knew her hands were clammy. Perspiration was forming on her forehead. Outside she could hear the wind wailing as it increased in velocity.

Lillian folded her hands and looked up at Cynthia. "You might as well sit down."

Cynthia bit her lip. The rest of her life would be determined by what she said in these next minutes. "I think I'm the one who should suggest the seating arrangements," she told Lillian. "Your father did leave this house to me. When you phoned, you talked about a settlement. Don't play games now. And don't try to intimidate me. Prison took all the shyness out of me, I promise you that. Where is Ned?"

"He'll be along any minute. Cynthia, those accusations you made to him are insane. You know that."

"I thought I came here to discuss receiving my share of Stuart's estate."

"You came here because I'm sorry for you and because I want to give you a chance to go away somewhere and begin a new life. I'm prepared to set up a trust fund that will give you a monthly income. Another woman wouldn't be so generous to her father's murderer."

Cynthia stared at Lillian, taking in the contempt in her eyes, the icy calm of her demeanor. She had to break that calm. She walked over to the window and looked out. The rain was beating against the house. Claps of thunder shattered the silence in the room. "I wonder what Ned would have done to keep me out of the house that night if it had been raining like this," she said. "The weather worked out for him, didn't it? Warm and cloudy. No other boats nearby. Only that one witness, and now I've found her. Didn't Ned tell you that she positively identified him?"

"How many people would believe that anyone could recognize a stranger after nearly thirteen years? Cynthia, I don't know whom you've hired for this charade, but I'm warning you—drop it. Accept my offer, or I'll call the police and have you arrested for harassment. Don't forget it's very easy to get a criminal's parole revoked."

"A *criminal's* parole. I agree. But I'm not a criminal, and you know it." Cynthia walked over to the Jacobean armoire and pulled open the top drawer. "I knew Stuart kept a gun here. But you certainly knew too. You claimed he had never told you that he'd changed his will and was leaving the Dartmouth half of his estate to me. But you were lying. If Stuart sent for me to tell me about his will, he certainly didn't hide what he was doing from you."

"He did *not* tell me. I hadn't seen him for three months."

"You may not have *seen* him, but you spoke to him, didn't you? You could have put up with Dartmouth getting half his fortune but couldn't stand the idea of splitting his money with me. You hated me for the years I lived in this house, for the fact that he liked me, while you two always clashed. You've got that same vile temper he had."

Lillian stood up. "You don't know what you're talking about."

Cynthia slammed the drawer shut. "Oh, yes, I do. And every fact that convicted me will convict you. I had a key to this house. You had a key. There was no sign of a struggle. I don't think you sent anyone to murder him. I think you did it yourself. Stuart had a panic button on his desk. He didn't push it. He never thought his own daughter would harm him. Why did Ned just *happen* to stop by that afternoon? You knew Stuart had invited me here for the weekend. You knew that he'd encourage me to go out with Ned.

Stuart liked company and then he liked to be alone. Maybe Ned hasn't made it clear to you. That witness I found keeps a diary. She showed it to me. She's been writing in it every night since she was twenty. There was no way that entry could have been doctored. She described me. She described Ned's car. She even wrote about the noisy kids on line and how impatient everyone was with them."

I'm getting to her, Cynthia thought. Lillian's face was pale. Her throat was closing convulsively. Deliberately, Cynthia walked back to the desk so that the sunburst pin was pointed directly at Lillian. "You played it smart, didn't you?" she asked. "Ned didn't start pouring money into that restaurant until after I was safely in prison. And I'm sure that on the surface he has some respectable investors. But today the government is awfully good at getting to the source of laundered money. *Your* money, Lillian."

"You'll never prove it." But Lillian's voice had become shrill.

Oh God, if I can just get her to admit it, Cynthia thought. She grasped the edge of the desk with both hands and leaned forward. "Possibly not. But don't take the chance. Let me tell you how it feels to be fingerprinted and handcuffed. How it feels to sit next to a lawyer and hear the district attorney accuse you of murder. How it feels to study the faces of the jury. Jurors are ordinary-looking people. Old. Young. Black. White. Well dressed. Shabby. But they hold the rest of your life in their hands. And, Lillian, you won't like it. The waiting. The damning evidence that fits you much more than it ever fitted me. You don't have the temperament or the guts to go through with it."

Lillian stood up. Her face was frozen in hatred. "Bear in mind there were a lot of taxes when the estate was settled. A good lawyer could probably destroy your so-called witness, but I don't need the scandal. Yes, I'll give you your half." Then she smiled.

"You should have stayed in Arizona," Ned Creighton said to Alvirah. The gun he was holding was pointed at her chest. Alvirah sat at the dinette table, measuring her chances to escape. There were none. He had believed her story this afternoon, and now he had to kill her. Alvirah had the fleeting thought that she'd always known she would have made a wonderful actress. Should she warn Ned her husband would be home any minute? No. At the restaurant she'd told him she was a widow. How long would Willy and Cynthia be? Too long. Lillian wouldn't let Cynthia go until she was sure there was no witness alive, but maybe if Alvirah kept him talking, she'd think of something. "How much did you get for your part in the murder?" she asked.

Ned Creighton smiled, a thin sneering movement of his mouth. "Three million. Just enough to start a classy restaurant."

Alvirah mourned the fact that she had lent her sunburst pin to Cynthia. Proof. Absolute, positive proof, and she wasn't able to record it. And if anything happened to her no one would know. Mark my words, she thought. If I get out of this, I'm going to have Charley Evans get me a backup pin. Maybe that one should be silver. No, platinum.

Creighton waved his pistol. "Get up."

Alvirah pushed back the chair, leaned her hands on the table. The sugar bowl was in front of her. Did she dare throw it at him? She knew her aim was good, but a gun was faster than a sugar bowl.

"Go into the living room." As she walked around the table, Creighton reached over, grabbed her notes and the beginning of her article and stuffed them in his pocket.

There was a wooden rocking chair next to the fireplace. Creighton pointed to it. "Sit down right there."

Alvirah sat down heavily. Ned's gun was still trained on her. If she tipped the rocker forward and landed on him, could she get away from him? Creighton reached for a narrow key dangling from the mantel. Leaning over, he inserted it in a cylinder in one of the bricks and turned it. The hissing sound of gas spurted from the fireplace. He straightened up. From the matchbox on the mantel he extracted a long safety match, scratched it on the box, blew out the flame and tossed the match onto the hearth. "It's getting cold," he said. "You decided to light a fire. You turned on the gas jet. You threw in a match, but it didn't take. When you bent down to turn off the jet and start again, you lost your balance and fell. Your head struck the mantel and you lost consciousness. A terrible accident for such a nice woman. Cynthia will be very upset when she finds you."

The smell of gas was permeating the room. Alvirah tried to tilt the rocker forward. She had to take the chance of butting Creighton with her head and making him drop the gun. She was too late. A viselike grip on her shoulders. The sense of being pulled forward. Her forehead slamming against the mantel before she fell to the stone hearth. As she lost consciousness, Alvirah was aware of the sickening smell of gas filling her nostrils.

"Here's Ned now," Lillian said calmly at the sound of door chimes. "I'll let him in."

Cynthia waited. Lillian still had not admitted anything. Could she get Ned Creighton to incriminate himself? She felt like a tightrope walker on a slippery wire, trying to inch her way across a chasm. If she failed, the rest of her life wouldn't be worth living.

Creighton was following Lillian into the room. "Cynthia." His nod was impersonal, not unpleasant. He pulled up a chair beside the desk where Lillian had an open file of printouts.

"I'm just giving Cynthia an idea of how much the estate shrank after the taxes had been settled," Lillian told Creighton. "Then we'll estimate her share."

"Don't deduct whatever you paid Ned from what is rightfully mine," Cynthia said. She saw the angry look Ned shot at Lillian. "Oh, please," she snapped, "among the three of us, let's say it straight."

134

Lillian said coldly, "I told you that I wanted to share the estate. I know my father could drive people over the edge. I'm doing this because I'm sorry for you. Now here are the figures."

For the next fifteen minutes, Lillian pulled balance sheets out of the file. Allowing for taxes and then interest made on the remainder, your share would now be five million dollars."

"And this house," Cynthia interjected. Bewildered, she realized that with each passing moment Lillian and Ned were becoming more visibly relaxed. They were both smiling.

"Oh, not the house," Lillian protested. "There'd be too much gossip. We'll have the house appraised, and I'll pay you the value of it. Remember, Cynthia, I'm being very generous. My father toyed with people's lives. He was cruel. If you hadn't killed him, someone else would have. That's why I'm doing this."

"You're doing it because you don't want to sit in a courtroom and take the chance on being convicted of murder, that's why you're doing it." Oh God, Cynthia thought. It's no use. If I can't get her to admit it, it's all over. By tomorrow Lillian and Ned would have the chance to check on Alvirah. "You can have the house," she said. "Don't pay me for it. Just give me the satisfaction of hearing the truth. Admit that I had nothing to do with your father's murder."

Lillian glanced at Ned, then at the clock. "I think at this time we should honor that request." She began to laugh. "Cynthia, I am like my father. I enjoy toying with people. My father did phone to tell me about the change in his will. I could live with Dartmouth getting half his estate but not you. He told me you were coming up—the rest was easy. My mother was a wonderful woman. She was only too happy to verify that I was in New York with her that evening. Ned was delighted to get a great deal of money for giving you a boat ride. You're smart, Cynthia. Smarter than the district attorney's office. Smarter than that dumb lawyer you had."

Let the recorder be working, Cynthia prayed. Let it be working. "And smart enough to find a witness who could verify my story," she added.

Lillian and Ned burst into laughter. "What witness?" Ned asked.

"Get out." Lillian told her. "Get out this minute and don't come back."

• • •

Jeff Knight drove swiftly along Route 6, trying to read signs through the torrential rain that was slashing the windshield. Exit 8. He was coming up to it. The producer of the ten o'clock news had been unexpectedly decent. Of course there was a reason. "Go ahead. If Cynthia Lathem is on the Cape and thinks she has a lead on her stepfather's death, you've got a great story breaking."

Jeff wasn't interested in a great story. His only concern was Cynthia. Now he gripped the steering wheel with his long fingers. He had managed to get her address as well as her phone number from her parole officer. He'd spent a lot of summers on the Cape. That is why it had been so frustrating when he had tried to prove Cynthia's story about stopping at the hamburger stand and gotten nowhere. But he'd always stayed in Eastham, some fifty miles from Cotuit.

Exit 8. He turned onto Union Street, drove to Route 6A. A couple of miles more. Why did he have the sense of impending doom? If Cynthia had a real lead that could help her, she could be in danger.

He had to slam on his brakes when he reached Nobscusset Road. Another car, ignoring the stop sign, raced from Nobscusset across 6A. Damn fool, Jeff thought as he turned right, then left toward the bay. He realized that the whole area was in darkness. A power failure. He reached the dead end, turned left. The cottage had to be on this winding lane. Number six. He drove slowly, trying to read the numbers as his headlights shone on the mailboxes. Two. Four. Six.

Jeff pulled into the driveway, threw open the door and ran through the pelting rain toward the cottage. He held his finger on the bell, then realized that because of the power failure it did not work. He pounded on the door several times. There was no answer. Cynthia wasn't home.

He started to walk down the steps, then a sudden unreasoning fear made him go back, pound again on the door, then turn the knob. It twisted in his hand. He pushed the door open.

"Cynthia," he started to call, then gasped as the odor of gas rushed at him. He could hear the hissing coming from the fireplace. Rushing to turn the jet off, he tripped over the prone figure of Alvirah.

Willy moved restlessly in the backseat of Cynthia's car. She'd been in that house for

138

more than an hour now. The guy who'd come later had been there fifteen minutes. Willy wasn't sure what to do. Alvirah really hadn't given specific instructions. She just wanted him to be around to make sure Cynthia didn't leave the house with anyone.

As he debated, he heard the screeching sound of sirens. Police cars. The sirens got closer. Astonished, Willy watched as they turned into the long driveway of the Richards estate and thundered toward him. Policemen rushed from the squad cars, raced up the steps and pounded on the door.

A moment later a sedan pulled into the driveway and stopped behind the squad cars. As Willy watched, a big fellow in a trench coat leaped out of it and took the steps to the porch two at a time. Willy climbed awkwardly out of the car and hoisted himself to his feet in the driveway.

He was in time to grab Alvirah as she staggered from the back of the sedan. Even in the dark he could see the welt on her forehead. "Honey, what happened?"

"I'll tell you later. Get me inside. I don't want to miss this."

In the study of the late Stuart Richards, Alvirah experienced her finest hour. Pointing her finger at Ned, in her most vibrant tones, she pronounced, "He held a gun to me. He turned on the gas jet. He smashed my head against the fireplace. And told me that Lillian Richards paid him three million dollars to set up Cynthia as the murderer."

Cynthia stared at her stepsister. "And unless the batteries in Alvirah's recorder are dead, I have both of them on record admitting their guilt."

The next morning, Willy fixed a late breakfast and served it on the deck. The storm had ended, and once again the sky was joyously blue. Seagulls swooped down to feast on surfacing fish. The bay was tranquil, and children were making castles in the damp sand at the water's edge.

Alvirah, not that much worse for her experience, had finished her article and phoned it in to Charley Evans. Charley had promised her the most ornate sunburst pin that money could buy, one with a microphone so sensitive it could pick up a mouse sneezing in the next room.

Now, as she munched a chocolate-covered doughnut and sipped coffee, she said,

"Oh, here comes Jeff. What a shame he had to drive back to Boston last night, but wasn't he wonderful telling the story on the news this morning, and all about how Ned Creighton is talking his head off to the cops? Buh-lieve me, Jeff will go places with the networks."

"That guy saved your life, honey," Willy said. "He's aces high with me. I can't believe I was curled up in that car like a jack-in-the-box when you had your head in a gas jet."

They watched as Jeff got out of the car and Cynthia rushed down the walk and into his arms.

Alvirah pushed her chair back. "I'll run over and say hello. It's a real treat to see how they look at each other. They're so in love."

Willy placed a gentle but firm hand on her shoulder. "Alvirah, honey," he begged, "just this once, for five minutes, mind your own business."

Plumbing
for
Willy

*I*f Alvirah Meehan had been able to look into a crystal ball and watch the events of the next ten days unfold, she would have grabbed Willy by the hand and raced out of the green room. Instead she sat and chatted with the other guests of the Phil Donahue show. Today the subject was not sex orgies or battered husbands but people who had messed up their lives by winning big in the lottery.

The Lottery Winners' Support Group had been contacted by the Donahue show, and now the worst-case guests had been chosen. Alvirah and Willy would be a counterpoint to the others, the interviewer told them. "Whatever she means by that," Alvirah commented to Willy after their initial interview.

For her appearance, Alvirah had had her hair freshly colored to the soft strawberry shade that softened her angular face. This morning Willy had told her that she looked exactly the same as she did when he'd first laid eyes on her at a Knights of Columbus dance more than forty years ago. Baroness Min von Schreiber had flown to New York from the Cypress Point Spa in Pebble Beach to select Alvirah's outfit for the broadcast. "Be sure to mention that the first thing you did when you won the lottery was come to the spa," she cautioned Alvirah. "Since that damn recession, business is not so brisk."

Alvirah was wearing a pale blue silk suit with a white blouse and her signature sunburst pin. She wished she'd managed to lose the twenty pounds she'd regained when she and Willy went to Spain in September, but still Alvirah knew she looked very nice. Very nice for her, that was. She had no illusions that with her slightly jutting jaw and broad frame she'd ever be tapped to compete in the Mrs. America contest.

There were two other sets of guests. Three coworkers in a pantyhose factory had shared a ten-million-dollar ticket six years ago. They'd decided their luck was so good that they should buy racehorses with their winnings and were now broke. Their future checks were owed to the banks and Uncle Sam. The other winners, a couple, had won sixteen million dollars, bought a hotel in Vermont, and were now slaving seven days a week trying to keep up with the overhead. Any leftover money was used to place classified ads trying to dump the hotel on someone else.

An assistant came to bring them into the studio.

Alvirah was used to being on television now. She knew enough to sit at a slight angle so she looked a little thinner. She didn't wear clunky jewelry that could rustle against the microphone. She kept her sentences short.

Willy, on the other hand, could never get used to being in the public eye. Even though Alvirah always assured him he was a grand-looking man, and people did say he looked like the late Tip O'Neill, he was happiest with a wrench in his hand, fixing a leaking pipe. Willy was a born plumber.

Donahue began in his usual breezy, slightly incredulous voice. "Can you believe it; after you win millions of dollars in the lottery you need a support group? Can you believe that you can be broke even though you have *big fat checks* still coming in?"

"Nah," the studio audience dutifully shrieked.

Alvirah remembered to tuck in her stomach, then reached for Willy's hand and entwined his fingers in hers. She didn't want him to look nervous on the television screen. A lot of their family and friends would be watching. Sister Cordelia, Willy's second oldest sister, had invited a whole crowd of retired nuns to the convent to see the show.

Three men observing the program with avid interest were not Donahue's usual viewers. Sammy, Clarence and Tony had just been released from the maximum security prison near Albany, where they'd been guests of the state for fifteen years for their part in the armed robbery of a Brink's truck. Unfortunately for them they never got to spend their six-hundred-thousand-dollar heist. The getaway car had blown a tire a block from the scene of the crime.

Now, having paid their debt to society, they were looking for a new way to get rich. The idea of kidnapping the relative of a lottery winner was Clarence's brainchild. That was why they were watching Donahue today from their seedy room in the shabby Lincoln Arms Hotel on Ninth Avenue and Fortieth Street. At thirty-five, Tony was ten years younger than the others. Like his brother Sammy, he was barrel chested, with powerful arms. His small eyes with hooded lids disappeared into folds of flesh. His thick dark hair was unkempt. He obeyed his brother blindly, and his brother obeyed Clarence.

Clarence was a total contrast to the others. Small, wiry, and soft-spoken, he emitted a chilling aura. With good reason people were instinctively afraid of him. Clarence had been born without a conscience, and a number of unsolved homicides would have been cleared from the books if he had talked in his sleep during his incarceration.

Sammy had never admitted to Clarence that Tony had been joyriding in the getaway car the night before the Brink's robbery and had run through a street littered with glass. Tony would not have lived to express his regret that he hadn't checked the tires.

One of the lottery winners who'd invested in the horses was whining, "There wasn't enough money in the world to feed those nags." His partners nodded vigorously.

Sammy snorted, "We're wasting our time with this. Those jerks can't rub two nickels together." He reached to turn off the set.

"Wait a minute," Clarence snapped.

Alvirah was speaking. "We weren't used to money," she explained. "I mean, we lived a nice life. We had a three-room apartment in Flushing and still keep it in case the state goes broke and tells us to take a flying leap for the rest of our checks. But I was a cleaning woman and Willy a plumber, and we had to be careful."

"Plumbers make a fortune," Donahue protested.

"Not Willy." Alvirah smiled. "He spent half his time fixing things free at rectories and convents and for people who were hard up. You know how it is. It's so expensive to get sinks and toilets and tubs working, and Willy felt that this was his way of making life easier for other people. He still does it."

"Well, surely you've had some fun with the money?" Donahue asked. "You're very well dressed."

Alvirah remembered to get in a plug for the Cypress Point Spa as she explained that, yes indeed, they had fun. They'd bought an apartment on Central Park South. They traveled a lot. They gave to charity. She wrote articles for the *New York Globe* and she'd been fortunate enough to solve some crimes along the way. She'd always wanted to be a detective. "Nevertheless," she concluded firmly, "every year since we've been winners we've saved more than half of every single check. And that money is all in the bank."

Clarence, followed by Sammy and Tony, joined in the vigorous applause of the studio audience. Clarence was smiling now, a thin, mirthless smile. "Two million bucks a year. Let's say almost half of that for taxes so that means they net a little over a million bucks a year and save half of that. They gotta have two million plus in the bank. That oughta keep us going for a while."

"We snatch her?" Tony asked, pointing at the screen.

Clarence withered him with a glance. "No, you dope. Look at the two of them. He's hanging on to her like she's a life preserver.

He'd fall apart and go running to the cops. We take him. She'll take orders and pay to get him back." He looked around. "I hope Willy enjoys staying with us."

Tony frowned. "We gotta keep him blindfolded. I don't want him picking me out of no lineup."

It was Sammy who sighed. "Tony, don't worry about it. The minute we get the money, Willy Meehan will be looking for leaks in the Hudson River."

Two weeks later, Alvirah was having her hair done at Louis Vincent, the salon around the corner from the Central Park South apartment. "Since the program was aired, I'm getting so many letters," she told Louis. "Do you know I even got one from the President? He congratulated us on our wise handling of our finances. He said we were a perfect example of liberal conservatism. I wished he'd invited us to a White House dinner. I've always wanted to go to one of those. Well, maybe someday."

"Just make sure I do your hair," Louis admonished as he gave a final touch to Alvirah's coiffure. "Are you having a manicure?"

Afterward, Alvirah knew she should have heeded the queer feeling that suggested she get back to the apartment. She would have caught Willy before he rushed into the car with those men.

As it was, when the doorman saw her half hour later, he broke into a relieved smile. "Mrs. Meehan, it must have been a mistake. Your husband was so worried."

Incredulous, Alvirah listened as José told her that Willy had come running from the elevator in tears. He'd yelled that Alvirah had had a heart attack under the dryer and had been rushed to Roosevelt Hospital.

"A guy was outside in a black Cadillac," José said. "He pulled into the driveway when I opened the door. The doctor sent his own car for Mr. Meehan."

"That sounds funny," Alvirah said slowly. "I'll get over to the hospital right away."

"I'll call a cab," the doorman told her. His phone rang. With an apologetic smile, he picked it up. "Two-eleven Central Park South." He listened, then, looking puzzled, said, "It's for you, Mrs. Meehan."

"Me?" Alvirah grabbed the phone and with a sinking heart heard a whispery voice say, "Alvirah, listen carefully. Tell the doorman

153

your husband is fine. It was all a misunder-
standing. He's going to meet you later. Then
go upstairs to your apartment and wait for
instructions.''

Willy had been kidnapped. Alvirah knew it.
Oh God, she thought. "That's fine," she managed to say. "Tell Willy I'll meet him in an
hour.''

"You're a very smart woman, Mrs. Meehan,'' the voice whispered.

There was a click in her ear. Alvirah turned
to José.

"Complete mistake, of course. Poor Willy.''
She tried to laugh. "Ah . . . ha . . . ha.''

José beamed. "In Puerto Rico I never once
hear about a doctor sending his car.''

The apartment was on the thirty-fourth floor
and had a terrace overlooking Central Park.
Usually Alvirah smiled the minute she
opened the door. The apartment was so
pretty, and if she said so herself, she had an
eye for furniture. All those years of cleaning
other people's houses had been an education in interior design. They'd bought the
apartment furnished—with white upholstery,
white carpets, white lamps, white tables,

154

white everything. After two months Alvirah felt like she was living inside a Clorox bottle. She gave everything to Willy's nephew and went shopping.

But today she took no comfort in the matching ivory couch and loveseat, Willy's deep comfortable chair with its own otto-man, the crimson and royal blue Oriental car-pet, the black lacquered table and chairs in the dining area, the late afternoon sun that danced across the blanket of autumn leaves in the park.

What good was any of it if anything hap-pened to Willy? With all her heart, Alvirah fiercely wished they'd never won the lottery and were back in their Flushing apartment over Orazio Romano's tailor shop. It was at this time she'd be coming home from clean-ing Mrs. O'Keefe's house and joking to Willy that Mrs. O'Keefe had been vaccinated with a phonograph needle. "Willy, she never shuts up. Even shouts over the vacuum. It's a good thing she isn't too messy. I'd never get the work done."

The phone rang. Alvirah rushed to pick up the extension in the living room, then changed her mind and in stumbling haste ran into the bedroom. The recording machine was there. She pushed the Record button as she picked up the phone.

It was the same whispery voice. "Alvirah?"

"Yes. Where's Willy? Whatever you do, don't hurt him." She could hear background sounds like planes taking off. Was Willy at an airport?

"We won't hurt him as long as we get the money and as long as you don't call the cops. You didn't call them, did you?"

"No. I want to talk to Willy."

"In a minute. How much money have you got in the bank?"

"Something over two million dollars."

"You're an honest woman, Alvirah. That's just about what we figured. If you want Willy back you'd better start making some withdrawals."

"You can have it all."

There was a low chuckle. "I like you, Alvirah. Two million is fine. Take it out in cash. Don't give a hint that anything is wrong. No marked money, baby. And don't go to the cops. We'll be watching you."

The airport sounds became almost deafening. "I can't hear you," Alvirah said desperately. "And I'm not giving you one cent until I'm sure that Willy is still alive."

"Talk to him."

Moments later a sheepish voice said, "Hi, honey."

Relief, total and overwhelming, flooded Alvirah. Her ever-resourceful brain, which had been inactive since José had told her about Willy getting in the "doctor's car," resumed its normal steel-trap efficiency.

"Honey," she yelled so that his abductors could hear, "tell those guys to take good care of you. Otherwise they won't get a plugged nickel."

Willy's hands were handcuffed together. His feet were tied. He watched as the boss, Clarence, put his thumb on the handset of the phone and broke the connection. "That's quite a woman you have, Willy," Clarence said. Then Clarence turned off the machine that played simulated airport background sounds.

Willy felt like a jerk. If Alvirah had really had a heart attack, Louis would have called him from the salon. He should have known that. What a dope he was. He looked around. This was some crummy dump. When he got in the car, the guy who was hiding in the backseat put a gun in his neck. "Try to make trouble and I blow you away." The gun was jostling against his ribs when they hustled him through the lobby and up in the rickety elevator of this crummy joint. It was only a couple of blocks from the Lincoln Tunnel. The windows were closed tight, but even so, the exhaust fumes from the buses and trucks and cars were overwhelming. You could practically see them.

Willy had sized up Tony and Sammy fast. Not too much upstairs. He might be able to give them the slip somehow. But when Clarence came in, announcing that he'd warned Alvirah to let the doorman think everything was hunky-dory, Willy felt his first real fear. Clarence reminded him of Nutsy, a guy he'd known as a kid. Nutsy used to shoot his BB gun into birds' nests.

It was obvious Clarence was the boss. He called Alvirah and talked to her about the ransom. He made the decision to put Willy on the phone. "Now," Clarence said, "put him back in the closet."

"Hey, wait a minute," Willy protested. "I'm starving."

"We're gonna order hamburgers and french fries," Sammy told him as he slipped a gag over Willy's mouth. "We'll letcha eat."

Sammy trussed Willy's feet and legs in a spiral sequence of cord and knots and shoved him into the narrow closet. The door did not seal against the frame, and Willy could hear the low-toned conversation. "Two million bucks means she has to go to twenty banks. She's too smart to leave more than a hundred thou in any of them. That's how much is insured. Figuring the forms she has to fill out and the bank taking its own good time in counting the money, give her three, four days to get it."

"She'll need four," Clarence said. "We get the money by Friday night. We tell her we're gonna count it and then she can pick up Willy." He laughed. "Then we send her a map with an X mark to show where to start dredging."

Alvirah sat for hours in Willy's chair, staring unseeingly as the late afternoon sun sent slanting shadows over Central Park. The last lingering rays disappeared. She reached to turn on the lamp and got up slowly. It was no use thinking of all the good times she and Willy had had these forty years or that just this morning they were going through brochures to decide on whether to take a camel trip through India or a balloon safari in western Africa.

I'm going to get him back, she decided, her jaw jutting out a little more aggressively. The first thing she had to do was to make a cup of tea. The next was to get out all the bankbooks and lay a plan for going from one bank to another and withdrawing cash.

The banks were scattered all over Manhattan and Queens. One hundred thousand dollars deposited in each of them and, of course, accumulated interest, which they took out at the end of the year and used to start a new account. "No double-your-money schemes for us," they'd agreed. In the bank. Insured. Period. When someone had tried to talk them into buying zero-coupon bonds that paid off in ten or fifteen years, Alvirah had said, "At our age we don't buy things that pay off in ten years."

She smiled, remembering that Willy had chimed in, "And we don't buy green bananas, either."

Alvirah swallowed a giant lump in her throat as she sipped the tea and decided that tomorrow morning she'd start on Fifty-seventh Street at Chase Manhattan, go across the street to Chemical, work her way along

Park Avenue starting at Citibank and then hit Wall Street.

It was a long night lying awake wondering if Willy was okay. I'm going to make them let me talk to him every night until I get all the money, she promised herself. That way they won't hurt him till I figure something out.

At dawn she was becoming tempted to call the police. By the time she got up, at seven, she'd decided against it. These people might have a spy in the building who would report if there was a lot of activity in the apartment. She couldn't take a chance.

Willy spent the night in the closet. They loosened the ropes enough for him to stretch out a little. But they didn't give him a blanket or pillow, and his head was resting on someone's shoe. There was no way to push it aside. There was too much junk in the closet. He dozed off occasionally. He dreamed his neck was embedded on the side of Mount Rushmore, directly below the sculpture of Teddy Roosevelt's face.

• • •

The banks didn't open till nine. By eight-thirty, Alvirah, in a burst of pressure-cooker energy, had cleaned the already clean apartment. Her bankbooks were in her voluminous shoulder bag. She had dug from the closet a frankfurter-shaped plastic carryall, the one remnant on Central Park South of the days when she and Willy spent their vacations taking Greyhound tours to the Catskills.

The October morning was crisp, and Alvirah was wearing a light green suit that she'd bought when she was on one of her diets. The waistband wouldn't close, but a large safety pin solved that problem. Automatically she fastened her sunburst pin with the concealed recorder on the lapel.

It was still too early to leave. Trying to keep up the positive thinking, that everything would be hunky-dory as soon as the money was paid, Alvirah reheated the kettle and turned on the radio to *CBS Morning News.*

For once the headlines were fairly mundane. There was no big-shot Mafia guy on trial. No fatal-attraction homicide. Nobody had been arrested for inside trading.

Alvirah sipped her tea and was about to hit the Off button when the newscaster announced that as of today, New Yorkers could use the device that recorded the phone numbers from which incoming calls were made within the 212 area code.

It took a minute for her to realize what that meant. Then Alvirah jumped up and ran to the utility closet. Among the electronic devices that she and Willy delighted in taking home from Hammacher Schlemmer was the recording machine that listed numbers on incoming phone calls. They'd bought it not realizing it was useless in New York.

Dear Lord and his Blessed Mother, she prayed as she ripped the box open, pulled out the recorder and with trembling fingers substituted it for the answering machine in the bedroom. Let them be keeping Willy in New York. Let them call from wherever they're hiding him.

She remembered to record an announcement. "You have reached the home of Alvirah and Willy Meehan. At the beep please leave a message. We'll get back to you real soon." She played it back. Her voice sounded unnatural, worried, full of stress.

She forced herself to remember that she had won the drama medal in the sixth-grade play at St. Francis Xavier School in the Bronx. Be an actress, she told herself firmly.

She took a deep breath and began again: "Hell-lo. You have reached the home . . ."

That's more like it, she decided when she listened to the new version. Then, clutching her shoulder bag, Alvirah headed for Chase Manhattan to begin to put together Willy's ransom money.

I'm gonna go nuts, Willy thought as he tried to flex arms that somehow managed to be both numb and aching. His legs were still firmly trussed together. He'd given up on them. At eight-thirty he heard a faint rapping sound and then a door opening. Probably what passed for room service in this dump. They brought up lousy food on paper plates. At least that was the way hamburgers had been delivered last night. Even so, the thought of a cup of coffee and a piece of toast set Willy's mouth to watering.

A moment later the closet door opened. Sammy and Tony were staring down at him. Sammy held the gun while Tony loosened Willy's gag. "Didja have a good night's sleep?" Tony's unlovely smile revealed a broken eyetooth. Willy longed to have his hands free for just two minutes. They itched to give

164

Tony a matching set of eyeteeth. "Slept like a baby," he lied. He nodded in the direction of the bathroom. "How about it?"

"What?" Tony blinked, his rubbery face drooping into puzzlement.

"He needs to go to the head," Clarence said. He crossed the narrow room and bent over Willy. "See that gun?" He pointed to it. "It has a silencer. You try anything funny and it's all over. Sammy has a very nervous trigger finger. Then we'll all be mad because you gave us so much trouble. And we'll have to take it out on your wife. Get it?"

Willy was absolutely certain that Clarence meant it. Tony might be dopey, Sammy might have an itchy trigger finger, but they wouldn't do anything without getting the okay from Clarence. And Clarence was a killer. Willy tried to sound calm. "I get it."

Somehow he managed to hobble to the bathroom. After he'd finished, Tony let him splash some water in his face. Willy looked around in disgust. The tile was broken, and the room looked as though it hadn't been cleaned in years. Flecks of rust-corroded enamel covered the tub and sink. Worst of all was the constant dripping from the water tank, faucets and shower head. "Sounds like

Niagara Falls in here," Willy commented to Tony, who was standing at the door.

Tony shoved him over to where Sammy and Clarence were sitting at a rickety card table, which was piled with containers of coffee and objects that resembled abandoned Egg McMuffin cartons. Clarence nodded to the folding chair next to Sammy. "Sit there." Then he whirled. "Shut that damn door," he ordered Tony. "That stinking dripping is driving me nuts. Kept me awake half the night."

A thought came to Willy. He tried to sound casual. "I guess we'll be here a couple of days. If you pick up a few tools for me, I can fix that for you." He reached for a container. "I'm the best plumber you ever kidnapped."

Alvirah was learning that it was much easier to put money in a bank than to get it out. When she presented her withdrawal slip at Chase Manhattan, the teller's eyes bulged. Then he asked her to step over to an assistant manager's desk.

Fifteen minutes later, Alvirah was still adamantly insisting that, no, she wasn't unhappy with the service. Yes, she was sure she wanted the money in cash. Yes, she understood what a certified check was. Finally she demanded emphatically, "Is it my money or isn't it?"

"Of course. Of course." They would have to ask her to fill out some forms—government regulations for cash withdrawals of over ten thousand dollars.

Then they had to count the money. Eyes popped when Alvirah told them she wanted five hundred hundred-dollar bills and one thousand fifty-dollar bills. That took a lot of counting.

It was nearly noon when Alvirah hailed a cab to cover the three blocks to the apartment, dump the money in a dresser drawer and start out again for the Chemical Bank on Eighth Avenue.

By the end of the day she'd managed to get only three hundred thousand of the two million she needed. Then she sat in the apartment, staring at the phone. There was a way to move quicker. In the morning she'd call the rest of the banks and tell them to expect her withdrawals. Start counting now, fellows.

At six-thirty the phone rang. Alvirah grabbed it as a phone number appeared on the recording machine. A familiar number. Alvirah realized the caller was the formidable Sister Cordelia.

Willy had seven sisters. Six of them had

gone into the convent. The seventh, now deceased, was the mother of Brian, whom Alvirah and Willy loved as a son. Brian, a playwright, was in London now. Alvirah would have turned to him for help if he'd been in New York.

But she wasn't about to tell Cordelia about Willy's abduction. Cordelia would have the White House on the phone, demanding that the President dispatch the standing army to rescue her brother.

Cordelia sounded a little peeved. "Alvirah, Willy was supposed to come over this afternoon. One of the old girls we visit needs to have her toilet fixed. It's not like him to forget. Let me talk to him."

Alvirah managed a he-har-har laugh that sounded even to her ears like the canned stuff you hear on lousy television shows. "Cordelia, it must have gone out of his mind," she said. "Willy is . . . he's . . . " She had a burst of inspiration. "Willy's in Washington to testify about the cheapest way to fix plumbing in the tenements the government is restoring. You know how he can do miracles to make things work. The President read that Willy is a genius at that and sent for him."

"The President!" Cordelia's incredulous tone made Alvirah wish she'd named Senator Moynihan or maybe some congressman. I never lie, she fretted. I don't know how.

"Willy would never go to Washington without you," Cordelia snorted.

"They sent a car for him." Well, at least that's true, Alvirah thought.

She heard the "hrrump" on the other end of the line. Cordelia was nobody's fool. "Well, when he gets back, tell him to get right over here."

Two minutes later the phone rang again. This time the number that came up was not familiar. It's *them,* Alvirah thought. She realized her hand was shaking. Forcing herself to think of the sixth-grade drama medal, she reached for the receiver.

Her hello was hardy and confident.

"We hope you've been banking, Mrs. Meehan."

"Yes, I have. Put Willy on."

"You can talk to him in a minute. We want the money by Friday night."

"Friday night! It's Tuesday now. That only gives me three days. It takes a long time to get all that together."

"Just do it. Say hello to Willy."

"Hi, honey." Willy's voice sounded subdued. Then he said, "Hey, let me talk."

Alvirah heard the sound of the receiver dropping. "Okay, Alvirah," the whispery voice said. "We're not going to call you again until Friday night at seven o'clock. We'll let you talk to Willy then and we'll tell you where to meet us. Remember, any funny business and in the future you'll have to pay to have your plumbing fixed. Willy won't be around to take care of it."

The receiver clicked in her ear. Willy. Willy. Her hand still gripping the phone, Alvirah stared at the number listed on the machine: 555-7000. Should she call back? But suppose one of them answered. They'd know she was tracing them. Instead she called the *Globe*. As she expected, her editor, Charley, was still at his desk. She explained what she needed.

"Sure, I can get it for you, Alvirah. You sound kind of mysterious. Are you working on a case you can write up for us?"

"I'm not sure yet."

Ten minutes later he called back. "Hey, Alvirah, that's some dump you're looking up. It's the Lincoln Arms Hotel on Ninth Avenue, near the Lincoln Tunnel. It's one step down from a flophouse."

170

The Lincoln Arms Hotel. Alvirah managed to thank Charley before she slammed down the receiver and headed out the door.

Just in case she was being watched she left the apartment house through the garage and hailed a cab. She started to tell the driver to take her to the hotel, then thought better of it. Suppose one of Willy's kidnappers spotted her? Instead she had him drop her at the bus terminal. That was only a block away.

Her kerchief covering her head, her coat collar turned up, Alvirah walked past the Lincoln Arms Hotel. Dismayed, she realized it was a pretty big place. She glanced up at the windows. Was Willy behind one of them? The building looked as though it had been built before the Civil War, but it was at least ten or twelve stories high. How could she ever find him in that place? Once again she wondered if she should call the cops and then remembered again the time some wife did call and the cops were spotted at the ransom drop and the kidnappers sped away. They found the body three weeks later.

No. She couldn't risk it. She *had* to get Willy back.

Alvirah stood in the shadows at the side of the hotel and prayed to St. Jude, the saint of lost causes. And then she spotted it. A sign in the window. HELP WANTED—Room service. 4:00 to 12:00 P.M. shift. She had to get that job, but not looking like this.

Ignoring the trucks and cars and buses that were barreling toward the tunnel entrance, Alvirah dashed into the street, grabbed a cab, and rattled off the address of the apartment in Flushing. Her brain was working overtime.

The old apartment had been their home for nearly forty years and looked exactly the same as it had the day they'd won the lottery. The dark gray overstuffed velour couch and matching chair, the green-and-orange rug the lady she cleaned for on Tuesdays had been throwing out, the mahogany-veneer bedroom set that had been Willy's mother's bridal furniture.

In the closet were all the clothes she'd worn in those days. Splashy print dresses from Alexander's. Polyester slacks and sweatshirts, sneakers and high-heeled shoes purchased at outlets. In the mirror cabinet in the bathroom she found the henna rinse that made her hair the color of the rising sun on the Japanese flag.

An hour later there was no vestige left of the gentrified lottery winner. Bright red hair wisped around a face now startling with the makeup she used to love before Baroness Min taught her that less is better. Her old lipstick exactly matched her flaming hair. Her eyelids were emblazoned with purple shadow. Jeans too tight across the seat, ankles hidden by thick socks and feet stuffed into well-worn sneakers, a fleece-lined sweatshirt with the skyline of Manhattan stenciled across the front finished the trans-formation.

Alvirah surveyed the overall result with sat-isfaction. I look like someone who'd apply for a job in that crummy hotel, she decided. Reluctantly she left her sunburst pin in a drawer. It just didn't look right on the sweatshirt, and she had the backup pin Char-ley had given her at the other apartment if she needed it. When she pulled on her old all-weather coat she remembered to switch her money and keys to the voluminous black-and-green tote bag that she'd always carried to her cleaning jobs.

Forty minutes later she was in the Lincoln Arms Hotel. The grimy lobby contained a bat-tered desk in front of a wall of mailboxes and four black Naugahyde chairs in advanced stages of disrepair. The stained brown carpet was pocked with gaping holes that revealed ancient linoleum flooring.

Never mind room service, they ought to look for a cleaning woman, Alvirah thought as she approached the desk.

The sallow-complexioned, bleary-eyed clerk looked up.

"Whaddaya want?"

"A job. I'm a good waitress."

Something that was more sneer than smile moved the clerk's lips. "You don't need to be good, just fast. How old are ya?"

"Fifty," Alvirah lied.

"You're fifty, I'm twelve. Go home."

"I need a job," Alvirah persisted, her heart pounding. She could feel Willy's presence. She'd have taken an oath that he was hidden somewhere in this hotel. "Give me a chance. I'll work free for three or four days. If you don't think I'm the best worker you ever had by, let's say Saturday, you can fire me."

The clerk shrugged. "So whadda I got to lose? Be here tomorrow at four sharp. Whaddaya say your name was?"

"Tessie," Alvirah said firmly. "Tessie Magink."

• • •

Wednesday morning Willy could sense the growing tension among his captors. Clarence flatly refused to allow Sammy to step outside the room. When Sammy complained, Clarence snapped, "After twelve years in a cell you shouldn't have no trouble staying put."

There was no sign of a chambermaid beating down the door to clean, but Willy decided the room probably hadn't been cleaned in a year anyhow. The three cotlike beds were lined up together, heads against the bathroom wall. A narrow dresser covered with peeling sheets of Con-Tact paper, a black-and-white television, and a round table with four chairs completed the decor.

On Tuesday night Willy had persuaded his captors to allow him to sleep on the bathroom floor. It was bigger than the closet, and, as he pointed out, if he stretched out that extra bit he would be able to walk when they exchanged him for the ransom. He did not miss the glances they exchanged at the suggestion. They had no intention of letting him go free to talk about them. That meant he had about forty-eight hours to figure out a way of being rescued from this fleabag.

At three in the morning, when he'd heard

Sammy and Tony snoring in harmony and Clarence's irritated but regular gasps, Willy had managed to sit up, get to his feet and hop over to the toilet. The rope that tethered him to the bathtub faucet allowed him just enough room to touch the lid of the water tank. With his manacled hands, he lifted it, laid it on the sink and reached into the grimy, rust-colored water of the tank. The result was that a few minutes later the dripping had become louder, more frequent and more insistent.

That was why Clarence had awakened to the distressing sound of constantly bubbling water. Willy smiled a grim, inner smile as Clarence barked, "I'm gonna go nuts. Sounds like a camel peeing."

When the room-service breakfast was being delivered, Willy was again securely tied and gagged in the closet, this time with Sammy's gun at his temple. From the hall outside the room, Willy could hear the faint croak of the obviously old man who was apparently the sole room-service employee. It was useless to even think about attracting his attention.

That afternoon, Clarence began stuffing towels around the bathroom door, but nothing could block out the sound of running water. "I'm getting one of my bad headaches," he snarled, settling down on the unmade bed. A few minutes later Tony began to whistle. Sammy shut him up immediately. Willy heard him whisper, "When Clarence gets one of his headaches, watch out."

Tony was clearly bored. His beady eyes glazed over as he sat watching television, the sound barely turned on. Willy sat next to him, tied to a chair, the gag loosened enough that he could talk through almost closed lips.

At the table, Sammy played endless games of solitaire. In late afternoon, Tony got bored with the television and snapped it off. "You got any kids?" he asked Willy.

Willy knew that if he had any hope of getting out of this dump alive, Tony would be his ticket. Trying to ignore the combination of cramps and numbness in his arms and legs, he told Tony that he and Alvirah had never been blessed with kids, but they thought of his nephew, Brian, as their own child, especially since Brian's mother—Willy's sister—had been called to her eternal reward. "I have six other sisters," he said. "They're all nuns. Cordelia is the oldest. She's sixty-eight going on twenty-one."

Tony's jaw dropped. "No foolin'. When I was a kid and kind of on the streets and picking up a few bucks separating women from their pocketbooks, if you know what I mean, I never once hit on a nun, even when they wuz heading for the supermarket, meaning they had cash. When I had a good hit I left a coupla bucks in the convent mailbox, sort of an expression of gratitude."

Willy tried to look impressed at Tony's largess.

"Will you shut up?" Clarence barked from the bed. "My head's splitting."

Willy breathed a silent prayer as he said, "You know, I could fix that leak if I just had a monkey wrench and a screwdriver."

If he could just get his hands on that tank, he thought. He could flood the joint. They couldn't very well shoot him if people were rushing in to stop the cascade of water he could loose.

Sister Cordelia knew something was wrong. Much as she loved Willy, she could not imagine the President sending for him in a private car. Something else; Alvirah was always so open you could read her like the headline of the *New York Post.* But when Cordelia tried to phone Alvirah Wednesday morning there was no answer. Then, when she did reach her at three-thirty, Alvirah sounded out of breath. She was just running out, she explained, but didn't say where. Of course Willy was fine. Why wouldn't he be? He'd be home by the weekend.

The convent was an apartment in an old building on Amsterdam Avenue and 100th Street. Sister Cordelia lived there with four elderly sisters and the one novice, twenty-seven-year-old Maeve Marie, who had been a policewoman for three years before realizing she had a vocation.

When Cordelia hung up after speaking to Alvirah she sat down heavily on a sturdy kitchen chair. "Maeve," she said, "something is wrong with Willy. I feel it in my bones."

The phone rang. It was Arturo Morales, the manager of the Flushing bank around the corner from Willy and Alvirah's old apartment.

"Sister," he began, sounding distressed, "I hate to bother you, but I'm worried."

Cordelia's heart sank as Arturo explained that Alvirah had tried to withdraw one hun-

179

dred thousand dollars from the bank. They were able to give her only twenty thousand but had promised to have the rest of the cash Friday morning; she'd told them she absolutely had to have it by then.

Cordelia thanked him for the information, promised never to hint that he'd violated bank confidentiality, hung up and snapped to Maeve Marie, "Come on. We're going to see Alvirah."

Alvirah reported to the Lincoln Arms Hotel promptly at four o'clock. She'd changed her clothes in the Port Authority. Now, standing in front of the desk clerk, she felt secure in her disguise. The clerk jerked his head to indicate that she was to go down the corridor to the door marked Stay Out.

It led to the kitchen. The chef, a bony seventy-year-old who bore a startling resemblance to forties cowboy star Gabby Hayes, was preparing hamburgers. Clouds of smoke rose from the spatters of grease on the grill. He looked up. "You Tessie?"

Alvirah nodded.

"Okay. I'm Hank. Start delivering."

There were no subtleties in the room-service department. Service consisted of the kind of brown plastic tray that was found in hospital cafeterias, coarse paper napkins, plastic utensils, sample-sized packets of mustard, ketchup and relish. Hank shoveled limp hamburgers onto buns. "Pour the coffee. Don't fill the cups too much. Dish out the french fries."

Alvirah obeyed. "How many rooms in this place?" she asked as she set up trays.

"Hundred."

"That many!"

Hank grinned, revealing tobacco-stained false teeth. "Only forty rented overnight. The by-the-hour trade ain't looking for room service."

Alvirah considered. Forty wasn't too bad. She figured there had to be at least two men involved in the kidnapping. One to drive the car, one to keep Willy from bopping him. Maybe even one more to make that first phone call. She needed to watch for big orders. At least it was a start.

She began delivering with Hank's firm reminder to collect on the spot. The hamburgers went to the bar, which was inhabited by a dozen or so rough-looking guys you wouldn't want to meet on a dark night. The second order she brought to the room clerk and hotel manager, who presided over the premises from an airless room behind the desk. Their heros were on the house. Her next tray, containing cornflakes and a double boilermaker, was for a disheveled, bleary-eyed senior citizen. Alvirah was sure the cornflakes were an afterthought.

Next she was sent with a heavy tray to four men playing cards on the ninth floor. Another card-game group on the seventh floor ordered pizzas. On the eighth floor, she was met at the door by a husky guy who said, "Oh. You're new. I'll take it. When you knock on the door, don't bang. My brother's got a bad headache." Behind him Alvirah could see a man lying on a bed, a cloth over his eyes. The persistent dripping sound from the bathroom reminded her overwhelmingly of Willy. He'd have that leak fixed in no time flat. There was clearly no one else in the room, and the guy at the door looked as though he could have cleaned the contents of the tray on his own.

In the closet, Willy could just about hear the cadence of a voice that made him ache to be back with Alvirah.

• • •

There were enough room-service calls to keep her busy from six until about ten. From her own observations and from the explanations of Hank, who grew increasingly garrulous as he began to appreciate her efficiency, Alvirah got to understand the setup. There were ten floors of rooms. The first six floors all had ten rooms and were reserved for the hourly guests. The upper-floor rooms were the largest, all with baths, and tended to be rented for at least a few days.

Over a plump hamburger that she cooked for him at ten o'clock, Hank told her that everybody registered under a false name. Everybody paid cash. "Like one guy who comes in to clean out his private mailboxes. He publishes dirty magazines. 'Nother guy sets up card games. Lots of fellows come in here and get a bag on when they're supposed to be on a business trip. That kind of stuff. Nothing bad. It's sort of like a private club."

Hank's head began to droop after he'd finished the last of his third glass of beer. A few minutes later he was asleep. Quietly, Alvirah went to the table that served as a combination chopping board and desk. When she brought down the money after each order was delivered, she'd been instructed to put it in the cigar box that served as cash register. The order slip with the amount was placed in the box next to it. Hank had explained that, at midnight, room service ended and the desk clerk tallied up the money, compared it with the receipts, and put the cash in the safe, which was hidden in the bottom of the refrigerator. The order slips were then dropped into a cardboard box under the table. There was a massive jumble of them in place now.

Some would never be missed. Figuring that the top layers had to be the most recent records, Alvirah scooped up an armful and stuffed them in her voluminous handbag. She delivered three more orders to the bar between eleven and twelve. In between deliveries, unable to stand the grimy kitchen, she set about cleaning it up as a bemused Hank watched.

After a quick stop at the Port Authority to change into her good clothes, scrub the rouge and purple eye shadow from her face and wrap a turban around her flaming hair, Alvirah stepped out of a cab at quarter of one. Ramon, the night doorman, said, "Sister Cordelia was here. She asked a lot of questions about where you were."

Cordelia was no dope, Alvirah thought

with grudging admiration. A plan was forming in her mind, and Cordelia was part of it. Even before she sank her tired body into the Jacuzzi that was bubbling with Cypress Point Spa oils, Alvirah sorted out the greasy order slips. Within the hour she had narrowed the possibilities. Four rooms consistently sent for large orders. She pushed away the gnawing fear that they were all occupied by card players or some other kind of gamblers and that Willy might be in Alaska right now. Her instinct had told her the minute she set foot in the hotel that he was nearby.

It was nearly three when she got into the double bed. Tired as she was, it was impossible to get to sleep. Finally she pictured him there, settling in beside her. "Nighty-night, Willy, lovey," she said aloud, and in her head heard him saying in response, "Sleep tight, honey."

Sister Cordelia arrived at seven o'clock on Thursday morning. Alvirah was prepared for her. She'd been up half an hour and was wearing Willy's plaid bathrobe, which had the faint scent of his shaving lotion. She had a pot of coffee on the stove.

"What's up?" Cordelia asked abruptly.

Over coffee and Sara Lee crumb cake, Alvirah told her everything. "Cordelia," she concluded, "I won't tell you I'm not scared, because that would be a lie. I'm scared to death for Willy. If someone is watching this place or maybe has a delivery boy keeping an eye out, and it gets back that strange people were coming and going, they'll kill Willy. Cordelia, I swear to you, I know he's in that hotel, and I have a plan. Maeve still has her gun permit, doesn't she?"

"Yes." Sister Cordelia's piercing gray eyes bored into Alvirah's.

"And she's still friends with the guys she sent to prison, isn't she?"

"Oh sure. They all love her. You know they give Willy a hand fixing pipes whenever he needs it, and they take turns delivering meals to our shut-ins."

"That's what I need. They look like the people who hang out in that place. I want three or four of them to check into the Lincoln Arms tonight. Let them get a card game going. That happens all the time. Tomorrow night at seven o'clock, I get the call where to leave the money. They know that I won't turn it over until I talk to Willy. To keep them from carrying him out of there, I want Maeve's

186

guys covering the exits. It's our only chance."

Cordelia stared grimly into space, then said, "Alvirah, Willy always told me to trust your sixth sense. I guess I'd better do it now."

By Thursday afternoon, Clarence's eyes were blinded with the crushing ache that was splitting his head from ear to ear. Even Tony was careful not to cross him. He didn't reach to turn on the television set but contented himself sitting next to Willy and in a hoarse whisper telling him the story of his life. He'd gotten up to age seven, the year he'd discovered how easy it was to shoplift in the candy store, when Clarence barked from the bed, "You say you can fix that damn leak?"

Willy didn't want to seem too excited, but the muscles in his throat squeezed together as he nodded vigorously.

"Whaddaya need?"

"A monkey wrench," Willy croaked through the gag. "A screwdriver. Wire."

"All right. Sammy, you heard him. Go out and get that stuff."

Sammy was playing solitaire again. "I'll send Tony."

Clarence bolted up. "I said *you.* That dopey brother of yours'll blab to the nearest guy where he's going, why he's going, who he's getting it for. Now go."

Sammy shivered at the tone, remembering how Tony had gone joyriding in the getaway car. "Sure, Clarence, sure," he said soothingly. "And listen, long as I'm out, how about I bring in some Chinese food, huh? Could taste good for a change."

Clarence's scowl faded momentarily. "Yeah, okay. Get lotsa soy sauce."

Alvirah dropped off the suitcase with her last bank pickup at twenty to four, barely time enough to rush to the Port Authority, change, and report to the job. As she trotted through the Lincoln Arms lobby she noticed a sweet-faced nun in traditional habit holding out a basket and quietly moving from one to the other occupants of the bar. Everybody threw something in. In the kitchen, Alvirah asked Hank about the nun.

"Oh her. Yeah. She spends it on the kids who live around here. Makes everybody feel good to toss her a buck or two. Kind of spiritual, you know what I mean?"

The chow mein was a welcome relief from hamburgers. After dinner, Clarence ordered Willy to go into the john and get rid of the dripping noise. Sammy accompanied him. Willy's heart sank when Sammy said, "I don't know how to fix nothing, but I know how *not* to fix it, so don't get smart."

So much for my big plan, Willy thought. Well, maybe I can stall it till I figure something out. He began by chipping at the years of accumulated rust around the base of the tank.

That night, orders were not as brisk as the night before. Alvirah suggested to Hank that she sort out all the old slips in the order box.

"Why?" Hank looked astonished. Why would anyone sort out useless slips?

Alvirah tugged at the sweatshirt she was wearing today. It said, I SPENT THE NIGHT WITH BURT REYNOLDS. Willy had bought it as a gag when they went to Reynolds' theater in Florida. She tried to look mysterious. "You never know," she whispered.

The answer seemed to satisfy Hank.

She hid the already sorted slips under the pile she dumped on the table. She knew what she was looking for. Consistent orders in quantity since Monday.

She narrowed it down to the same four rooms she'd selected from her earlier sorting.

At six o'clock it suddenly got busy. By eight-thirty she'd delivered food to three of the four suspect rooms. Two contained the ongoing card games. One was now a crap game. She had to admit that none of the players looked like kidnappers.

Room 802 did not phone for an order. Maybe the guy with the bad headache and his brother had checked out. At midnight a discouraged Alvirah was about the leave, when Hank grumbled, "Working with you is easy. The new day guy quit, and tomorrow they're gonna bring in the kid who fills in. He screws up all the orders."

Breathing a grateful prayer of thanks, Alvirah immediately volunteered to come in for the seven-to-one morning shift as well as her usual four to twelve. She reasoned that she could still rush to the banks that had promised to have the cash for her between twelve-fifteen and three.

"I'll be back at seven," she promised Hank.

"So will I," he complained. "The day cook quit too."

On the way out, Alvirah noticed some familiar faces hanging around the bar. Louie, who'd served seven years for bank robbery and had a black belt in karate; Al, who'd been a strongman for a pawnbroker and served four years for assault; Lefty, whose specialty was hot cars. She smiled inwardly. Maeve was coming through for her—these were her men.

True to their training, even though Alvirah was sure they'd seen her, neither Louie, Al, nor Lefty gave any sign of knowing her.

Willy had reduced the dripping to its original annoying level, then an irritable Clarence had shouted in for him to knock off the hammering. "Leave it where it is. I can put up with that much noise for another twenty-four hours."

And then what? Willy wondered. There was one hope. Sammy was bored with observing him fiddling around with the water tank. Tomorrow Sammy would be more careless. That night Willy insured the further need of his services by again hopping over to the water tank and adjusting the drip-drip level.

In the morning, Clarence's eyes were feverish. Tony started talking about an old girlfriend he planned to look up when they got to the hideout in Queens, and no one told him to keep his mouth shut. Meaning, Willy thought, they're not worried about me hearing them.

When breakfast was delivered, Willy, securely stashed in the closet, jumped so suddenly that the gun in Sammy's hand almost went off. This time he didn't hear just a cadence of a voice that reminded him of Alvirah. It was clearly her ringing tone asking Tony if his brother's headache was any better.

A startled Sammy hissed in Willy's ear, "You crazy or somethin'?"

Alvirah was looking for him. Willy had to help her. He had to get back into the bathroom, work on the water tank, tap the wrench to the cadence of "And the Band Played On," their song, the one the band was playing when he first asked Alvirah to dance at the K of C hall over forty years ago.

He got his chance four hours later when, at Clarence's furious command, wrench and screwdriver in hand and a jittery Sammy beside him, he resumed his task of jointly fixing and sabotaging the water tank.

He was careful not to overdo. He reasonably told a protesting Sammy that he wasn't making that much noise, and anyhow, this place would probably love to have one decent john. Scratching his four-day growth of beard, squirming in his wrinkled clothing, Willy began to send off signals three minutes apart. "Ca-sey would WALTZ with the STRAW-ber-ry BLONDE tap-tap TApppp TApppp TApppp."

Alvirah was delivering pizza to 702 when she heard it. The tapping. Oh God, she prayed, oh God. She placed the tray on the uneven tabletop. The occupant of the room, a nice-looking fellow in his thirties, was coming off a binge. He pointed up, "Wouldn't that kill you? They're renovating or something. Take your pick. Sounds like Niagara Falls or New Year's Eve up there."

It has to be 802, Alvirah decided, thinking of the guy on the bed, the doorkeeper, the open bathroom door. They must shove Willy in the closet when they order room service.

Even though she was so excited her heart was thumping through the sweatshirt that read DON'T BE A LITTERBUG, she took time to caution the drinker that booze would be his ruination.

There was a phone in the hallway by the bar. Hoping she wasn't being observed by the desk clerk, Alvirah made a hurried call to Cordelia. She finished by saying, "They'll be phoning me at seven o'clock."

At quarter of seven that night, the occupants of the bar of the Lincoln Arms Hotel were awed at the sight of six mostly elderly nuns, in traditional floor-length habit, veil, and wimple, entering the lobby. The desk clerk jumped up and made a shooing motion toward the revolving door behind them. Alvirah watched, tray in arms, as Maeve, the appointed spokesperson, stared down the desk clerk.

"We have the owner's permission to ask for donations on every floor," Maeve told him.

"You got no such thing."

Her voice dropped to a whisper. "We have Mr. ———'s permission."

194

The clerk's face paled. "You guys shut up and get out your loot," he yelled at the occupants of the bar. "These here sisters are gonna pass the hat."

"No, we're starting upstairs," Maeve told him.

Alvirah protectively brought up the rear as the bevy of nuns, led by Cordelia, entered the elevator.

They went directly to the eighth floor and clustered in the hallway where Lefty, Al and Louie were waiting. At exactly seven o'clock Alvirah knocked on the door. "Room service," she called.

"We didn't order nothin'," a voice snarled.

"Someone did, and I've got to collect," she shouted firmly.

She heard scuffling. A door slammed. The closet. They were hiding Willy. The door opened a crack. A nervous Tony instructed, "Leave the tray outside. How much?"

Alvirah kept her foot firmly in the door as the oldest nuns materialized behind her. "We're collecting for the Lord," one of them whispered.

Clarence had the phone in his hand. "What the hell's going on out there?" he shouted.

"Hey, that's no way to talk to the sisters,"

Tony protested. Reverently he stepped aside as they drifted past him into the room.

Sister Maeve brought up the rear, her hands folded in the sleeves of her habit. In an instant, she circled behind Clarence, yanked her right hand out and held a gun against his temple. In the crisp tone that had made her a superb cop, she whispered, "Freeze, or you're dead."

Tony opened his mouth to yell a warning, but it was obliterated as Lefty karated him into unconsciousness. Lefty then insured Clarence's silence with a judicious rap on the neck that made him collapse beside Tony on the floor.

Louie and Al herded the reluctant Sister Cordelia and her elderly flock into the safety of the hallway. It was time to rescue Willy. Lefty had his hand ready to strike. Sister Maeve had her gun pointed. Alvirah threw open the closet door as she bellowed, "Room service."

Sammy was standing next to Willy, his gun in Willy's neck. "Outside, all of you," he snarled. "Drop that gun, lady."

Maeve hesitated for a moment, then obeyed.

"Outside!" Sammy barked.

He's trapped and he's desperate, Alvirah thought frantically. He's going to kill my Willy. She forced herself to sound calm. "I've got a car in front of the hotel," she told him. "There's two million dollars in it. Take Willy and me with you. You can check the money, drive away and then let us out somewhere." She turned to Lefty and Maeve, "Don't try to stop us or he'll hurt Willy. Get lost all of you." She held her breath and stared at Willy's captor, willing herself to seem confident as the others left the room.

Sammy hesitated for an instant. Alvirah watched as he turned the gun to point toward the door. "It better be there, lady," he snapped. "Untie his feet."

Obediently she knelt down and yanked at the knots in the ropes binding Willy's ankles. She peeked up as she undid the last one. The gun was still pointed at the door. Alvirah remembered how she used to put her shoulder under Mrs. O'Keefe's piano and hoist it up to straighten out the carpet. One, two, three. She shot up like an arrow, her shoulder whamming into Sammy's gun hand. He pulled the trigger as he dropped the gun. The bullet released flaking paint from the drooping ceiling.

Willy threw his manacled hands around Sammy, bear-hugging him until the others rushed back into the room.

As though in a dream, Alvirah watched Lefty, Al and Louie free Willy from his handcuffs and ropes and use them to secure the abductors. She heard Maeve dial 911 and say, "This is Officer Maeve O'Reilly, I mean Sister Maeve Marie, reporting a kidnapping, attempted murder and successful apprehension of the perpetrators."

Alvirah felt Willy's arms around her. "Hi, honey," he whispered.

She was so filled with joy she couldn't speak. They gazed at each other. She took in his bloodshot eyes, stubble of beard and matted hair. He studied her garish makeup and DON'T BE A LITTERBUG sweatshirt. "Honey, you're gorgeous," Willy said fervently. "I'm sorry if I look like one of the Smith Brothers."

Alvirah rubbed her face against his. The tears of relief that were welling in her throat vanished as she began to laugh. "Oh, sweetie," she cried, "you'll always look like Tip O'Neill to me."

A
Clean
Sweep

*T*he phone rang, but Alvirah ignored it. She and Willy had only been home long enough to unpack, and already the answering machine had picked up six messages. They'd agreed that tomorrow would be time enough to catch up with the outside world.

It's nice to be home, she thought happily as she stepped out onto the terrace of their Central Park South apartment and looked down at the park, where now in late October the leaves had turned into a blazing rainbow of orange and crimson and yellow and russet.

She went back inside and settled on the couch. Willy handed her a cocktail, a Manhattan in honor of being back in the city, and carried his own to his big easy chair. He lifted his glass to her. "To us, honey."

Alvirah smiled fondly at him. "I have to say all that sightseeing does wear me out. I'm going to rest my hands and feet for at least two weeks," she said.

"Agreed," Willy nodded and then added sheepishly, "Honey, I still think riding those mules in Greece was a little much. I felt like a broken-down Hopalong Cassidy."

"Well, you *looked* like the Lone Ranger," Alvirah assured him. She paused, looking lovingly at her husband. "Willy, we've had so much fun, haven't we? If it weren't for the lottery I'd still be cleaning houses and you'd be fixing busted pipes."

And once again they sat in silent wonder, marveling over the wonderful event that had made a clean sweep of their former life. The dates of their birthdays and wedding anniversary were the numbers they'd always played, a dollar a week for ten years until the unbelievable moment when the lottery ticket with those numbers was pulled and they found themselves the sole winners of the forty-million-dollar prize.

As Alvirah said, "Willy, for us, life began at sixty, well, not quite sixty." So far among their travels, they'd been to Europe three times, to South America once, had taken the Trans-Siberian Railway from China to Russia and now had just returned from a cruise around the Greek islands.

The phone rang. Alvirah glanced at it. "Don't be tempted," Willy begged. "We need to get our breath. It's probably Cordelia, and she'll have a job for me, fixing the plumbing at the convent or something. It can wait a day."

They listened to the answering machine. It was Rhonda Alvirez, secretary of the Manhattan chapter of the Lottery Winners' Support Group. Rhonda, a founding member of the group, had won six million dollars in the lottery and been persuaded by a cousin to invest her first big check in his invention, a fast-acting drain cleaner. As it turned out, the only thing the cousin's cleaner whooshed down the drain was Rhonda's money.

That was when Rhonda started the support group, and when she read about how well Alvirah and Willy had handled their windfall, she begged them to be honorary members and regular guest lecturers.

Rhonda had already left one message. Now she got right to the point. "Alvirah, I know you're home. The limo dropped you off an hour ago. I checked with your doorman. Please pick up. This is important."

"And you think Cordelia's bad," Alvirah murmured as she obediently reached for the phone.

Willy watched her expression change to disbelief and concern and then heard her say, "Of course we'll talk to her. Tomorrow morning at ten. Here. Fine."

When she hung up she explained, "Willy, we're going to meet Nelly Monahan. From what Rhonda tells me she's a very nice woman, but much more important, she's a lottery winner who's been shafted by her ex-husband. We can't let that happen."

The next morning at nine o'clock, Nelly Monahan prepared to leave her three-room apartment in Stuyvesant Town, the East Side housing development that she'd moved into over forty years ago as a twenty-two-year-old bride. Even though the rent was now ten times more than the fifty-nine dollars a month that had been the starting figure, the flat was still a terrific bargain, provided, of course, that you could spend nearly six hundred dollars a month for shelter.

But now that she was retired and living on a tiny pension and her monthly social security check, it had become painfully obvious to Nelly that she might have to give up the apartment and move in with her cousin Margaret in New Brunswick, New Jersey.

To Nelly, a dyed-in-the-wool New Yorker, the prospect of spending her final years away from the Big Apple was appalling. It had been bad enough that her husband, Tim, had walked out on her, but to give up the apartment broke her heart. And then to learn that Tim's new wife had produced that winning lottery ticket! It was just too much. That was when her neighbor suggested that Nelly call the support group, and now she had a meeting with Alvirah Meehan, who, Rhonda assured her, was a problem solver who got things done.

Nelly was a small, round, nondescript

woman with vaguely pretty features and lingering traces of brown in her gray hair, whose natural wave framed her face and softened the lines that time and hard work had etched around her eyes and mouth.

With her hesitant voice and shy smile, Nelly gave the outward appearance of being a pushover, but nothing could have been further from the truth. People who tried to take advantage of her soon learned that Nelly had a spunky streak and an implacable sense of justice.

Until her retirement at age sixty, she had worked as a bookkeeper for a small company that manufactured venetian blinds and, some years earlier, was the one who realized that the owner's nephew was bleeding the place dry. She'd persuaded her boss to make the nephew sell his house and pay back every dime he'd stolen or risk becoming a guest of the Department of Correction of New York.

And once, when a teenager tried to grab her pocketbook as he rode past her, she'd poked her umbrella into the spokes of his bicycle, causing him to go sprawling on the road with a sprained ankle. She alternately shouted for help and lectured the would-be mugger until the police came.

But these episodes paled compared to being cheated out of her nearly two-million-dollar share of the lottery money by her husband of forty years and her successor, Roxie, the new Mrs. Tim Monahan.

Nelly knew that Alvirah Meehan and her husband Willy lived in one of the fancy Central Park South buildings, so she dressed carefully for her meeting with them, selecting a brown tweed suit she'd bought on sale at A&S. She'd even gone to the extravagance of having her hair washed and set.

Promptly at 10:00 A.M. she was announced by the doorman.

At ten-thirty, Alvirah poured a second cup of coffee for their guest. For half an hour she'd deliberately kept the conversation general, talking about their shared backgrounds and changing life in the city. From her experience as an investigative columnist for the *New York Globe,* she'd learned that relaxed people tended to be better witnesses.

"Now let's get down to business," she said, touching the sunburst pin on the lapel of her jacket and turning on the recorder in it. "I'm going to be honest," she explained. "I'll be recording our conversation because sometimes when I play it back I pick up something that I missed."

Nelly's eyes sparkled. "Rhonda Alvirez told me you used that recorder to solve crimes. Well, let me tell you, I've got a crime for you, and the criminal's name is Tim Monahan."

She went on to explain, "In the forty years I was married to him, he could never hold a job because he always found a reason to file suit against his current employer. Tim spent more time in small claims court than Judge Wapner."

Nelly then enumerated the long list of defendants who had tangled with Tim, including the dry cleaner accused of putting a hole in an ancient pair of trousers, the bus company whose vehicle's sudden stop Tim said caused whiplash, the secondhand car dealer who refused to fix his car after the warranty expired, and Macy's, which was sued for a broken spring he discovered on a La-Z-Boy recliner Nelly had given him years before.

In her gentle voice she continued to tell them that Tim always considered himself a bit of a ladies' man and would gallantly rush to open doors for attractive girls while she, Nelly, walked behind him like the invisible woman. It had been especially annoying when he sang the praises of Roxie Marsh, who owned the catering outfit he worked for occasionally. Nelly had met the woman once and recognized that Roxie was the type who buttered up her help and then paid them slave wages.

She went on to explain also that while Tim drank a little too much, was a pain in the neck and looked particularly silly when he tried to act like Beau Brummell, he was nevertheless company of a sort, and after forty years she was used to him. Besides that she loved to cook and always enjoyed Tim's hearty appetite. It hadn't been perfect, but they had stuck it out.

Until they did or didn't win the lottery.

"Tell me about it," Alvirah ordered.

"We played the lottery every week, and one day I woke up feeling particularly lucky," Nelly explained earnestly. "It was the last chance to get in on the lottery for an eighteen-million-dollar pot. Tim was between jobs, and I gave him a dollar and told him to be sure to pick up a ticket when he bought his newspaper."

"And did he?" Alvirah asked quickly.

"Absolutely! When he got back, I asked him about it and he said yes, he'd bought it."

"Did you see the ticket?" Willy asked quickly.

Alvirah smiled at her husband. Willy was frowning. He seldom lost his temper, but when he did he looked and sounded remarkably like his sister Cordelia. Willy would have no use for a man who cheated his wife.

"I didn't ask to see it," Nelly explained as she swallowed the last of her coffee. "He always held the ticket in his wallet. Besides, there was no need. We always played the same numbers."

"So do we," Alvirah told her. "Our birthdays and wedding anniversary."

"Tim and I took ours from the street addresses of the houses we grew up in—1802 and 1913 Tenbroeck Avenue in the Bronx, and 405 East Fourteenth Street, the number of our building all these years. That came out to be 18-2-19-13-4-5.

"Tim didn't say one word about picking different numbers. That was on Saturday. The next Wednesday I was watching the TV when our number was pulled, and you can't imagine my shock."

"Yes I can," Alvirah told her. "I had cleaned for Mrs. O'Keefe the day we won, and let me tell you, she'd had all her grandchildren in the day before and the place was a mess. I was bone tired and soaking my feet when our numbers were pulled."

"She kicked over the pail," Willy explained. "We spent our first ten minutes as multimillionaires mopping up the living room."

"Then you do understand," Nelly sighed. She went on to explain that Tim had been out that night, working his occasional job as a bartender for Roxie the caterer. Nelly had sat up waiting for him and to celebrate had made his favorite dessert, a crème brûlée.

But when he got home, a tearful Tim handed her the ticket he was holding. It wasn't the numbers they always played. Every single one was different. "I decided to change our luck," Tim told her.

"I thought I'd have a heart attack," Nelly said. "But he felt so terrible that I ended up telling him it didn't matter, that it just wasn't to be."

"And I bet he ate the crème brûlée," Alvirah snapped.

"Every speck. He said every man should be so lucky as to have a wife like me. Then a few weeks after, he walked out on me and moved in with Roxie. He told me he'd fallen in love with her. That was a year ago. The divorce came through last month and he married Roxie three weeks ago.

"They'd announced that there were four

winners of the eighteen-million-dollar pot, and I didn't realize that one of them hadn't shown up to collect. Then last week, on the very last day before the ticket expired, Roxie, now the second Mrs. Tim Monahan, showed up at the redemption window and claimed she'd just happened to realize she had the fourth ticket, the ticket with the numbers Tim and I always played."

"Tim was working for Roxie the night your number won, and he had the ticket in his wallet?" Alvirah asked, to confirm her suspicion.

"Yes, that's the point. He had big eyes for her all along and probably showed the ticket to her."

"And she's a flirt who saw her big chance," Willy said. "That's disgusting."

"If you want to know what disgusting is, I'll show you the picture of the two of them in the *Post* saying how lucky they were that Roxie happened to find her ticket," Nelly's voice quivered into a near sob. Then she got a flinty look in her eye, and her jaw moved out an inch. "It's not justice," she said. "There's a retired lawyer, Dennis O'Shea, living down the hall from me, and I spoke to him about it. He did some research and learned that there are a couple of other cases on record where one spouse or the other pulled that scam and the court decided that the one holding the ticket is the owner. He said that it was a disgrace and a horror and a terrible shame, but legally I was out of luck."

"How did you happen to go to a meeting of the Lottery Winners' Support Group?" Alvirah asked.

"Dennis sent me. He'd read about all the people who lost all the money they made on the lottery in bad investments and thought it might help me to be around kindred souls."

Righteous wrath in her voice and a certain mulish expression around her mouth, Nelly summed up her luckless saga. "Tim moved out on me faster than you can say abracadabra, and now the two of them will live the life of Reilly while I move in with my cousin Margaret because I can't afford to stay where I am. Margaret only asked me to live with her because she likes my cooking. She talks so much I'll probably be stone deaf in a year."

"There's got to be a way to help," Alvirah decreed. "Let me put on my thinking cap. I'll call you tomorrow."

• • •

At nine o'clock the next morning, Nelly sat at the dinette table in her Stuyvesant Town apartment, enjoying a warm bagel and a cup of coffee. It may not be Central Park South, she thought, but it's a wonderful place to live. Since Tim took off, she'd made little changes in the apartment. He'd always insisted on keeping that big, ugly recliner of his right by the window, but since he'd taken it with him when he moved out, she'd rearranged the rest of the furniture the way she'd always secretly wanted and then she'd made bright new slipcovers for the couch and wing chair and bought a lovely hooked rug for next to nothing from neighbors who were moving.

Looking now at the autumn sun streaming in, and seeing how cheerful and inviting the place was, she reflected on how more and more she'd come to realize that Tim had been a lifelong drag and that she really was better off without him.

The trouble was that she couldn't make ends meet without his pitiful income, and try as she did, she couldn't find a job. Who wants to hire a sixty-two-year-old woman who can't use a computer? Answer: nobody.

Margaret had already called this morning. "Why don't you give the apartment up on the first and save a month's rent? I'm having the back bedroom painted for you."

How about the kitchen? Nelly wondered. I bet that's where you really expect me to spend my time.

It was all so hopeless. Nelly took a sip of her excellent, fresh-brewed coffee and sighed.

Then Alvirah called.

"We've got a plan," she said. "I want you to go and see Roxie and Tim and get them to admit they shafted you."

"Why would they admit it?"

"Get one of them mad enough to brag that they put one over on you. Do you think you can do that?"

"Oh, I can get Roxie's goat," Nelly said. "When they got married last month, I found a picture of Tim at Jones Beach where he looks like a beached whale and I had it framed and sent it to her. On it, I wrote, 'Congratulations and good riddance.' "

"I like you, Nelly," Alvirah chuckled. "You're a woman after my own heart. Here's the plan. One way or another you're going to make a date to see them and you're going to wear an exact copy of my sunburst pin. My editor had a couple of extras made for me."

"Alvirah, your pin looks valuable."

"It's valuable because it has the recorder in it. You're going to turn it on, get them to admit that they cheated you, and then we're going to get your lawyer friend, Dennis O'Shea, to sign a complaint to Matrimonial Court that you were cheated out of marital assets."

A faint hope stirred in Nelly's ample bosom. "Alvirah, do you really think there's a chance?"

"It's about the only chance," Alvirah said quietly.

For several minutes after getting off the phone, Nelly sat deep in thought. She remembered how a couple of years ago when Tim's mother was dying, the old woman had asked him to tell the truth: Hadn't he been the one who set the garage on fire when he was eight years old? He'd always denied it, but that day, seeing she was breathing her last, he broke down and confessed. I know how to get to him, Nelly thought as she reached for the phone.

Tim answered. When he heard her voice he sounded irritated. "Listen, Nelly, we're packing up to go to Florida for good, so what's up?"

Nelly crossed her fingers. "Tim, I've got bad news. I don't have more than another month." And I don't, she thought. At least not in Stuyvesant Town.

Tim sounded at least somewhat concerned. "Nelly, that's too bad. Are you sure?"

"Very sure."

"I'll pray for you."

"That's why I'm calling. I have to say I've had some pretty nasty thoughts about you in these weeks since Roxie turned in the lottery ticket."

"It was her ticket."

"I know."

"I mean I used to tell her how we played those numbers and she tried them for luck that week and I tried some other combination."

"Her numbers?"

"I forget," Tim said quickly. "Look, Nelly, I'm sorry, but we're leaving tomorrow, and the movers are coming in the morning. I've got a lot to do."

"Tim, I have to see you. I'm trying to get my soul in readiness, and I've hated you and Roxie so much I have to see you face to face and talk to you. Otherwise I'll never die in peace." More straight truth, Nelly thought.

From the background, she heard a strident voice yell, "Tim, who the hell is that?"

Tim lowered his voice and said quickly, "We're leaving on a noon plane tomorrow. Be here at ten o'clock. But Nelly, I have to tell you. I can only spare fifteen minutes."

"That's all I want, Tim," Nelly said, her voice even softer than usual. She hung up the phone and dialed Alvirah. "He's giving me fifteen minutes tomorrow morning," she said. "Alvirah, I could kill him."

"That won't do you any good," Alvirah said. "Come on over this afternoon and I'll show you how to work the pin."

The next day at nine o'clock, Nelly was about to put on her coat when the doorbell rang. It was Dennis O'Shea, the nice retired lawyer who lived down the hall in 8F. He'd moved there about six months ago. A number of times he'd fallen in step with her when they met at the elevator. He was on the small side, maybe five seven or so, with a neat, compact build, kindly eyes behind frameless glasses, and a pleasant, intelligent face.

He'd told her that his wife had died two years ago, and when he'd retired from the

Legal Aid Society at age sixty-five, he decided to sell the house in Syosset and move back to the city. He split his time now between the apartment and his cottage on Cape Cod.

Nelly could tell that, like her, Dennis had a strong sense of justice and didn't like the underdog to be pushed around. That was why she'd had the courage to ask him for advice when Roxie turned in the winning ticket.

This morning, Dennis looked worried. "Nelly," he said, "are you sure you know how to turn on that recorder?"

"Oh, sure, you just sort of run your hand over the fake diamond in the center."

"Show me."

She did.

"Say something."

"Go to hell, Tim."

"That's the spirit. Now play it back."

She snapped the cassette out of the pin and put it in the machine Alvirah had also given her and then pushed the replay button. Nothing happened.

"I guess you told your friend Alvirah Meehan about me," Dennis said. "She called a few minutes ago and explained what's going on. She said that you seemed to have trouble turning on the recorder."

Nelly felt her fingers tremble. She hadn't been able to sleep all night. Her share of the winnings was just maybe, possibly within her grasp. But if this didn't work, it was all over. She hadn't shed one tear all this year, but right now, looking at the concern on Dennis O'Shea's face, she felt her eyes fill up. "Show me what I'm doing wrong," she said.

For the next ten minutes they tried turning the recorder on and off, saying a few words, then playing it back. The trick was to snap that little switch firmly. Finally Nelly said, "I have it. Thanks, Dennis."

"My pleasure. Nelly, you get them on record saying they cheated you, and I'll have them in Matrimonial Court so fast they won't know what hit them."

"But they're moving to Florida."

"The lottery checks are issued in New York. Let me worry about that part of it."

He waited with her at the elevator. "You know what bus to take."

"It's not that far to Christopher Street. I'll walk at least one way."

• • •

Alvirah had a busy morning. At eight she started vigorously cleaning the already spotless apartment. At quarter to nine she had looked up Dennis O'Shea's phone number and called him, explaining her worry that Nelly might not have the hang of using the recorder; then she got back to polishing the polished. To Willy, it was an unmistakable sign that she was deeply concerned.

"What's eating you, honey?" he asked finally.

"I have a bad feeling," she admitted.

"You're afraid Nelly won't be able to handle the recorder?"

"I'm worried about that, and I'm worried that she may not be able to get them to say a word, and most of all I'm worried that they tell her everything and she doesn't get it on tape."

Nelly was meeting her ex-husband and Roxie at ten. At ten-thirty Alvirah sat down and stared at the phone. At ten thirty-five it rang. It was Cordelia, looking for Willy. "One of our old girls has a leak in her kitchen ceiling," Cordelia said. "The whole apartment is starting to smell mildewed. Send Willy right over."

"Later, Cordelia. We're waiting for an important message." Alvirah knew there was no getting off without explaining the problem.

"You should have told me before," Cordelia snapped. "I'll start praying."

By noon Alvirah was a total wreck. She called Dennis O'Shea again. "Any word from Nelly?"

"No. Mrs. Meehan, Nelly told me that Tim Monahan was only going to give her fifteen minutes."

"I know."

Finally, at twelve-fifteen, the phone rang. Alvirah grabbed it. "Hello."

"Alvirah."

It was Nelly. Alvirah tried to analyze the tone of her voice. Strained? No. Shocked. Yes, that's what it was. Shocked. Nelly sounded as though she was in a trance.

"What happened?" Alvirah demanded. "Did they admit it?"

"Yes."

"Did you get it on tape?"

"No."

"Oh, that's terrible. I'm so sorry."

"That's not the worst of it."

"What do you mean, Nelly?"

There was a long pause, then Nelly sighed. "Alvirah, Tim's dead. I shot him."

222

• • •

Five hours later, Alvirah and Willy posted bond after Dennis O'Shea, Nelly's self-appointed lawyer, pled her not guilty to charges of second-degree murder, first-degree manslaughter and carrying a concealed weapon. Nelly rose from her trancelike lethargy only long enough to say in a surprised voice, "But I did kill him."

They took her home. Half a Sara Lee crumb cake, neatly enveloped in plastic, was on the kitchen counter. "Tim always loved that cake," Nelly said sadly. "He looked awful today even before he died. I don't think Roxie cooked much for him."

Alvirah was feeling wretched. All this had been her big idea. Now Nelly was facing long years in prison. At her age that could mean the rest of her life. Yesterday Nelly had said that she could kill Tim. And I joked about it, Alvirah thought. I told her that wouldn't do any good. I never thought she meant it. How did she happen to have a gun?

She put on the kettle. "I think we'd better talk," she said. "But first I'll make a nice strong cup of tea for you, Nelly."

• • •

Nelly told her story in a flat, emotionless voice. "I decided to walk down to Christopher Street, to get my thoughts together, you know what I mean? I took the pin off and put it in my pocketbook. It's so pretty I was afraid I'd get mugged for it. Then on Tenth Street and Avenue B, I saw a couple of kids. They couldn't have been more than ten or eleven. Can you believe one of them was showing the other a gun?"

She stared ahead. "Let me tell you, I saw red. Those boys were not only playing hookey but treating that gun like a cap pistol. I marched up to them and told them to hand it over."

"You what?" Dennis O'Shea blinked.

"The one who wasn't holding the gun said, 'Shoot her,' but I think the other kid must've thought I was an undercover cop or something," Nelly continued. "Anyhow, he looked scared and handed it to me. I told them that kids their age should be in school and should play stickball, the way boys did when we were growing up."

Alvirah nodded. "So you had the gun with you when you went to see Tim and Roxie?"

"I couldn't take time to turn it in at the police station. Tim was only giving me fifteen

224

minutes. As it turned out, I didn't need more than ten.''

Alvirah saw that Willy was about to ask a question. She shook her head. It was obvious that Nelly was about to relive the scene in her mind. "All right, Nelly," she said softly. "What happened when you were with them?"

"I was a couple of minutes late. They're making a movie on Christopher Street, and I had to push through a lot of people who were gawking at the actors. The movers were just leaving when I got there. Roxie let me in. I don't think Tim had told her I was coming. Her mouth sort of dropped open when she saw me. The living room was empty except for Tim's old recliner, and he was camped in it, as usual. Didn't even get up like a gentleman. Then Mrs. Tim Monahan the Second, bold as brass, says to me, 'Get lost.'

"I was so nervous by then that I looked right at Tim and just blurted out everything I had rehearsed, that I only had a month left and that I wanted his forgiveness for being so angry at him, that it didn't matter about the ticket, that I was glad he had someone to take care of him. But before I died, just like his mother, I wanted to hear the truth.''

"You told them that!" Willy exclaimed.

225

"You're smart," Alvirah breathed.

"Anyhow, Tim had a funny look on his face, like he was going to laugh, and he said that it had been bothering him from the start. That yes, he had bought the winning ticket and switched it with Roxie and he had kept it in a safe-deposit box at the bank on West Fourth Street until he took it out and gave it to Roxie to cash in last month and he was sorry for my trouble and I was a fine, generous woman."

"He admitted it just like that!" Alvirah said.

"So fast that I almost collapsed, and he was laughing when he said it. Now I'm pretty sure that he was just making fun of me. I realized I didn't have the pin on and I opened my pocketbook and started to fumble for it and Roxie yelled something about the gun and I took it out to explain and it went off and Tim went down like a load of blubber. And after that it's all vague. Roxie tried to grab the gun, and the next thing I knew I was in the police station."

She reached for her cup. "So I guess I don't have to worry about keeping this apartment or about going to my cousin's in New Brunswick. Do you think they'll send me to the same prison where they keep that woman who had her husband shot because she wanted to keep the dog when they were divorced?"

She put the cup down and slowly stood up. As Alvirah and Willy and Dennis O'Shea watched, her face crumbled. "Oh my God," she said, "how could I have shot Tim?"

Then she fainted.

The next morning, Alvirah came back from visiting Nelly in the hospital. "They're going to keep her for a few days," she told Willy. "It's just as well. The newspapers are having a field day. Take a look." She handed him the *Post.* The front page showed an hysterically weeping Roxie watching Tim's corpse being carried from the apartment.

"According to this, Roxie claims that Nelly just showed up and started shooting."

"We can testify that she had made an appointment with Tim," Willy said, "but Nelly did say that Roxie didn't seem to expect her." His forehead furrowed as he considered the situation. "Dennis O'Shea phoned while you were out. He thinks it would be a good idea to plea-bargain."

227

Alvirah flicked a piece of lint from the sleeve of her smartly tailored pantsuit. It was an outfit she usually enjoyed wearing. It was only a size 14 and she could close the button at the waist of the slacks without too much yanking. But today nothing could give her comfort. Nelly may have been cheated out of her lottery ticket, but I'm the one who gave her a ticket to prison, she thought.

"I've been thinking that if I could possibly find those kids Nelly took the gun from, it would at least prove that she didn't intend to go there with it. I made her describe them to me."

The thought of action brought a little relief. "I'd better change into some old duds so I can just hang around. That isn't a great neighborhood."

An hour later, wearing ancient jeans, a tired Mickey Mouse sweatshirt, and her sunburst pin, Alvirah took up her vigil on the corner of Avenue B and Tenth Street. The boys Nelly had described were about ten or eleven years old. One was short and thin with curly hair and brown eyes, the other was taller and heavyset. They both had duck haircuts and wore gold chains and an earring.

The odds of just running into them were

small, and after thirty minutes Alvirah began to systematically work her way through the neighborhood stores. She bought a newspaper in one, two apples in another, aspirin in the drugstore. In each place she began a conversation. It was with the shoemaker that she finally hit pay dirt.

"Sure I know those two. The little guy is big trouble. The other isn't a bad kid. They usually hang around that corner." He pointed out the window. "This morning the cops were picking up truants and taking them back to school, so I guess they won't be here till three o'clock."

Delighted with the information, Alvirah rewarded the shoemaker by purchasing an assortment of polishes, none of which she needed. As he slowly counted out change, he explained that he'd dropped and stepped on his reading glasses, but that at a distance he could see a gnat sneeze. Then, glancing past her, he exclaimed, "There are the kids you're looking for." He pointed across the street. "They musta sneaked out of school again."

Alvirah spun around. "Forget about the change," she called as she dashed out of the store.

• • •

An hour later she dejectedly related to Willy and Dennis O'Shea what had happened. "When I talked to them, they'd just seen Nelly's picture in the *Post* and recognized her. Those little skunks were on their way to the police station to report that Nelly came up to them and asked where she could buy a gun because she needed one right away and offered them a hundred bucks. They claim they didn't know where to get one but later some other kid bragged about selling one to her."

"That's a damn lie," Dennis said flatly. "Just before Nelly left her apartment yesterday morning she checked her wallet. I couldn't help but notice she didn't have more than three or four dollars in it. Why would those kids lie like that?"

"Because Nelly took their gun away," Alvirah told him, "and this is their chance to get even." She realized she did not know why Dennis had been sitting in the living room talking to Willy when she arrived home.

But when he told her the reason, she was sorry she'd asked. The autopsy was complete. One bullet had grazed Tim's forehead.

The other two had lodged in his heart, and from the angle of entry it was clear they'd been fired after he was lying on the floor. The district attorney had called Dennis to tell him the plea bargain was now first-degree aggravated manslaughter with a minimum of fifteen years in prison. Take it or leave it. "And when I spoke to him he hadn't heard from those kids," Dennis concluded.

"Does Nelly know about this yet?" Alvirah asked.

"I saw her this morning just after you left. She intends to check out of the hospital tomorrow and get her affairs in order. She said she has to pay for her crime."

"I kind of hate to bring this up," Willy offered, "but is it possible that Nelly did buy the gun and was mad enough to mean to kill Tim?"

"She pointed the gun at his heart when he was on the floor?" Alvirah exclaimed. "I can't believe it."

"I don't think she did it deliberately," O'Shea agreed. "But she did kill him. Her prints are on the gun." He got up. "I'd better call and get the plea bargain in motion. I'll see if they'll give Nelly a little time before she has to start serving her sentence."

"He likes Nelly," Willy observed when he'd let Dennis O'Shea out.

"He's the kind of man she should have been with all these years," Alvirah agreed. Suddenly she felt old and tired. I'm just a meddling fool, she thought. Once again she could hear herself advising Nelly to go see Tim. And she could also hear Nelly saying, "I could kill him."

Willy patted her hand, and she looked up at him gratefully. He was her best friend as well as the best husband in the world. Poor Nelly had put up with a guy who couldn't hold a job, who fought with everyone, who drank too much, and who was the size of a beached whale.

Why the heck did Roxie marry him?

For the ticket, of course.

That night Alvirah could not sleep. Over and over she considered every single detail, and it all added up to one thing: fifteen years in prison for Nelly Monahan. Finally, at two o'clock, she got out of bed, being careful not to disturb Willy, who was clearly in the second stage of sleep. A few minutes later, armed with a steaming pot of tea, she sat at the dining table and played back the recording she had made of the first meeting with Nelly and then her confession after they bailed her out.

She was missing something. What was it? She got up, went to the desk, got a spiral notebook and pen, returned to the table and rewound the tape. Then as she played it back, she took notes.

When he got up at seven o'clock, Willy found her poring over her notes. He knew what she was doing. He put on the kettle and settled at the table across from her. "Can't figure out what you're missing," he commented. "Let me take a look."

A half hour passed. And then Willy said, "I can't see anything. But reading about Tim's recliner makes me think of old Buster Kelly. Remember he had a recliner too. Even insisted on moving it into the nursing home with him."

"Willy, say that again."

"Buster Kelly insisted on moving his recliner—"

"Willy, that's it. Tim was sitting in his recliner when Nelly went to the apartment." Alvirah reached across the table and grabbed her notebook. "Look. Nelly says that the moving men were just pulling away when she got there. Why didn't the recliner go with

them?'' She jumped up. "Willy, don't you see? Tim had a reason for telling Nelly he'd cheated her. I bet you anything Roxie had just told him to go stuff it. She stuck with him until he handed her the lottery ticket and she turned it in. Then she didn't need him anymore."

The more she said, the surer Alvirah was that she'd hit the nail on the head. Her voice rose in excitement as she continued. "Tim was trying to keep Nelly from claiming a share in the ticket and never thought that Roxie would double-cross him. I'll bet her telling those moving men to leave the recliner was the first notice he'd gotten that Roxie was going to dump him."

"And by admitting to Nelly that he'd cheated her, he thought he'd get the ticket back and have half the money. It makes sense," Willy agreed.

"Nelly didn't kill Tim. That first bullet just grazed his forehead. Roxie didn't grab her hand to take the gun away but to aim it at Tim."

They stared at each other. Willy's eyes shone with admiration. "Smartest redhead in the world," he said. "There's just one problem, honey. How are you going to prove it?"

How was she going to prove it? Alvirah made a list of where to start. She wanted to talk to the movers who had cleared out Roxie's apartment. Tim had told Nelly that he'd kept the lottery ticket in a safe-deposit box in a bank around the corner from Christopher Street. She wanted to find it and see when he took out the box and whose name was on it. Finally she wanted to talk to the superintendent of the building where Roxie and Tim had their little love nest.

Yet even as her brain busily worked away, it was with an overriding sense that she was spinning wheels. The fact remained that it would be almost impossible to prove that Roxie had guided Nelly's hand.

At nine o'clock she called Charley Evans at the *Globe,* and explained her needs. At ten he called back. Stalwart Van company had picked up the contents of Roxie and Tim's apartment, he reported. The three guys assigned to the job were working on East Fiftieth Street today. The Greenwich Savings Bank on West Fourth had a safe-deposit box in the name of Timothy Monahan. He rented it last year and closed it out three weeks ago. "They're willing to talk to you."

Alvirah wrote swiftly, said, "Charley, you're a doll," then hung up and turned to Willy. "Come on, honey."

Their first stop was at East Fiftieth Street, where the Stalwart Van movers were dismantling an apartment. They hung around the van until the three returned, struggling under the weight of a nine-foot breakfront.

Alvirah waited until they hoisted it into the cavelike back of the truck, then introduced herself. "I won't take a minute of your time, but it's important I ask a few questions." Willy opened his wallet and displayed three twenty-dollar bills.

They cheerfully explained that Tim hadn't been in the apartment when they got there. In fact, when he did come back just before ten, they could tell he wasn't expected. Roxie had yelled, "I told you to get a haircut. You look like a slob."

The burly mover chuckled. "Then he said something about having an appointment at ten that he didn't think she'd like, and she said, 'What appointment, to fix yourself a drink?' "

"We were on the way out the door and the guy yelled for us to come back and get his recliner and the wife told us to just get going," the smallest mover, the one who had carried the heaviest part of the breakfront, volunteered.

"And in court it wouldn't prove anything," Willy reminded Alvirah an hour later when they left the Greenwich Savings Bank, having confirmed that Tim Monahan rented the safe-deposit box a year ago, the morning after the disputed winning ticket was drawn, and visited it only once, the day he gave it up three weeks ago. That day he'd been accompanied by a flashy-looking woman. The clerk identified Roxie's picture. "That's the one."

"He went into the vault and gave up that safe-deposit box half an hour before they showed up at the clerk's office to turn in the ticket," Alvirah said, every inch of her throbbing with frustration.

"I know they did," Willy agreed, "but—"

"But legally it doesn't prove anything. Oh, Willy, it may not do any good, but let's try to get a look at the apartment they lived in."

They turned the corner and were treated to a crowd of spectators pressing against stanchions as they watched Tom Cruise catch up with a fleeing Demi Moore and spin her around.

"Nelly said they were filming a scene here

the other day," Alvirah commented. "Well, we've got better things to do than gawk."

She was at the door of 101 Christopher Street when a familiar voice yelled, "Aunt Alvirah."

She and Willy spun around as a thin young man with half-glasses on the end of his nose expertly made his way to them.

"Brian, as I live and breathe."

Brian was the son of Willy's deceased sister, Madaline. Now a successful playwright, to Willy and Alvirah he was the son they never had.

"I thought you were in London," Alvirah said as she hugged him.

"I thought you were in Greece. I just got back, and they wanted some additional dialogue. I wrote the screenplay for this epic." He nodded to the cameras down the street. "Look, I've got to get back over there. I'll catch you later."

An overhead camera anchored to a van was being positioned down the block. Subconsciously Alvirah made note of it as she rang the superintendent's bell at 101.

Ten minutes later she and Willy were being shown the three-bedroom apartment where the late Tim Monahan had breathed his last.

"You're in luck," the superintendent informed them. "Roxie just called yesterday to say she didn't want the apartment anymore, so nobody knows it's available. And you're the kind of tenants the management wants," he added virtuously as he thought of Alvirah's check for a thousand dollars nestled in his hip pocket.

"You mean she wasn't going to give it up when she moved to Florida?"

"No. She said it might be needed, but she'd switched it to Tim's name."

The late Tim Monahan's battered recliner caught the morning sun. The rest of the room was empty. The remains of the chalk marks on the floor the police had made to indicate where Tim's body had lain were still visible.

A shadow passed over the chair. Startled, Alvirah turned and was treated to the sight of the Mirage Films van with the camera passing outside. "That's it," she said.

The next morning, Nelly Monahan sat on a chair in her room in Lenox Hill Hospital, waiting to be discharged. On her lap she had a lined pad on which she was making notes of everything she had to do before she went to prison. A saddened Dennis O'Shea had told her that the district attorney would only let her plead guilty to a lesser offense if she would accept fifteen years in prison without the possibility of parole.

"It's only justice," she'd told him quietly. "I must pay for what I did." Then when he took her hand, she'd winced. Her wrist was sore, probably because Roxie had tried so hard to wrestle the gun from her, and there was a scrape on her index finger from where she'd scratched it trying to turn on the recorder in the pin.

Then Dennis said he thought they should go to trial and he'd represent her, but she said it wouldn't be right for her to get off. She had taken a life.

"Give up apartment," Nelly wrote now. "Turn off phone."

She looked up. A smartly dressed Alvirah was at the door. "You look nice, Alvirah," she said admiringly. "Do you know what color the prison uniforms are? It's funny. Last night I was just lying awake thinking about things like that."

"Don't worry about prison uniforms," Alvirah told her. "It ain't over till it's over. Now I'm going to take you home in a taxi, and I called Dennis and said you are *not,* repeat, *not* going near the district attorney's office or signing anything until I put my plan in action, starting with interviewing the heartbroken widow of the late Tim Monahan."

Roxie Marsh Monahan debated about what to wear for her meeting with Alvirah Meehan. It was exciting to think of having a whole article written about her in the *Globe.* She'd loved the story in the *Post* but was sorry she hadn't had her hair done Monday the way she'd planned. It had looked a little stringy in the picture of her watching Tim's body being carried out. But on the other hand, she'd been crying hysterically, so maybe it was better that her hair was going every which way. Kind of rounded out the effect.

She glanced around. The junior suite in the Omni Park Hotel was very attractive. She'd rented it the day of the shooting. The district attorney's office had asked her to stay in New York for a short time while all the facts of the case were settled. They'd told her that Nelly was undoubtedly going to cop a plea, so there wouldn't be any trial.

Roxie decided that in a way she'd miss

New York, but she loved golf and in Florida could play it every day without worrying about rattling dishes for some dreary party. Catering was hell. God, she didn't think she'd ever cook so much as a string bean for herself again.

She smiled. She'd been wrapped in a warm glow of anticipation ever since that dumb bunny Tim had handed her the ticket just as they went into the lottery office. Actually, Tim wasn't so dumb. That first night when he'd showed her the winning ticket she'd offered to hold it for him. No way, he'd told her. He wanted to make sure that they were really compatible.

She'd been stuck with having to look at that dopey face every day, listen to him snore at night, see him plopped in that shabby recliner with a beer in his hand, act happy when he slobbered all over her with clumsy kisses. She'd earned every nickel of two hundred thousand or so bucks less taxes she had coming in each year for the next twenty years.

She held up the two black suits she'd bought in Annie Sez yesterday. One had gold buttons. The other, sequin lapels. Gold buttons it would be. The sequins looked a little too festive. Roxie dressed, put on her customary bangles and turquoise rings. She knew she didn't look fifty-three. She knew that with her blond hair and snazzy figure, she was still very attractive. And now she could afford to stay that way.

It all added up to catching a really interesting guy.

Thank you, Tim Monahan. Thank you, Nelly Monahan. Incredible the way I snatched victory from the jaws of defeat, Roxie exulted. Her one blunder had been to tell Tim the truth when he saw that the movers were leaving and his recliner was still squatting in the living room. She should have bluffed it out somehow. She certainly would have kept her mouth shut if she'd known that Nelly Monahan would ring the doorbell seconds after she told Tim to jump in the lake, that he wasn't going with her. As Roxie reshaped her lips, the phone rang. Alvirah Meehan was in the lobby.

"Our angle is to talk about how the winning lottery ticket has led to such tragedy for you," Alvirah sympathized as she sat opposite Roxie a few minutes later.

243

Roxie dabbed at her eyes. "I'm sorry I ever found it in my makeup drawer. I came across it under a box of Q-tips and I'd just read an article about how a lot of people don't realize they have a winning ticket and never know they might have been millionaires and the number to call was listed, so I laughed and I said to Tim, 'Wouldn't it be a gasser if this was a lucky ticket?' "

Alvirah turned slightly so that the recorder in her sunburst pin wouldn't miss a word. "And what did he say?"

"Oh, that silly darling said, 'Don't waste the phone call unless it's an eight hundred number.' " Roxie squeezed tears from her eyes. "I'm sorry now I did."

"You'd rather be catering, wouldn't you?"

"Yes," Roxie sobbed. "Yes."

Alvirah never used vulgar language, but a familiar vulgarity almost escaped her lips. Instead, through gritted teeth, she managed to say, "I have just a few more questions and then our photographer wants to take some pictures."

Roxie's sobs ended abruptly. "Let me check my makeup."

Mel Levine, the top photographer from the *Globe,* had his marching orders: *Get good close-ups of her hands.*

• • •

Willy's oldest living sibling, Sister Cordelia, did not like to be left out of anything. Knowing that Alvirah was involved with Nelly Monahan, the woman who had shot her ex-husband in the presence of his second wife, made Cordelia decide to pay an unannounced visit to Central Park South.

Accompanied by Sister Maeve Marie, a young policewoman turned novice, Cordelia had arrived at the apartment and was ensconced in the wing chair in the living room when Alvirah arrived home. Since the chair was upholstered in handsome crimson velvet and Cordelia still wore an ankle-length habit and short veil, Alvirah had the immediate and familiar thought that if a woman pope were ever elected, she would look like Cordelia.

"Cordelia just dropped by," Willy explained, his right eyebrow lifted. That was a signal he hadn't brought Cordelia up to date on their plans.

"I hope it's not an inconvenience, Alvirah," Sister Maeve Marie apologized. "Sister Superior felt you might need our help." Maeve had the slender, disciplined body of an athlete. Her face, dominated by wide gray eyes, was strikingly handsome. Like Willy's, her expression was saying, "Sorry, Alvirah, but you know Cordelia."

"So what's going on?" Cordelia asked, getting straight to the point.

Alvirah knew there was absolutely no other choice than to tell her the truth, the whole truth and nothing but the truth. She sank down on the couch, wishing she'd had time for a peaceful cup of tea with Willy before the visit. "We have to get Nelly off. It's my fault that she went to see Tim, and I can't let her spend the rest of her life in prison."

Cordelia nodded. "So what are you going to do about it?"

"Something you may not like. Brian wrote a screenplay for Mirage Films."

"I know that. I hope he can trust them not to put a lot of smut in it. What's that got to do with Nelly Monahan, poor soul?"

"The day of the shooting, Mirage was filming a scene right outside the building where Roxie and Tim Monahan lived. We're going to try to make Roxie believe that the camera caught her twisting Nelly's hand and pointing the gun at Tim."

"You're going to fake it?" Cordelia exploded.

"Exactly. Brian got the producer to agree

to cooperate. Mel, the *Globe* photographer, took a lot of pictures of Roxie today. Besides that, we have pictures of her when Tim's body was being carried out. We've got to find a model who in a blurry long shot resembles Roxie. We'll dress her in the same kind of striped pantsuit Roxie was wearing and do a close-up of her grabbing Nelly's hand. I still have to talk Nelly into this, but I'll manage it."

Willy gave her an encouraging nod and continued the explanation. "Cordelia, we've already put a deposit on the apartment. The only furniture in the room was Tim's recliner, and it's still there. The chalk marks where the body was lying are visible. I'll take Tim's part. I mean I'll stretch out on the floor by the recliner. Nelly said Tim was wearing a gray sweat suit and moccasins."

Sister Maeve Marie's eyes were snapping with excitement. "When I was a cop we called that 'testalying.' I love it."

Willy looked at Cordelia. He knew Alvirah had every intention of carrying out her scheme. Even so, it would help if Cordelia wouldn't try to throw a monkey wrench in the plans. Alvirah was worried enough about having set up the scheme that got Nelly in so much trouble. When Cordelia didn't approve of a course of action, she had an uncanny way of convincing you it was destined for failure.

Cordelia frowned momentarily, then her brow cleared. "God writes straight in crooked lines," she said. "When are we going to film?"

Alvirah felt a wave of relief. "As soon as possible. We've got to find an actress who can impersonate Roxie." As she spoke she was looking at Sister Maeve Marie. Like Roxie, Maeve was tall and had a good figure. Like Roxie, her hands were well shaped with long fingers.

"I'm very glad you two came," she said heartily.

Two days later they were ready to close the trap. In the Christopher Street apartment where Tim Monahan had gone to his Maker, Brian was directing the action.

"Uncle Willy, just lie down there. We had to erase the chalk marks, but we penciled in the outline."

Obediently Willy stretched out by the recliner.

Brian and the cameraman stepped outside, and Brian peered through the lens, then consulted the picture of the dead Tim that the editor at the *Globe* had managed to get copied by bribing an aide in the medical examiner's office.

"You don't look fat enough," Brian decreed.

"Good news," Willy mumbled.

The problem was solved when Brian took off his sweater and stuffed it under Willy's sweatshirt.

Nelly was standing in the corner. She was wearing the blue suit and print blouse she'd worn when she visited Tim and Roxie. In her purse she was carrying a gun that looked just like the one that she had taken from the boys the other day.

Only four days ago, she thought. It doesn't seem possible. She peeked over at Dennis O'Shea, who gave her an encouraging smile. Then she glanced at Sister Maeve, who looked unnervingly like Roxie. She had on a blond wig and an exact copy of the striped suit Roxie had been wearing when she became the widow Monahan. An outsized turquoise ring reached the knuckle of her index finger. Acrylic blood-red fingernails accentuated her long fingers, and wrinkles and liver spots had been painted on the backs of her hands. Just like Roxie, Nelly thought with a touch of satisfaction as she glanced down at her own smooth skin.

Sister Cordelia was watching the proceedings with her arms folded. She reminded Nelly of the nuns she'd had in parochial school.

Brian asked if she was ready. When she nodded that she was, he said, "Then go to the door, Nelly. Try to do everything just as you did it the other day."

She looked at Willy. "Then you can't be dead yet."

As he struggled to his feet, she went to the door. "Roxie let me in," she explained. "Tim was sitting in his chair. I could tell he was very upset, but I thought it was at me or maybe even because I had told him about being terminal. Anyhow, I just walked past Roxie and went over to him and just blurted out that I wanted the truth before I died . . ."

"Do it," Brian ordered. "Maeve, you go to the door."

Nelly had rehearsed the speech she made to Tim so much that it wasn't hard to stand over the recliner and deliver it again. It wasn't hard to superimpose Tim's face over Willy's. But Willy looked concerned.

"You should start smiling," she instructed. "It was very mean of you, and you shouldn't have smiled when I told you I was dying."

Oh my God, Alvirah thought. Maybe I'm barking up the wrong tree.

"But then I forgave you because right away you admitted that you'd switched the ticket." Nelly opened her purse. "And I almost fainted because I remembered I didn't have the sunburst pin on and I opened my purse and started fumbling in it like this and Roxie saw the gun." She paused. "Wait a minute. Roxie was yelling at Tim to shut up, but when she opened the door for me, she had just said something else to him."

"It's not important," Brian said quickly. "We're not doing audio."

Nelly felt as though she were watching the replay of a videotape. It was all coming back. She grabbed the pin at the bottom of her purse and, like an echo, she could hear Roxie scream about the gun.

"I let go of the pin and grabbed the gun and pulled it out and tried to show it to her. Tim jumped up. The gun went off. Tim yelled ... what did he yell ... 'Nelly, don't go wacko. We'll split the ticket.' Then he dove for the floor."

He dove for the floor, Alvirah thought. He didn't fall. He *dove.*

It was all clear to Nelly. She thought she'd shot him and started to faint, then felt a hand close on hers, her wrist being wrenched. That's why my wrist hurts. That's the way it happened. I'm sure of it now.

But Tim had said something else, she thought. What was it? . . . Roxie, he said something to Roxie.

She felt Sister Maeve twist her hand and point the gun down at Willy, now acting out his part on the floor. *That was when I fainted.*

She let her knees cave in and sank to the floor.

"That was very good, Nelly," Brian said. "I can't believe we did it on a first take, but I think we have it. We'll just play it back to be sure, then hope to God Roxie won't see through the trick."

Nelly sat up. She reached for her purse and dug in it for the pin, which she had failed to return to Alvirah. "I wonder," she said.

Alvirah experienced that wonderful moment when instinctively she knew something important was about to happen. "What is it, Nelly?" she asked.

"Just now it was as though I was hearing Dennis teaching me how to turn on the pin. He told me that I had to give it a hard snap with this finger." She held up the index finger of her right hand.

"And that finger has been bothering me since I was here the other day. Do you think I might have turned on the recorder just before I tried to show Roxie the gun? I never checked it. Do you think it might have picked up Tim's voice pleading for his life?"

"Saints preserve us," Cordelia breathed.

The switch of the recorder in the pin Alvirah had given Nelly was still in the On position. The battery was dead, of course, but Alvirah expertly took out the tiny cassette, switched it to her pocket machine, rewound it and pushed the playback button.

Cordelia's lips moved in silent prayer as Alvirah turned it on. The sound began immediately. A shot, Tim's voice telling Nelly not to go wacko. Nelly saying, "Oh my, oh my. Oh, I'm sorry," then a harsh voice, Roxie's voice, "Tim, you bastard."

And finally Tim's pleading, "Roxie, don't. Roxie, don't shoot me!"

Alvirah felt Willy's arm around her. "You've done it again, honey."

Two nights later, Nelly insisted on cooking the celebration dinner for the six of them: Alvirah and Willy, Sisters Cordelia and Maeve Marie, and Dennis and herself.

As a former policewoman, Maeve had insisted that, with the weight of evidence, the district attorney should be brought in on the scam, and one of his best undercover agents, posing as the cameraman who'd captured the shooting, had contacted Roxie.

When Roxie saw the videotape and heard Tim's voice pleading with her not to shoot him, she'd immediately offered the undercover agent whatever he wanted to sell it to her. Then, under his skillful questioning, she admitted everything. Now Roxie was under indictment and Nelly was vindicated and declared the rightful owner of the lottery ticket.

Dennis had brought champagne. With moist eyes, Nelly acknowledged their toast and then raised one of her own. "To all of you and to Brian. I'm sorry he has to be in

Hollywood tonight, what with the earthquakes and everything."

"It's all so unbelievable," she said a few minutes later as she watched Dennis carve the succulent saddle of lamb she'd prepared with her own special recipe. The rest of the meal consisted of tomato-and-onion salad, mashed potatoes, crisp green beans, flaky biscuits, mint jelly, warm apple pie and coffee.

Nelly beamed as she accepted their compliments.

At nine o'clock Cordelia and Maeve got up to go. "Willy, I'll see you first thing in the morning," Cordelia ordered. "Bring your toolbox. I've got a bunch of jobs for you."

"We're ready to go, too. We'll drop you off," Willy told her.

"I'm not setting foot out of here until I help Nelly clean up," Alvirah announced firmly, then felt Willy's shoe tap hers.

She turned, following his gaze. Nelly and Dennis were smiling into each other's eyes.

"It's time to go home, honey," Willy said firmly as he put his hands on the back of her chair.

The
Lottery
Winner

"*A*lvirah. Come at once. I need you desperately!"

Alvirah's eyes snapped open. In a split second she emerged from a comfortable dream in which she was at a state dinner at the White House to the reality of being awakened at three in the morning by a pealing telephone, followed by the panicky voice of Baroness Min von Schreiber.

"Min, what's wrong?" she cried.

Willy grunted awake beside her. "Honey, what's the matter?" he mumbled.

Alvirah laid a soothing hand across his lips. "Sshhh." Then she repeated, "Min, what's wrong?"

Min's tragic groan rushed across the continent from the Cypress Point Spa in Pebble Beach, California, to the luxury apartment on Central Park South. "We are going to be ruined. There is a jewel thief among the guests. Mrs. Hayward's diamonds have disappeared from the wall safe in her cottage."

"Saints preserve us," Alvirah said. "What is Scott doing about it?" Scott Alshorne, the sheriff of Monterey County, had befriended Alvirah when she helped solve a murder at the spa a few years earlier.

"Oh, dear me, it's so complicated. We cannot call Scott," Min said, her voice uneven. "Nadine Hayward is hysterical. She doesn't dare admit to her husband that the insurance lapsed on the diamonds. She persuaded him to give the handling of their personal insurance policies to her son by her first marriage so he'd get the commission, and he gambled the premium check away. The insurance company would be responsible because her son was their agent, but then *he* would be prosecuted, and she can't bring herself to file a claim and have him sent to prison. So she has some wild idea of having paste copies made of the diamonds to fool her husband."

By now Alvirah was fully awake. "Having paste copies worked in "The Necklace" by de Maupassant. I wonder if Mrs. Hayward has read it."

"De MOWpassant, not de MOPpassant," Min corrected. Then she sighed heavily. "Alvirah, it is ridiculous to let anyone get away with stealing four million dollars' worth of jewelry. We can't just ignore this. Another theft could occur. You must rush here. I need you. You must take charge of identifying the culprit. As my guest, of course. And bring Willy. He could use the exercise classes. I shall assign him a personal trainer."

Fifteen hours later the limousine carrying Willy and Alvirah passed the Pebble Beach Club, then the estates lining Shore Drive. It rounded the bend, passing the tree that gave the Cypress Point Spa its name. Driving through the ornate iron gates of the spa, the car wound its way toward the main house, a rambling three-story ivory stucco mansion with pale blue shutters. Even though she was exhausted, Alvirah's eyes were snapping with anticipation.

"I love this place," she told Willy. "I hope Min gave us Tranquility. It's my favorite cottage. I remember the first time I came here. It was right after we won the lottery, and the prospect of spending a week hobnobbing with all the celebrities made me think I'd died and gone to heaven."

"I know, honey," Willy said.

"It was the beginning of finding out how the other half lives. What a lesson! Why—" Alvirah stopped suddenly, realizing she'd been about to remind Willy that when she'd helped to solve a murder at the spa, she'd almost gotten herself killed doing it.

It was obvious Willy remembered. He put his hand over hers and said, "Honey, I don't want you to get yourself in trouble worrying about somebody's lost jewelry."

"I won't. It will be fun to help out, though. It's been too quiet lately. Oh, look, there's Min."

The car had pulled up to the front door. Min came sweeping down the steps to greet them, her arms outstretched. She was wearing a blue linen dress that clung to her full but excellent figure. Her hair, not a shade different than it must have been twenty years ago, was twirled in an elaborate French twist. She was wearing pearl and gold earrings and a matching necklace; as always, she looked as though she had stepped out of a page in *Vogue.*

"And to think she's five years older than me," Alvirah muttered in awe. Behind Min, a stately Baron Helmut von Schreiber descended, his military carriage making him seem taller than his five feet seven. His perfectly trimmed goatee drifted a bit in the breeze as his welcoming smile revealed perfect teeth. Only the crinkles around his blue-gray eyes hinted that he was in his early fifties.

The chauffeur hopped out to open the door, but Min beat him to it. "You are true friends," she gushed, her arms open to embrace them. Suddenly she stopped and stared. "Alvirah, where did you buy that suit? It is well cut, but you must not wear beige. It washes you out." Then she stopped again, shaking her head this time. "Oh, but all of that will wait."

The chauffeur was directed to take the luggage to Tranquility cottage. "A maid will un-pack for you," Min informed them. "We must talk."

Obediently they followed her up to her sumptuous office on the second floor of the mansion. Helmut closed the door and went over to the sideboard. "Iced tea, beer, some-thing stronger?" he asked.

Alvirah always was tickled by the fact that absolutely no liquor was allowed on the premises of Cypress Point Spa—except in Min and Helmut's private quarters. She opted for iced tea. Willy looked pathetically grateful at the thought of a beer. Really, she thought, it had been mean to roust him out of bed in the middle of the night, but it was the only way they could make the nine o'clock flight.

Even then, they hadn't been able to get in first class, and each of them was squeezed into a middle seat, between other people. Willy's first words when they got off the plane were, "Honey, I didn't know how much I'd gotten used to the good life."

Sipping the iced tea, Alvirah got right to the point. "Min, exactly what happened? When was the robbery discovered?"

"Late yesterday afternoon. Nadine Hayward arrived on Saturday, so she'd been here three days. Her husband is staying at their condo in the Pebble Beach Club. He's in a golf tournament there. They're going on to San Francisco for a charity ball, so Nadine brought all her best jewelry and put it in the wall safe in her cottage."

"She's been here before?" Alvirah asked.

"Regularly. Ever since she married Cotter Hayward, she comes to the spa whenever he's in one of his tournaments. He's a fine amateur golfer."

Alvirah frowned. "That's what's been throwing me. There was another woman named Hayward one of the times I was here —a couple of years ago. She was Mrs. Cotter Hayward too."

"That was the first wife, Elyse. She still visits the spa, but usually not at the same time as Nadine. Even though she loathes Cotter, she was not happy about being replaced, especially since she unfortunately introduced the new wife to him."

"They fell in love under this roof," Helmut said with a sigh. "These things happen. But to complicate matters, Elyse is also a guest this week."

"Wait a minute," Alvirah said. "You mean

to tell me that Elyse and Nadine are both here?"

"That's exactly it. Naturally we have placed them at tables distant from each other in the dining room and arranged their schedules so they should never be in the same exercise classes."

"Alvirah, honey, I think you're getting off the subject," Willy suggested. "Why don't you stick to finding out about the robbery and then maybe we can go over to the cottage and catch a nap?"

"Oh, Willy, I'm sorry." Alvirah shook her head. "I'm so inconsiderate. Willy needs more sleep than I do, and he couldn't close an eye on the plane. His seat was between two kids who were playing checkers on his tray table. The parents wouldn't let them sit together because they fight so much."

"Why didn't the parents sit with them?" Min asked.

"They had their hands full with three-year-old twins, and you know how good hearted Willy is."

"The robbery," Willy prompted.

"This is what happened," Min said. "At five o'clock Nadine had gone to the salon to have her hair recombed. She got back to Repose cottage at ten minutes of six to find it torn apart. All the drawers had been rifled, her suitcases pulled out. Someone, or perhaps several people, had thoroughly searched every inch of the cottage."

"What were they looking for?" Alvirah asked.

"The jewelry, of course. You know how everyone gets dressed up for the evening. The women love to show off their gems to each other. Nadine had worn a diamond necklace and bracelet the night before. Someone was looking for those pieces but couldn't know that she also had the Hayward tiara, rings and two other bracelets with her as well." Min sighed then burst out, "Why did the stupid woman have to bring everything she owned? Surely she couldn't wear all of that to the charity ball."

Helmut patted her hand. "Minna, Minna, I cannot allow you to let your blood pressure rise. Think beautiful thoughts." He took up the story. "What is odd is that the intruder apparently stumbled onto the safe only after searching through everything else. It is hidden behind the picture of Minna and myself in the sitting room of the cottage."

"Wait a minute," Alvirah interrupted. "You

267

just said that you thought someone must have seen Nadine wearing the jewelry the night before. Did she leave the spa that evening?"

"No. She was at what we jokingly call the cocktail hour, then at dinner, then at the Mozart recital in the music room."

"Then the only people who would have seen her are the other guests and the staff, and every one of them would know enough to look for the safe. All the cottages have one now." Alvirah sucked in her breath and smoothed the skirt of the beige suit she had been sure would find approval in Min's eyes. I did forget that she said beige washes me out, she thought ruefully. Oh, well.

She resumed her train of thought. "That's something else. Was the safe jimmied?"

"No. Someone knew the combination Nadine had set."

"Or was a professional and knew how to find it," Willy added. "What makes you think the thief isn't a thousand miles away right now?"

Min sighed. "Our only hope is that if it was an inside job and Alvirah can track down the perpetrator, we may be able to force him or her to return the gems. All the guests are known to us. Their reputations are impeccable. There are only three new staff members, and their movements are absolutely accounted for." Min looked suddenly ten years older. "Alvirah, this is the sort of problem that can ruin us. Cotter Hayward is a very difficult man. He will not only prosecute Nadine's son, but I also wouldn't put it past him to find some reason to hold us responsible for the theft."

"When is Nadine supposed to leave for San Francisco and the charity ball?" Alvirah asked.

"On Saturday. That gives you three days to perform a miracle."

A two-hour nap and a luxurious shower revived Alvirah. Anxious for Min's approval, she settled at the dressing table and applied her makeup carefully. Not too much blush, she thought, don't go over the lip line, just a touch of eyeliner, use dark powder to soften the contour of jaw and nose. She was glad to hear Willy singing in the shower. He was feeling better as well.

On the bed she had laid out a handsome caftan that Min had selected for her during her last visit to the spa. After she slipped into it she fastened on her sunburst pin and got out her notebook. While Willy dressed, she jotted down the information Min had given her, breaking it into categories.

When she was finished, she had several immediate questions. Why was Elyse Hayward, the first Mrs. Cotter Hayward, here? Coincidence? Helmut had indicated that Elyse usually avoided being at the spa at the same time as her former friend, Nadine.

Interesting, Alvirah thought.

The three new staff members worked in the Roman Bath, which was the newest attraction at the spa. It had taken two years to complete, but was truly splendid, a replica of the one in Baden-Baden. Two of the newcomers were masseuses, the third was an attendant in the resting room. But Min had said that their movements were accounted for. Even so, Alvirah decided, I'll go to the Roman Bath and at least take a look at the three of them.

Willy appeared at the door of the sitting room. "Do I pass inspection to mingle with the swells?"

His fine head of wavy white hair framed his genial features and warm blue eyes. A handsome navy sports jacket hid the paunch that reappeared whenever they dined lavishly on a cruise. "You look splendid," Alvirah beamed.

"So do you. Hurry up, honey. I can't wait to have one of Min's fake cocktails."

The veranda was already filled with guests. Violin music from inside the mansion drifted through the open windows. As they walked up the path, Alvirah said, "Now remember, Min is going to introduce us to Nadine Hayward. Nadine knows we're here to help and that later on we're going to stop back at her cottage and get a real chance to talk to her."

Since they'd won the lottery, Alvirah had been coming to the spa at least once a year. Willy would sometimes pick her up at the end of her week and they'd go on to take a trip, but this would be his first overnight stay.

"Honey, what have I got to say to those people?" he'd ask when she'd urge him to accompany her. "The guys talk about their golf game or bat the breeze about the cutups they were in their Ivy League schools or how their companies are investing in Asia. Do I tell them that I was born in Brooklyn, went to

P.S. 38 and was a working plumber until we struck it rich in the lottery? Do you think they care that my hobby now is to trot around the world with you and, when we're in New York, to fix pipes and sinks and toilets for people who need help?"

"There isn't one of them who wouldn't die happy knowing he has two million dollars a year less taxes coming in," was Alvirah's answer. Still she admitted to herself that she *was* a little concerned that somebody might try to put Willy down with one of those sweetly chilling remarks that could cut like a knife. Anyone tried that on her and she could give as good as she got, but Willy was too kind to zing anyone.

Five minutes later she realized she needn't have worried. Willy was deep in conversation with the CEO of American Plumbing, explaining to him exactly why his biggest competitor's highly touted new line of hydro-flush toilets were totally impractical for the average home. As Alvirah watched, the CEO's expression became more and more delighted.

Tanned, tinted and handsomely dressed men and women were clustered in little groups. Alvirah chuckled over a remark she overheard one woman make to another: "Darling, you don't know me well enough yet to dislike me."

Then Min plucked at her sleeve. "Alvirah, I want you to meet Nadine Hayward."

Alvirah turned swiftly. She didn't know what she'd expected, but it wasn't this very pretty, sweet-faced, blue-eyed blonde with a peaches-and-cream complexion. She could pass for thirty and probably is in her early forties, Alvirah decided, but boy, she must be nervous. She looks as though she got dressed during a fire drill. Nadine Hayward was wearing a lime green shantung outfit with wide trousers and a waist-length jacket. It had obviously cost a fortune, but it looked all wrong. The middle button of the jacket wasn't fastened. Black pumps were a discordant note against the silvery sheen of the outfit. Nadine's dark blond hair was carelessly twisted into a chignon. A single strand of pearls was slipping under the neckline of the pale green shell.

As Alvirah watched, Nadine's expression changed to sheer panic. "Oh, my God! My husband is coming," she murmured.

"I thought you said he was attending a golf dinner at the club," Min hissed.

"He was supposed to, but . . ." Nadine's voice trailed off, and she clutched Min's arm.

Alvirah glanced at the path. A tall man was winding his way up toward the veranda. "When he heard Elyse was here he told me I wouldn't see him till Saturday," Nadine whispered through now bloodless lips.

Around them people were chatting and laughing. But Alvirah caught several sets of eyes appraising them. The tension emanating from Nadine Hayward was palpable.

"Smile," she ordered firmly. "Button your jacket . . . Fix your pearls . . . That's better."

"But he doesn't know the jewelry's missing. He'll wonder why I'm not wearing any of it," Nadine moaned.

Cotter Hayward was at the stairs. Sotto voce, Alvirah urged, "For your son's sake, you've got to fake this until I get a chance to help you out."

At the mention of her son, an expression of pain came into Nadine's eyes, then was gone. "I did a bit of acting way back," she said. Now her smile seemed genuine, and a moment later when her husband came up the steps and touched her arm, her reaction of astonished pleasure was flawless.

I don't like this guy, Alvirah thought as Hayward curtly acknowledged the introduction to her, then turned to his wife. "I imagine they'll let me stay for dinner here," he said. "I have to get back in time for the speeches, but I wanted to see you."

"You are most welcome," Min said. "Would you and Nadine prefer to have a small table to yourselves, or did you want to join her at her group table?"

"No groups, please," Hayward said dismissively.

He dyes his hair, Alvirah thought. Good job, but I can tell. Nobody in his fifties is that blond. But Cotter Hayward was a handsome man, no getting around that.

It was Min and Helmut's firm rule that their guests share tables of eight. The only exception was if a guest had a visitor and needed a chance to talk privately. In that case, never more than once a week, a table for two was available.

Tonight, Alvirah was delighted to see that Min had placed her and Willy at the group table with Elyse, the first Mrs. Cotter Hayward, who turned out to be a brittle, pencil-thin, auburn-haired fashion plate in her mid-forties. A handsome older couple from Chicago named Jennings; a stunning woman in her late thirties, Barra Snow, a model whom Alvirah instantly recognized from the Adrian Cosmetics ads; Michael Fields, an ex-congressman from New York; and Herbert Green, the plumbing CEO, were the other diners at table eight.

Alvirah managed to maneuver it so that she was only one seat away from Elyse Cotter. It quickly became obvious to her that Elyse was extremely vocal about both her former husband and her former friend. "Nadine doesn't look like Sparkle Plenty tonight," she observed caustically. "I wonder if that's a matter of choice or if Cotter has started using his favorite line about keeping the jewelry in a bank vault because he worries about a robbery. If so, it means he's met someone else and Nadine's days are numbered." Her smile was not pleasant. "I should know."

"Nadine was wearing some of the Hayward jewelry the other night," Barra Snow said. "You had dinner served in your cottage, Elyse."

Alvirah perked up her ears and switched on the recording device in her sunburst pin. Had it been just an accident that Cotter Hayward's first wife mentioned a robbery? She'd

276

have to call Charley Evans, her editor at the *Globe,* and ask him to send her some background on all the Haywards from the newspaper morgue.

Let's see, she thought as she selected a tiny loin lamb chop from the silver platter the waitress was holding, when I was here four years ago, Elyse was still married to Cotter, so Nadine hasn't been in the picture too long. It's obvious Elyse was born with a silver spoon in her mouth, but I can tell from her voice that Nadine isn't a graduate of Miss Porter's. Wonder how she got so close to the Haywards in the first place?

"Honey, you're still holding the serving fork," Willy prodded.

At a table near the picture window overlooking the pool and gardens, Nadine and Cotter Hayward ate in almost total silence. When Cotter spoke it was usually to complain.

Then came the question Nadine dreaded. "How come you're not wearing any decent jewelry? Every other woman in this place is showing off her trophies; surely yours must be some of the finest."

Nadine managed to keep her voice even.

"I didn't think it was in the best taste to dangle them in front of Elyse. After all *she* was wearing them when she came here a few years ago."

Her fingers damp with perspiration, she watched her husband's reaction and inwardly collapsed with relief when he nodded. "I suppose you're right. Now I've got to get back. Those after-dinner speeches will be starting."

As he got up, he leaned over quickly and brushed her cheek with an impatient kiss. The way he would have kissed Elyse toward the end of their marriage, Nadine thought. Oh dear God, what am I going to do?

She watched him walk across the spacious room and then was astonished to see Elyse hurrying toward him. Even though Nadine could only see the back of his head, Cotter's body language was obvious. He stopped abruptly, went rigid, and then after Elyse spoke to him, pushed her aside and hurried out.

Nadine was sure that Elyse had reminded him that the final divorce payment was owed to her next week. Three million dollars. Cotter was infuriated at the prospect of paying it. And I'm paying for it as well, Nadine thought.

After what Elyse cost him, the prenuptial I signed will leave me penniless if he gets angry enough about the jewelry to divorce me . . .

Now what did Elyse have to say to her ex? Alvirah wondered, as she nibbled on a tiny cookie and tried to make the rainbow sherbet last. From where she was sitting she could see the expression of savage satisfaction on the divorcée's face and the angry dark red flush that colored Cotter Hayward's features.

"My, my," Barra Snow murmured with a slight smile. "I didn't know fireworks were on the menu."

"Do you know the Haywards well?" Alvirah asked casually.

"We have mutual friends and occasionally are in the same place."

Willy jumped up to hold Elyse Hayward's chair as she returned to the table, a grim smile on her face. "Well, I made his day," she said with obvious delight. "There's nothing that drives Cotter crazier than parting with money." She laughed. "His lawyers have been trying to negotiate a settlement. Instead of a final three-million-dollar payment next

week, they'd like me to accept annual install-
ments for the next twenty years. The answer
I gave them is that I didn't win a lottery, I
divorced a rich man.''

That's for our benefit, Alvirah thought. ''It
depends on the annual installment,'' she
murmured.

Herbert Green, the plumbing executive,
chuckled. ''I like your wife,'' he told Willy.

''So do I.'' Willy had just finished his sherbet. ''That was a great dinner, but I have to
say I'd like to top it off with a Big Mac.''

Barra laughed. ''I'm glad you feel like that.
My sister was awarded a McDonald franchise
in her divorce. I wasn't that lucky.''

''Neither will Nadine be when Cotter tires
of her,'' Elyse volunteered. ''Here's her settlement.'' She touched her thumb to the tip of
her forefinger to form a perfect circle. Her
meaning was very clear. ''Nadine's a perfect
example of why we should obey the ninth
commandment.''

''Thou shalt not covet thy neighbor's wife,''
Willy said.

''Or *husband*.'' Elyse laughed. ''Nadine's
problem is that she was unlucky enough to
get mine.''

• • •

Nadine Hayward did not wait for the recital in the music room. Instead she slipped away from the dining room with the first people to leave and made her way to her cottage, which was one of the farthest from the main house.

It's Wednesday night, she thought. Saturday morning Cotter will come for me. I'll have to tell him about the robbery. He'll want to know why I didn't call the police immediately. Then I'll have to tell him that Bobby didn't pay the insurance premium to the company. And Bobby will be prosecuted.

I can't let that happen.

If only I hadn't come here four years ago and met Cotter.

It was the thought she had been trying to avoid.

As she turned off the main path to her cottage, Nadine was filled with self-loathing and regret that she had ever met Cotter. My one extravagance, she thought, coming here after Robert died, and I had to meet him.

Her first husband had been Robert Crandell, a distant cousin of Elyse's, handsome and bright and witty and loving. And a gambler. She'd married him at twenty, divorced him when Bobby was ten. It was the only way to separate herself from his debts. But they'd remained friends. More than friends. I always loved him, she thought now.

He'd been killed nearly five years ago, driving too fast on a rain-slick highway, still a gambler, still untrustworthy. But he'd left an insurance policy that was enough to take care of Bobby's college education, and it was the relief of discovering this fact, coupled with the emotional drain of his death, that impelled Nadine to treat herself to a week at Cypress Point Spa.

When she was still married to Robert, she'd occasionally met Cotter and Elyse at family events. By the time she met them again, at the spa, it was clear that they were barely speaking to each other. Three months later, Cotter phoned. "I'm in the process of a divorce," he'd announced, "because I haven't been able to stop thinking about you."

Thoughtful. Charming. Oh, how Cotter could turn on the charm. "You've never had it easy, Nadine," he said. It's time someone took care of you. I know what you went through with Robert. It's a miracle he wasn't murdered. Those bookies play rough when you welsh on debts. I bailed him out from time to time. I don't think you knew that."

He had never bailed Robert out, Nadine thought as she put the key in the door of her cottage. Cotter never bailed anyone out.

Before she could turn the key, the door opened and the frightened face of her twenty-two-year-old son stared down at her. Then Bobby threw his arms around her. "Mom, help me. What am I going to do?"

Alvirah and Willy lingered over decaf espresso with the other guests at their table, hoping to pick up more gossip, but to Alvirah's disappointment Elyse dropped the subject of her ex-husband.

"Are you attending the recital, Mrs. Meehan?" Barra Snow asked.

"We're still on New York time," Alvirah said. After Elyse's crack about the lottery, it was on the tip of her tongue to say that they were going to hit the sack, but she decided against it. "I think we'd better retire," she finished.

At a demure pace, Alvirah led Willy through the dining room; as soon as they were outside, however, she quickened her step. "Let's go," she said. "I'm dying to talk to Nadine. From what I'm learning about Cotter Hayward's attitude toward money, there's no doubt that he won't be talked out of reporting the theft to the insurance company."

When they arrived at Nadine's cottage, they were surprised to hear the murmur of voices through the open window. "I wonder if the husband came back," Alvirah whispered, but at her knock the door was opened by a handsome young man who even in the half-light she could see was the image of Nadine.

Sitting opposite them on the pale blue and white sofas in the harmoniously decorated sitting room, Willy and Alvirah waited as Nadine told Bobby that the Meehans knew all about the theft and were there to help.

It was clear to Alvirah that Bobby was desperately worried, but even so she did not like it when he tried to justify his own chicanery. "Mom, I swear to you this is the first time I ever cashed a premium check," he said, his voice shrill. "I'd made a bet. It was a sure thing."

" 'A sure thing.' " Nadine's voice broke into a near sob. "Your father's words. I heard them for the first time when I was nineteen years old. I don't want to hear them anymore."

"Mom, I was going to reinstate the policy, I swear."

"Wasn't there a notice of termination sent?" Alvirah asked.

Bobby looked away. "I knew it was coming."

"And destroyed it?" Alvirah persisted.

"Yes."

"That's also a criminal offense," she said severely.

"Bobby," Nadine cried, "I persuaded Cotter to switch the jewelry insurance to you because you'd gotten the job with Haskill. Then I persuaded him to let you live in the New York apartment."

So like his father, she thought. The repentant face, the dejected slump of the shoulders.

It was as though Bobby knew what she was thinking. "Mom, I'm not like Dad, not that way. Any time I bet before, it was with my money."

"Not always. I've covered some of your losses."

"But never a lot. Mom, if you can talk Cotter into not prosecuting, I swear, never, never again. I don't want to go to prison."

Bobby buried his face in his hands.

Nadine put her arms around him. "Bobby,"

she said. "Don't you see? I'm helpless to stop him."

Then she paused. "Or am I?"

An hour later, when Willy and Alvirah were settled in bed, Alvirah began to think aloud. "Nadine's son, Bobby, is what I would call spineless and more than a little selfish. I mean, when you think about it, his mother persuaded Cotter Hayward to switch the insurance policy on the jewelry to him so he'd get the commission, then he gambles away the premium. And my feeling is that he's more worried about the prospect of going to prison than he is about the fact that the fallout of all this might mean the end of Nadine's marriage."

"Uh-huh," Willy agreed, his tone sleepy.

"Not that I think Cotter Hayward is any prize," Alvirah continued. "He reminds me of Mr. Parker. You remember I cleaned for the Parkers on Wednesdays until they moved to Florida. I think she died. The nice ones always die, don't they, and the mean old birds hang around forever. Anyhow—picky, picky, picky! That's the way he was. And *cheap!* One day Mr. Parker yelled at his poor wife for giving away an old suit of his. He had a closet full of clothes but couldn't stand to let so much as an odd sock get away."

Willy's even breathing was his only comment.

"The only way to save Bobby Crandell from prison is to find the thief," Alvirah mused aloud. "The thing is that the night of the robbery, Nadine locked the front door of the cottage, but since Bobby said he was able to get in through the sliding glass door of the sunroom tonight, it stands to reason that anyone else could have done the same thing. Nobody really worries about locks around here."

And then a thought shot through her mind that made her gasp. How heavy a gambler was Bobby Crandell? He knew his mother had the jewelry with her. Nadine had told them that the combination she always set when she used a wall safe in a spa or hotel was the year of her birth, 1-9-5-3. Bobby probably knew that.

Alvirah pondered the notion that Bobby Crandell might have been in deep trouble because of gambling debts. Suppose his life had been threatened if he didn't produce the money he owed? Suppose he owed very big

287

money? Suppose he decided to steal the jewelry even though he had already stolen the premium money? Maybe he was desperate enough to hope that his mother could persuade Cotter Hayward not to file a claim for the missing jewelry, she thought.

Alvirah had another question to ask herself before she fell asleep. Why did Cotter Hayward suddenly decide to have dinner with Nadine tonight?

The call came at eleven o'clock, shortly after he had retired. Still wide awake, Cotter Hayward reached for the receiver and barked a greeting.

Hayward got out of bed and dressed in chinos and a sweater. Then, as an afterthought, he made a martini. I probably shouldn't have one, he told himself sourly. But given the way his night had gone, he could certainly use it.

At quarter of twelve he left his condo on the grounds of the Pebble Beach Club and, walking in the shadows, made his way to the sixteenth hole. Standing in the wooded area off the green, he waited.

The faint snap of a twig alerted him to an approaching presence. He turned around, expectantly. Just then the clouds parted. In the instant before he died, Cotter Hayward lived a lifetime. He saw his assailant, realized that it was a golf club that was about to descend on his skull and even had time to recognize how much of a fool he had been.

At 5:45 A.M. Alvirah was dreaming that they were sailing from Southampton on the *QE2.* Then she realized that the sound she was hearing was not a ship's bell but the peal of the telephone. It was Min.

"Alvirah, please come up to the main house immediately. There is a problem."

Alvirah struggled into a pale yellow Dior sweat suit and matching sneakers, as Willy blinked sleep from his eyes. "What's the matter now?" he asked.

"I don't know yet. Oh darn if I didn't put this top on backwards."

Willy squinted in the direction of the clock. "I thought people came to this place to relax."

"Some people do. Hurry up and get dressed so you can go with me. I've got a bad feeling."

A few minutes later Alvirah's bad feeling

was compounded by the presence at the spa's main entrance of a car bearing the logo of the sheriff of Monterey County. "Scott's here," she said tersely.

Scott Alshorne was in Min's office. Min and Helmut were still in dressing gowns. Even though they both seemed distraught, Alvirah could not resist a moment of total admiration for the way the two of them could look like fashion plates even when roused from bed in the predawn hours. Min's robe was a shimmering pink satin with a lace-edged collar and delicately corded sash. Helmut's maroon knee-length silk robe was trimly handsome over matching pajamas.

Fortunately Sheriff Alshorne never changed. His teddy-bear body, his craggy and tanned face, his white, unmanageable hair and piercing eyes were still the same. He was as warm when he embraced a friend as he was implacable when he was trailing a criminal.

He hugged Alvirah and shook hands with Willy. Then, dispensing with small talk, he said, "Cotter Hayward's body was found on the grounds of the Pebble Beach Club an hour ago by a maintenance man."

"Saints preserve us," Alvirah gasped, even

as she thought, Which one did it, Nadine or Bobby?

"Vicious blows with a heavy object. Whoever killed him wanted to make sure he was dead." Scott looked at Alvirah appraisingly. "From what Min tells me, you're not here just to be pampered."

"Not exactly." Alvirah's mind was racing. "Does Nadine know about her husband?"

"Scott came directly here," Min said. "We will accompany him when he tells her. Helmut's medical services may be required. I only wish I knew where to reach Nadine's son so he can rush to her side."

"Bobby's—" Willy was interrupted by a warning glance from Alvirah.

The exchange was not lost on Scott Alshorne. "Do you know this Bobby?" he asked.

"We've met," Alvirah hedged, then realized it would be useless to conceal from Scott the fact that Bobby Crandell had been in Nadine's cottage at ten o'clock last night.

"Is he staying with his mother?" Scott queried.

"He was going to last night," Alvirah admitted. "Nadine is in one of the two-bedroom cottages."

Scott stood up, suddenly looming over the

others. "Alvirah, my good friend," he said, "let's get something straight. There was a major theft on these premises three days ago. I should have been notified—*immediately*. Min has given me the background, but that doesn't justify her decision to go along with Nadine Hayward and conceal the crime. What you people don't seem to understand is that we should have been collecting samples for DNA testing at the safe. Now it's too late."

He moved closer to Alvirah. "Instead of sending for me, she sent for you. Now we have not only a grand larceny theft but a first degree murder on our hands. I want any information you've picked up since you arrived here yesterday. Do I make myself clear?"

"I want to make *myself* clear too," Willy said, and his tone was icy. "Don't bully my wife."

"Oh, honey, Scott's not bullying me," Alvirah said soothingly. "It's just his version of the Miranda warning." She looked up at Scott. "I know what you're thinking—that Nadine and Bobby are the likely suspects. But I also know you're a big man and will keep an open mind. I met Cotter Hayward a few years ago when he was here with his then-wife, Elyse. They weren't exactly lovey-dovey at the time, and, believe me, from what I saw last night that lady hated him. But she had nothing to gain by killing him, or at least not as far as I know. Then again, I bet Cotter Hayward had a lot of enemies, so before you jump to conclusions, take a good look at some of the men in that golf tournament and find out which of them might have had a reason to hate him too."

Min pointed to the clock. "It is going on to six-thirty," she said nervously. "The morning walk will be starting in fifteen minutes. We must let Nadine know what has happened."

"And I think Elyse should find out, too, before the rumors start flying," Alvirah suggested. "If you'd like, I'll go to her cottage and talk to her."

"Not without me," Scott snapped, and then added with a reluctant grin, "All right, Alvirah. You can come along when we see Hayward's widow."

Min and Helmut rushed upstairs to change into jogging suits, and then the somber procession left the main house. Willy elected to go to their own cottage. "I'll only be in the way," he said.

Maids carrying breakfast trays passed

them as they walked down the winding path to Nadine's cottage. Alvirah could feel their curious stares.

As it turned out, Helmut's medical services were indeed needed. Nadine was in the sitting room when they arrived. She looked as though she had not closed her eyes all night. Alvirah noticed immediately that her robe was inside out. Must have put it on in a real hurry, she thought. Why?

Nadine's peaches-and-cream complexion went ashen when she saw them. "What's wrong? Has anything happened to Bobby?"

So that's it, Alvirah thought. Bobby's taken off and she doesn't know where he's gone. She watched as Min and Helmut stood protectively by Nadine as Scott told her that her husband had been the victim of foul play.

Nadine said nothing. Then she sighed and slumped over in a dead faint.

"If Nadine was a wreck, you should have seen Bobby," Alvirah told Willy an hour later. "He came in while Helmut was trying to revive his mother, and I guess he thought she was dead. He'd been crying, you could see that. He pushed Helmut aside and kept saying, 'Mom, it's my fault, I'm sorry. I'm sorry.' "

"Did he mean sorry about stealing the premium, or had they had an argument?" Willy asked.

"That's what I'm trying to figure out. When Nadine came to and Helmut gave her a sedative and put her to bed, Scott talked to Bobby. But all he said was that he couldn't sleep and got up to go for a jog. Then he said he didn't have another word to say until he hired a lawyer."

Willy whistled soundlessly. "That doesn't sound like an innocent man talking."

Alvirah nodded reluctantly. "You can tell he's not really a bad kid, Willy, and he certainly loves his mother, but I do think he's the kind who doesn't think things through. I mean, I hate to say it, but I could see him deciding that if Cotter Hayward were out of the way, his mother would never have to report the missing jewelry."

Willy handed her a cup of coffee. "You haven't had anything to eat. The maid left a thermos and what passes for a muffin. You need a magnifying glass to see it on the plate."

"Nine hundred calories a day, honey.

That's why people look so good when they leave here." Alvirah devoured the muffin in one bite. "But you know what was interesting? When we went to tell Elyse about her ex-husband, she went hysterical."

"I thought she couldn't stand him."

"So did I. And maybe she couldn't. But she knew that Cotter Hayward was so afraid of dying that he would never make a will. He has no children, so that means—"

". . . that Nadine may be a very wealthy widow," Willy finished. "And I guess now her son can afford to hire a good lawyer."

At twelve o'clock, Scott returned to the spa with a search warrant for Nadine's cottage. By then the media were camped outside the compound and police barricades had been erected to hold them back.

Sheriff Alshorne was besieged for a statement. He got out of his car and stood before the cameras and microphones. "The investigation is proceeding," he said. "The autopsy is presently taking place. You will be kept informed of developments."

Questions were shouted at him: "Sheriff, is it true that Mrs. Hayward's son has retained a lawyer?" "Is it true that Mrs. Hayward's jewelry was stolen a few days ago and you were not informed?" "Is it true that Mr. Hayward had a confrontation with his ex-wife last night at dinner?"

"No comment," Scott said tersely in response to each question hurled at him. He got back in his car and snapped, "Step on it," to his deputy. They were waved past the barricade and escaped onto the spa grounds. "I wonder how many of the employees will sell their inside stories to the scandal sheets," he fumed as they headed to the widow's cottage.

Nadine was dressed and, although deathly pale, she was completely composed. "I understand," she said tonelessly when Scott showed her the search warrant. "I don't know what you're looking for and I'm very sure you won't find anything incriminating, but go ahead."

"Where is your son?" Scott asked.

"I sent him over to the Roman Bath. The massage and swim treatment will be good for him."

"He does understand that he is not to leave the premises?"

"I gather you made that quite clear. Now

if you'll excuse me, I'll be in Baroness von Schreiber's office. She is helping me make arrangements for my husband's cremation when his body is released."

The search of the cottage was thorough and the results were nil. Exasperated, Scott studied the wall safe. "This is a pretty good one," he commented to a deputy. "It wasn't jimmied, so that means if it wasn't a professional safecracker, whoever took those gems had the combination."

"The son?"

"He was in his New York office Wednesday morning. The jewelry disappeared Tuesday afternoon. We're checking the red-eye flights, but of course he may not have used his own name if he was on one of them."

It was in the second bedroom, the one in which Bobby had slept, that Scott found something that he felt was significant—Nadine's pocket-sized phone directory, wedged open by the base of the telephone to the *H* page. The first five telephone numbers were listings for Cotter Hayward, his office, his boat, the New York apartment, the New Mexico ranch, the Pebble Beach condo.

"Bobby was in here last night," Scott said. "Cotter was at the Pebble Beach condo. I wonder if our friend Bobby placed a call to him and arranged a private meeting."

It was the custom of the Cypress Point Spa that luncheon was served informally at tables around the pool. Most of the guests were dressed in tank suits and robes. The ones who had completed the morning program and were planning on an afternoon of golf on the spa's newly installed nine-hole course were suitably garbed for a few hours on the links.

Alvirah had no intention of following either a beauty or exercise regime, and she'd never held a golf club. Nonetheless, she changed hastily into the dark blue tank suit and pink terry-cloth robe that were part of the standard equipment of every cottage. She had prevailed on Willy to likewise clad himself in the bathing trunks and short robe that were standard for male guests.

"We don't want to stand out," she'd urged him. "I need to get a feel of what people are saying about the murder."

She realized it probably would look tacky

to wear her sunburst pin on the robe. Even the women who looked like Christmas trees at the evening "cocktail" party wouldn't do that. Nevertheless she fastened the pin to her lapel. She turned the recording device on as they approached the pool. She didn't want to miss a word of what people would be saying about the murder.

Alvirah was surprised to see Elyse sitting at one of the tables with Barra Snow and other guests. "Come on, honey," she hissed to Willy, noting that there were still two seats available at the table.

Now appearing totally composed, Elyse had eschewed the spa-issue tank suit and robe and was wearing a striped cotton shirt, white skirt and golf shoes. "A terrible shock," she was saying to the woman who had just approached the table to speak to her. "After all, I was married to Cotter for fifteen years, and at least some of those times were happy. Thanks to him I took up golf, and for that I'll always be grateful. He was an excellent teacher. That's what really kept us together so long. I think that long after we were sick of each other we still enjoyed playing golf together."

"Are you sure you want to play this after-

300

noon? We can get someone to fill in the foursome."

The woman who was talking to Elyse was another one of the slim, tanned, elegant types with an almost-English accent. She only looks familiar because she's a clone of half the women here, Alvirah decided after studying her a few moments.

Barra Snow answered for Elyse. "I'm certain Elyse will be better off if she plays with us. I've already asked a caddy to get her clubs from her car. She mustn't just sit and brood."

"I am not brooding," Elyse contradicted sharply. "Really, Barra, if you insist on offering sympathy, save it for Nadine. I hear that Bobby was with her last night, and I gather she wasn't expecting him. I'd love to know what kind of scrape he's in now. Nadine had to beg money from Cotter to bail him out the last time. He's going to be just like his father, that boy."

Alvirah remembered that Elyse was a distant cousin of Bobby's late father. How did she know that Nadine bailed Bobby out? she wondered. Did she hear that from Cotter? She thought about Elyse's hysterical reaction to the news of the death. Was it just because Nadine will inherit a lot of money, or was there a love/hate relationship with her ex-husband? Interesting, she decided.

The Jennings woman who had been at their table the night before hurried over. "I just heard on the television that the rumor is that Nadine's jewelry was stolen the other day. Isn't that incredible?"

"The jewelry," Elyse gasped. "The Hayward jewelry! My God, did Cotter know that? That stuff was in his family for three generations. They never gave it to the wife, you know. She was just allowed to wear it. His father was married four times, and the joke was that all four wives had their portraits done in the same pieces. They were known as the Hayward chorus line. I thought Nadine would finally be the one to keep everything. Cotter was the last of the line."

She's thrilled it's been stolen, Alvirah thought, or else she's a good actress.

A genial-looking man in the uniform of a spa caddy approached the table, a golf bag over his shoulder. "I have your clubs, Mrs. Hayward," he said, as he put the bag down, "but I think I'd better clean the sand wedge off. The sleeve is missing, and it's a bit sticky."

"That's ridiculous," Elyse snapped. "All the clubs were cleaned before they were put back in the bag."

Sticky? Alvirah's antennae began to vibrate. She jumped up and said, "I'll take a look at that, please."

She took the golf bag from the startled caddy and looked down into it. Being careful not to touch any of the clubs, she leaned over and studied the one that did not have a sleeve covering it. The curved steel head of that club was matted with dark brown stains. Even with her naked eye it was possible to see bits of skin and hair sticking to the metal.

"Somebody call Sheriff Alshorne," Alvirah said quietly. "Tell him I think I've found the murder weapon."

Two hours later, Alvirah and Willy were visited in their cottage by Sheriff Scott Alshorne.

"That was good work, Alvirah," Scott admitted somewhat grudgingly. "If that caddy had cleaned the club, valuable evidence would have been lost."

"DNA?" Alvirah asked.

Alshorne shrugged. "Maybe. We do know

that it was the murder weapon, and we know it came from the ex-wife's golf bag, which was in the trunk of her unlocked car in the parking area."

"Meaning anyone could have taken it and replaced it," Willy commented.

"Anyone who knew it was there," Alvirah said. "Right, Scott?"

"Yes."

"I didn't touch that club, but it looked like it must have made a pretty nasty weapon. Am I right?"

Alvirah's forehead was furrowed, always a sign that, as she put it, she had her thinking cap on.

"Yes, it made a formidable weapon," Scott agreed. "The sand wedge is the heaviest golf club."

"I didn't know that. If I were going to bop someone on the skull with a golf club I'd have grabbed just any one of them, I think."

"Alvirah," Scott said, shaking his head, "maybe I'll just have to hire you. Yes, I've come to the same conclusion. Someone who's either a golfer or *knows* about golf chose that club for his or her encounter with Cotter Hayward last night."

"And you're concentrating on Bobby Cran-dell, aren't you?"

He shrugged. "Or his mother, for all the reasons you know."

Alvirah thought about Bobby, the scared handsome young face, the attempt to justify himself by pointing out that he'd always covered his own losses until now. She figured it was closer to the truth that Nadine had always bailed him out, and he had come running to her expecting her to be able to do it again. Last night Alvirah had seen with her own eyes that he realized *this* time his mother was powerless to save him. And it was pretty obvious that Nadine would do anything rather than see her son go to prison. She'd as much as said that . . .

"It looks bad for both of them," she said slowly, "but you know something, Scott? They're both innocent. I feel it in my bones."

They were in the sitting room of the cottage. The sliding glass door was open, and a refreshing cool breeze from the Pacific had cleared the midday heat.

Running footsteps sounded from the patio outside, then suddenly Nadine was pushing open the sliding screen. "Alvirah, help me," she sobbed. "Bobby is going to confess to murdering Cotter. Stop him, please stop him." Then she saw the sheriff. "Oh my God!" she wailed.

Scott stood up. "Mrs. Hayward, I'd better go find your son and hear what he has to say. And I suggest you look into your own heart and decide why he suddenly felt the need to confess to murder."

Flanked by Scott Alshorne and two sheriff's deputies, Bobby Crandell was taken to the Monterey County police station. A few minutes later, Alvirah and Willy accompanied Nadine, as they followed in the spa limo.

Nadine was no longer sobbing. Wordless on the brief drive, when they reached the station she demanded to see the sheriff. "I have something very important to tell him," she said.

Alvirah sensed immediately what Nadine was going to do. "Nadine, I want you to get a lawyer before you say one word."

"A lawyer can't help me. No one can."

They were escorted to a waiting room, where they sat until Scott sent for them an hour later. By then Alvirah was so worried that she almost forgot to turn on the recorder in her sunburst pin.

"Where is Bobby?" Nadine demanded when they were finally escorted to Scott's office.

"He's waiting for his confession to be typed up."

"He has nothing to confess to," Nadine cried. "I—"

Scott interrupted her. "Mrs. Hayward, don't say another word until you listen to me. You've heard of the Miranda warning?"

"Yes."

Alvirah felt Willy's hand reach to comfort her as Scott read the Miranda warning to Nadine, gave it to her to read, asked her if she understood it.

"Yes, yes, and I know I'm entitled to have a lawyer."

"Very well." Scott turned to a deputy. "Get the stenographer. Alvirah, you and Willy wait outside."

"Oh no, please let them stay." Nadine was trembling.

Alvirah put an arm around her. "Let me stay with her, Scott."

Nadine's confession was straightforward. "I phoned Cotter at the condo. I told him I had to talk to him."

"What time was that?"

"I . . . I'm not sure. I was in bed. I couldn't sleep."

"What did you want to talk to him about?" Scott asked.

"I was going to tell him about the jewelry being stolen and beg him not to report it. Alvirah, you're so smart. I thought maybe, just maybe, you'd find out who took it. I *did* wear some of the pieces the other night. A number of people admired them and all those same people are here. Maybe everything is in a safe in one of the cottages."

"Did he agree to meet you?" Scott asked.

"Yes, on the golf links."

"Why not in the condo?" Alvirah asked. "You're his wife."

"He . . . he said he felt like a walk and that would make it just about halfway for the two of us. He told me exactly how to get there."

"Why did you bring a golf club?" Scott asked.

Nadine bit her lip. "Cotter could become quite violent. I was afraid that if he became enraged . . . And that's just what happened. When I told him about the theft and the premium, he was so angry. He raised his hand and tried to hit me. I backed off and raised the club and . . ." Her voice trailed off. Then she whispered, "I don't remember hitting him, but then he was lying there, and I knew he was dead."

"You put the golf club back in Elyse Hayward's car?"

"Yes. I just wanted to get rid of it."

"Why *her* car?"

"I knew she had clubs there. I'd seen her with them. On the way out of the spa, I cut through the parking lot."

Not only his forehead, but Scott's entire face appeared to be creased in thought. "You make a more credible confession than your son did," he said. "I'm sorry for you, Mrs. Hayward. You'd have done Bobby a much bigger favor letting him face the music for cashing the insurance premium check. He could have handled it. He was willing to face the gas chamber rather than let you be arrested for your husband's murder. I can tell you now that his confession didn't hold water."

Scott stood up. "When your statement is typed up and signed, you'll be formally arraigned. As of now, you are under arrest on suspicion of murder in the first degree."

Alvirah and Willy had gone to the police station with Nadine and now they returned from it with Bobby. A study in misery, he sat hunched in the car, his chin resting on his clasped hands, his eyes half closed. Alvirah's maternal instincts coursed through her entire being. He hurts so much, she thought, and he's blaming himself. Finally she spoke to him: "Bobby, you'll stay in your mother's cottage, won't you?"

"Yes, if Baroness von Schreiber allows it. My mother was only supposed to stay till Saturday."

"I know Min will have a place for you." She turned to Willy. "I think you and Bobby should stick together the rest of the day. Take him over to the gym or the pool."

She closed her lips, not wanting to promise what she couldn't deliver. But as the limo cruised along the Seventeen Mile Drive, she decided to say her piece. "Bobby, I know you didn't kill Cotter Hayward and I'm just as sure your mother didn't kill him, either. She thinks she's protecting you, just as you thought you were protecting her. Now I want the truth. What happened after Willy and I left you the other night?"

The faintest hope brightened Bobby's face. He brushed back the dark blond hair that was so like his mother's. "Mom and I were pretty wrung out. She said that she knew Cotter would start thinking about her not wearing any of the jewelry at dinner, and it might be better if she told him what had

310

happened instead of waiting till Saturday. We both went to bed. I could hear her crying for a while, but I didn't know whether I should go to her. Then I fell asleep."

He glanced nervously at the front seat, then realized that Alvirah had pushed the button that raised the privacy glass between them and the chauffeur. "I woke up about five o'clock and looked in on Mom. She wasn't in her room. I found her address book and called Hayward's condo, but there wasn't any answer. I was scared and decided to go over there. I was afraid that she'd gone to see him and that maybe something had happened to her. I jogged over, but when I got there I saw police cars; a maintenance man told me what had happened. After that, I just kind of panicked. That's why I confessed to the murder. Because if my mother did it, she did it for me."

Alvirah looked at the young man, his face a mask of misery. "I don't believe she did it. Bobby," she said, "I told Sheriff Alshorne that there may have been other people who had a good reason to kill your stepfather. Now my job is to find out which one did it."

• • •

There was a large manila envelope waiting for Alvirah in the cottage. It was the material she had requested from Charley Evans, her editor at the *New York Globe,* volumes of newspaper and magazine clippings and stories about Cotter Hayward. Alvirah almost forgot that she had missed lunch as she began to dive into them, then she remembered the breakfast mini-muffin and realized that her looming headache was not caused by stress alone. She phoned room service.

Ten minutes later a smiling waitress appeared with a glass of spring water, a pot of herb tea and a carrot and cucumber salad, the luncheon menu of the day. Alvirah thought longingly of a nice, juicy hamburger, then remembered Barra Snow's remark about her sister getting a McDonald franchise in her divorce settlement. She half smiled, thinking that at this moment she felt as though she could eat the sister's profits in one sitting.

Alvirah found that the voluminous material on Cotter J. Hayward actually did make fascinating reading. He had been born in Darien, Connecticut, the grandson of the inventor of a circuit carrier for long-distance telephone calls who had sold his invention to AT&T for sixty million dollars.

"Huge money in those days," Alvirah thought as she made a note on her pad. That was when Cotter the first bought the jewelry for his wife. Because he was a notorious skinflint, the purchase made headlines. The jewelry was passed on to his son, Cotter the second, the playboy whose four wives each in turn got to wear it. But while the jewels may have remained intact, his lavish living and matrimonial settlements much diminished the family fortune.

Cotter the third, Nadine's late husband and Elyse's late ex-husband, seemed to be something of a chip off both blocks. There were dozens of pictures of him in his younger days, escorting film stars and debutantes. He had married Elyse when he was thirty-five, and like his grandfather, was known for his parsimony. He did his own investing and was rumored to be worth over one hundred million dollars, but no real figures were available.

He must have been a terrific golfer, Alvirah decided. Many of the pictures of him were taken on the golf course, playing with people like Jack Nicklaus and former President Ford. The older pictures showed him and Elyse, arm in arm, dressed for golfing, sometimes accepting awards together. The most recent pictures, those taken in the last three years, showed him with Nadine at social events, but there wasn't a single one of her at the golf outings.

One picture in particular caught Alvirah's eye. It showed Elyse and Barra Snow being awarded matching trophies at a charity outing at the Ridgewood Country Club in New Jersey and Cotter Hayward as chairman of the outing presenting them. That was only six weeks ago, she thought.

Cotter's smile that day seemed very genuine as he stood between the women. Elyse was smiling up at him. Love/hate, Alvirah thought. It's what Elyse felt for her ex. She read the caption under the picture and then raised her eyes. Oh my, she thought. Oh my.

Reaching for the phone she called Charley at the *Globe,* thanked him for the material he'd sent and requested him to have other material faxed as soon as possible. "I know it's eight o'clock in New York, but if you could put someone on it right away, I'll ask Min to let me have a key to the office so I can collect it tonight. Thanks a lot."

Her next job was to play back the recordings she had made at the dinner table last night, at Nadine's cottage and at lunch. As she listened, she made notes.

An exhausted Willy came in at six o'clock. "We swam, we did those exercise machines. Bobby knows all about using them. Then we had a glass of orange juice together and talked. He's a nice young fellow, honey, and knows his mother is in this situation because of him. I tell you, if somehow the real murderer can be found and Nadine gets off, Bobby Crandell won't so much as buy a lottery ticket again." Then Willy noticed the piles of clippings sorted on the table. "Any luck?"

"Not really, but I'm not sure. Anyhow, dinner should be interesting."

To Alvirah's relief, their entire table was in attendance. She'd been afraid that Elyse might decide to have dinner served in her cottage. But the first Mrs. Hayward, still icy in her composure, was elegantly dressed in a dark blue ankle-length sheath.

Barra Snow was wearing a white silk pantsuit that showed off her silver-blonde beauty. But she's not as gorgeous as her pictures in those ads, Alvirah thought—little lines were visible around Barra's eyes and mouth.

The discussion seemed to focus on Nadine's arrest. "I hope she realizes that if she's convicted, she won't collect a dime of Cotter's money," Elyse said, an unmistakable note of satisfaction in her voice.

"As you say, the ninth commandment must be obeyed," Alvirah prodded. "I mean when you think about it, if you and Mr. Hayward had patched things up four years ago . . . I guess you did that a lot didn't you? Fight and make up, fight and make up? Then *you'd* be his widow. Instead of that, he turned to Nadine. I'm sorry for you too. We all hate to lose a husband, but there's nothing the matter with being a rich widow."

"I really don't appreciate your observations, Mrs. Meehan," Elyse said sharply. "I've been made aware of your reputation as an amateur detective, but please spare me your ruminating."

Alvirah made herself look distressed. "Oh, I'm so sorry. I didn't mean to offend you." She hoped she looked properly penitent. "I'm just so sorry for Nadine. I mean, she's not a golfer. She has such fair skin, and her son told Willy that she is the world's worst athlete. She's more the artistic type, I think. Anyhow, what I mean is that it was just bad luck for everybody that Cotter and you didn't make up, wasn't it? And bad luck for her that, of all things, she carried *your* golf club when she went to meet him. I certainly hope she wasn't trying to throw suspicion on you. But then sometimes murderers get so rattled they make mistakes."

Elyse pointedly ignored Alvirah and her comments and began chatting exclusively with the Jennings couple, while Barra flirted halfheartedly with the former congressman. Over dessert, Alvirah was dismayed to hear that Elyse was leaving on Saturday.

"I just want to get a million miles away," Elyse said. "This place is totally depressing, and I never played worse golf. I *knew* I'd be lousy today."

Then Barra said, "I'm leaving too. There was a call from my agency. I have to do some retakes in New York on a photo shoot for Adrian. I'm canceling my second week here."

Alvirah found it hard not to stare at Elyse. The microphone was on, and later she'd have to listen to every word they'd said at dinner. Elyse had given something away. What was it?

The nightly entertainment was a slide show and lecture on fourteenth-century Spanish art. As people drifted into the back parlor where chairs had been placed, Alvirah asked Min for a key to her office. "I've got more faxes coming later, and I want to see them tonight."

Min's warm smile was for the benefit of observers. When she spoke, her voice was anxious. "Six guests canceled their next week's reservation. They are furious at the way the media is swarming outside the gates. Alvirah, why couldn't Nadine have killed Cotter with one of his *own* golf clubs? Why did she have to take one from these premises? Was she trying to make it look as though Elyse had committed the crime?"

"That's what's been bugging me," Alvirah replied, nodding. "I don't get it either. Why replace a club with blood all over it unless you want it to be found?"

The next morning, at Alvirah's request, Scott Alshorne came to Tranquility cottage for morning coffee. "Are you satisfied?" she asked him point-blank. "I mean totally, completely satisfied that Nadine killed her husband?"

Scott studied the contents of his cup. "Good coffee."

"You didn't answer Alvirah's question," Willy told him sternly.

Alvirah smiled to herself. She knew Willy was still a little miffed at Scott for the way he'd talked to her yesterday.

"I'm not sure I can," Scott said slowly. "Nadine has confessed. She had a motive, a very strong motive. There are two local telephone charges on the bill for her cottage. One was made on the ninth. That was Wednesday. One was made on the tenth. That was yesterday and would be consistent with her saying she called Cotter Hayward Wednesday night and Bobby saying he tried to reach Cotter early Thursday morning. So what have I got to doubt about her statement?"

"Sheriff, have you ever spread a rumor to flush out a killer?" Alvirah asked. "I mean defense attorneys in California do it all the time to protect their clients, so why not do it when it might accomplish some good?"

As he shook his head, she said persuasively, "Scott, it all has to do with the jewelry. Don't you see that? The jewelry is still missing. Let's suppose Nadine knew that Cotter Hayward was getting ready to dump her and staged a robbery so that at least she'd come

319

out of the marriage with jewelry she thought she could find a way to sell. The minute she called Bobby to report the loss and found out that he'd let the policy lapse, all she had to do was cancel the robbery. She called Bobby before she told Min about it. And let me tell you, when I met her, Nadine was frantic."

"All right, she didn't steal her own jewelry. I'll buy that."

"Are you sure Bobby was still in New York the afternoon of the theft?"

"Yes. We had his movements verified."

"Then somebody else stole that stuff, and dollars-to-doughnuts that person is the killer. Scott, go along with me on this, please."

It was a beautiful day. The morning sun beamed warm and bright over the Olympic-sized pool and the surrounding tables with their rainbow-colored umbrellas. At one of the tables a portable radio was tuned in to a local newscast, its volume on high. Riveted attention had replaced the quiet languor of guests who'd mixed a morning of exercise with facials and seaweed wraps and massages.

The voice on the radio was reporting that

there was a rumor that the sheriff had been keeping a lid on important evidence. Several clear footprints had been discovered in the wooded area near the sixteenth hole, where Cotter Hayward had been murdered. The sheriff was said to believe that they were the footprints of the killer, who apparently had been hiding and waiting for Hayward. What made this discovery especially significant was that these footprints, while clearly those of a woman, were definitely larger than the confessed killer's size, which was five and a half.

"And the shocker," the broadcaster continued, "is that the stolen jewelry was actually paste copies, which Hayward had made when he switched insurance policies. He was always concerned that Bobby Crandell would do exactly what he *did*—cash the premium check and let the policy lapse. So it looks as if whoever stole the Hayward jewelry is stuck with fool's gold."

Alvirah was not able to sit at Elyse Hayward's table this afternoon, but she did manage to capture a spot at one next to it. She switched on her recorder and turned her chair toward Elyse, then in a voice that was sure to carry, said: "That's not the whole story. You know I nose around a little, and I hear they're so sure the killer is a guest here that the sheriff is getting a court order to check the shoe sizes of all the women at the spa. If he finds a match, the judge will let him search the cottage and belongings to look for the jewelry."

"That's illegal," someone protested.

"This is California," Alvirah reminded her. She leaned backwards as far as she dared without toppling over and was able to hear with her own ears Elyse saying very quietly, "How like Cotter. How very like Cotter." Then she pushed her chair away from the table and excused herself.

Alvirah knew that a woman detective dressed as a spa maid would be following Elyse. She had another plan, however. When it was time to leave for the afternoon appointments, she quietly followed Barra Snow to her cottage, slipped around to the patio and, flattening herself against the side of the sliding glass door, peered in.

She pulled her head back as Barra looked around, then she inched forward just far enough to see Barra shove aside the portrait of Min and Helmut and dial the combination of her safe. A moment later she pulled out a

322

plastic bag, the sparkling contents of which were heaped together.

"I thought so!" Alvirah breathed. "I *thought* so! Now Barra has to get rid of them . . ."

She stepped back. Barra's cottage, like Nadine's, was one of the farthest from the main house, a bit remote, with a wooded area behind it. Where was Barra going to try to dump the stuff? Alvirah wondered.

I was sure it was Elyse, Alvirah thought, but then when I asked Charley Evans to send me the file photos from that outing at the Ridgewood Country Club, I started seeing a different picture. In a couple of the photos, the way Cotter and Barra are looking at each other tells a lot. Then on the tape, it's so clear that Barra persuaded Elyse to go golfing yesterday. Barra was the one who sent the caddy for the clubs, knowing all along what he would find. She didn't seem to care whether Elyse was implicated, or if Nadine remained the prime suspect. Either way, no one would think her involved in the murder.

Alvirah's suspicions had been deepened when Barra had said she had to go back for a photo shoot. Alvirah knew that wasn't true. The caption under the picture referred to her as the ex-Adrian model. That's what had caught Alvirah's eye.

Plus she had made that crack about her sister getting a McDonald's franchise in her divorce settlement . . . What had Barra said? *"I* wasn't that lucky." I bet she hasn't got much money at all, Alvirah told herself.

The question remained, however, did she do the robbery on her own? And how did she know the combination of Nadine's safe.

There was only one person who could have given it to her, Alvirah realized—Cotter Hayward. Would he have stolen his own jewelry to get the insurance money to pay off that final three million to Elyse?

It was quiet inside the cottage. Barra must be going crazy trying to figure where to dump the jewelry she believes is worthless, Alvirah thought. Then her reverie was abruptly broken as something small and hard was pressed into her back, and she heard Barra Snow murmur, "You're much too clever for your own good, Mrs. Meehan."

Scott Alshorne was in a bad mood. He did not like the idea of allowing false rumors to swirl around during a murder investigation.

Therefore, it was not hard to look coldly furious when once again he got out of his car at the gates of the spa to confront the media.

"I have no comment about the alleged footprints in the vicinity of the murder scene," he said, his tone frosty. "I will not discuss the rumor that the stolen jewelry consisted of paste copies of the Hayward gems. I will actively pursue discovery of the source of any leaks from my office to the media."

And that much at least is true, he thought as he pushed his way past the microphones and cameras back to the car. The grounds of the spa had a deserted feeling. Scott knew that after luncheon was served, the serious business of beauty resumed with a vengeance. Min was always after him to take a full day of treatment as her guest. Just what I need, he thought irritably, to be wrapped in seaweed.

He went directly to Min's office where Walt Pierce, one of his deputies, Min, Helmut and Willy were awaiting him. "Where's Alvirah?" he asked.

"She should be here any minute," Willy told him evasively.

"Meaning she's up to something," Scott

said, congratulating himself that he had assigned Liz Hill, a woman deputy, to keep track of Alvirah.

He turned to Pierce. "Any reports yet?"

"Darva called in," Pierce told him. She followed Elyse Hayward to her cottage. She's got her under observation now."

"Any indication that Hayward has the jewelry?" Scott demanded.

"She went straight for the safe," Pierce informed him. "She had a bottle of gin hidden in it."

"Gin!" Min exclaimed. "It is part of our code of honor that guests will not conceal liquor in the safe. The maids are instructed to report any evidence of spirits in the cottages, but of course they do not have access to the safes."

"How can our guests lose weight if they imbibe?" Helmut sighed. "How can they retain the fresh bloom of youth?"

You manage, Willy thought.

"Darva has Elyse Hayward under surveillance with her binoculars. She says Hayward is crying and laughing and drinking. In other words, she's tying one on," Pierce continued.

"There goes Alvirah's theory," Scott said.

"If Elyse Hayward had the jewelry, she'd be trying to unload it. The last thing she'd be doing is getting drunk. Walt, what have you heard from Liz?"

"Mrs. Meehan is hiding on the patio of Barra Snow's cottage. Liz can't see the interior, just the front side opposite the patio, but so far no activity."

"How long has Liz been there?" Scott asked.

"About fifteen minutes."

The walkie-talkie Pierce was holding buzzed. He snapped it on and said, "What's up?" Then his tone changed. He looked at Min. "Deputy Hill wants to know if there's another entrance to Barra Snow's cottage."

"Yes," Min said. "That cottage has a sliding glass door from the master bedroom to the back patio."

Scott grabbed the walkie-talkie. "What's the matter?" He listened, then asked, "Are you wearing a maid's uniform? . . . All right. . . . Go up to the cottage. Make an excuse to go inside, then report back."

Willy felt the familiar sickening lurch in the pit of his stomach that always grabbed him when he began to worry about Alvirah.

A moment later the walkie-talkie buzzed

again. Deputy Hill made no attempt to speak softly, and they could all hear her. "Barra Snow and Mrs. Meehan are gone. They must have left through the back door. That's only a few feet from the woods. Snow must have opened the wall safe. The picture in front of it is pushed aside."

"We're on the way," Scott told her. "Try to pick up their trail."

Willy grabbed his arm. "Where do those woods end?"

"At the Pebble Beach Club," Min told him. "If Barra has the jewelry, she must be planning to get rid of it somewhere in those woods. It would be almost impossible to find. There are more than eighty acres, and much of it is dense and even swampy in places." Then, noting the look on Willy's face, she added hastily, "but Alvirah may simply be following her. I'm sure she is fine."

Alvirah stumbled through the thick undergrowth, prodded on by the gun in her back. The lush vegetation clawed at her ankles, and countless insects buzzed around her face. I attract mosquitoes, she thought. If there was only one mosquito in the world it would find me.

"Move faster," Barra ordered.

If I could just distract her, Alvirah thought, looking about for something to use as a club, anything with which to defend herself.

She deliberately stumbled and fell to her knees, then used the moment to catch her breath. "Where are you taking me?" she demanded, looking up at Barra Snow.

She found it difficult to reconcile this hard-eyed, thin-lipped woman with the sophisticated, amusing one she'd sat at the same table with these past few days. It was as though Barra had donned a mask. Or maybe, Alvirah thought, her other face was the mask.

"You killed Cotter Hayward, didn't you?" she asked. "You stole the jewelry?"

Snow pointed the gun at her. "Get up," she ordered. "Unless you want to die here."

Alvirah scrambled to obey. She had the presence of mind to turn on the recorder in her pin as she got to her feet. Then, hoping Barra wouldn't notice, she slid the small shoulder bag down her arm, and as she began to move, let it drop.

"That's better. Keep going."

"All right. All right." Alvirah dragged her feet, hoping to leave some trace of a trail. It was stifling in this place, with no breeze penetrating the dense foliage. She could hardly breathe. But no matter what, she needed to get a confession on record. "Tell me something," she panted. "Did you kill Cotter?"

"Alvirah, you're so smart, you must have it all figured out. Just shut up and MOVE!"

Alvirah felt the gun again, this time at the back of her head. "The way I figure it, you stole the jewelry and tried to make it look like a break-in by throwing all that stuff around. You must have really wondered why Nadine didn't report the theft."

"I'm going as fast as I can," she gasped. "Don't keep sticking that thing in my neck."

Then she continued, "The question is, why did you kill Hayward? He was meeting you on the golf course, wasn't he? My bet is that you were supposed to hand the jewelry over to him. Am I right?"

"Yes, you're right."

Fury and frustration resounded in Barra Snow's voice.

Moments later, the woods thinned suddenly, and they came upon a swampy area. Alvirah felt mud oozing beneath her feet. Directly ahead of them was a pond, all slimy water and vegetation. We have to be getting near the grounds of the Pebble Beach Club,

she thought. What does she think she's going to do now?

"I bet he gave you the combination for Nadine's safe and was going to claim the insurance money to pay off Elyse," she volunteered.

"Right on all counts," Barra said. "You can stop now."

Alvirah turned. "The thing is, why did you kill him? Was it because of the way Elyse talked about him being so cheap and Nadine being left penniless if she ever divorced him? Maybe you thought you were better off with that?" She pointed to the bag of jewelry Barra was carrying.

"Right again, Alvirah." This time Barra Snow pointed the gun at Alvirah's heart. "And when I tell them that I saw you dash past my cottage following a man who looked like one of the caddies at the Pebble Beach Club, they'll start looking for the killer here, not at the spa. And I'll be back at the spa in time for my facial.

"By the time they find you—if they find you, since that pond is deep, and the mud sucks you down like quicksand—I'll be far away from here.

"Now take these fake jewels in your

clammy little hands. I want to get rid of both them and you." As Alvirah obeyed, Barra stepped back and aimed the gun once again at Alvirah's heart.

As he ran to Barra's cottage, Scott ordered that squad cars be sent to both sides of the woods and that deputies begin the search for Barra and Alvirah. "They could have gone anywhere," he snapped. "Walt, we'll split up until more help comes. Min, you and the Baron and Willy stay out of it."

Ignoring the sheriff's command, Willy plunged into the thickets shouting for Alvirah. That woman is a killer, he said to himself, and she's getting desperate. If she knows Alvirah is following her, it's better if she realizes other people are around as well, that she can't get away with another murder.

Willy realized that the sheriff and the deputy had gone off in another direction from the one in which his instincts told him to head. Maybe I'd better veer over in the direction of the ocean, Willy thought, worried now that his instincts might be wrong. Maybe Barra Snow would try to get Alvirah down to the beach.

Then he saw it. Alvirah's pocketbook. He was sure she'd dropped it on purpose. Then he was able to make out where some grass was trampled. Yes, this *was* the right direction.

He charged ahead, reaching the clearing in time to see what was happening but not in time to stop Barra Snow.

As Barra pulled the trigger, Alvirah swerved, then felt a sharp pain coming from the vicinity of her sunburst pin. As she toppled backwards into the water, she thought, My God, I've been shot.

Willy lunged through the mud and grabbed Barra's arm just as she pointed the gun at the spot where Alvirah was starting to sink. The shot exploded into the air as he wrenched the gun from her hand, tossed it into the water, then pushing her down, leaped after it.

"I've got you, honey," he said, lifting Alvirah's head. "I've got you."

Alvirah felt a pain in her shoulder. The pin, she thought. My sunburst pin took the bullet. She had been saved by ducking—and sheer luck! Barra's aim had been thrown off by her movement, and the bullet had merely grazed the pin. She felt the pain radiating from the point of impact, but again thought in wonder, I'm all right. I know I'm all right. And I've still got the jewelry.

She managed not to faint until she had the satisfaction of seeing Scott come charging into the clearing in time to collar Barra Snow, who was struggling furiously to extract herself from the mire.

"I think the occasion calls for breaking the cardinal rule of the Cypress Point Spa," Helmut said, as a maid carrying champagne and glasses on a tray followed him into Tranquility cottage.

Alvirah's arm was in a sling. She was comfortably ensconced on a sofa in the sitting room and beaming amiably at Min, Scott, Nadine and Bobby. Willy, still pale with worry over her narrow escape, was hovering over her like a mother hen.

"I think you need rest, honey," he said for the fifteenth time in the last five hours.

"I'm fine," Alvirah said, "and forever thankful that I insisted on wearing my pin 'just in case.' Heaven knows I never thought 'just in case' would include getting shot at. The pin's pretty well destroyed, but the recording is still okay. I got Barra Snow cold." She beamed at the thought.

Scott Alshorne shook his head. Once again he found himself counting his blessings that Alvirah Meehan lived a continent away. She attracted trouble, no question about it.

He grudgingly admitted to himself, though, that Alvirah's scheme to spread the rumors about the footprints at the crime scene and the paste jewelry had certainly worked. If he hadn't gone along with it, Nadine Hayward would still be in jail, sticking to her story that she had murdered her husband—just to protect her son. And Barra Snow would be packing her bags and heading home, leaving behind a murdered man and taking with her four million dollars' worth of stolen jewelry.

He accepted a glass of champagne when offered one, and when Helmut proposed the toast to Alvirah, Scott gladly joined in acknowledging her valor. Nevertheless, with an eye to the future, he decided it was time to say his piece.

"Alvirah, my good friend, you have saved the day again. But I would implore you to realize that if a deputy had not been following you—"

"Who *you* put on my tail," Alvirah interrupted. "That was very clever of you, Scott."

"Thank you. I would like to point out that you came within an inch of losing your life today, and all because you did not simply ask for help when you followed Barra Snow."

Alvirah's attempt to look chagrined was not convincing. "I'll be honest," she said. "I was betting mostly on Elyse being the murderer. It just made sense. And let me tell you, there really *was* a love/hate relationship between her and Cotter Hayward."

"Looking back, I agree," Nadine said quietly. "Apparently one of the things that attracted Cotter to me was that I *didn't* play golf. I gather he and Elyse would get into constant screaming matches about each other's games. But after four years I think he was bored with me and missed that kind of companionship."

"Except that he was getting it from Barra, not Elyse," Scott interjected. "When Elyse Hayward learned what happened this afternoon, she admitted that she honestly thought Cotter Hayward was getting interested in being with her again. Then she sensed there was someone else in the picture, but she hadn't guessed that it was Barra."

Scott turned to Nadine. He half smiled when he saw the blissfully peaceful look on her face and the absolute happiness emanating from her son, Bobby. But then he forced himself to look stern. "Nadine, you and Bobby lied for each other. It was easy to see through Bobby's attempts to cover for you, but please realize you could have gone to the gas chamber if a judge or a jury had believed your story. Fortunately, Alvirah did not, and I had gut-level doubts about it as well."

"But you did leave your cottage after you went to bed the other night," Alvirah said. "That's why Bobby went looking for you. I never did hear where you went."

Nadine looked embarrassed. "I did make a call to Cotter, but when he answered, I was so upset I just hung up. Then I went over to the lap pool and settled into one of the beach chairs. I knew no one would see or hear me there, and I didn't want Bobby to hear me crying. I guess I was so exhausted I fell asleep."

"So *that's* why there was a blanket on one of those chairs," Min breathed. "I am glad to hear it. When it was reported to me, I did not know what to think."

"I have a point to make," Alvirah said, and

now she looked stern. "Nadine, I gather you're now a very wealthy woman. I'll say this right in front of Bobby. You won't do him any favors if you ever cover gambling debts for him."

"I agree," Bobby said. He looked at Nadine. "Mom, I don't deserve you."

Min arose. "I must get to the main house. Tonight I lecture on the need for quiet meditation as part of the overall process of achieving beauty."

This time Willy spoke up. "Min, with all due respect, thanks for your hospitality, but in the interest of achieving a little peace, we're heading back to New York in the morning. You can let someone on the waiting list know that Tranquility cottage is available."

Bye, Baby Bunting

*I*t was December 20th, and although later on Alvirah would call it the most awful day of her life, when it began she could not have felt more festive.

At 7:00 A.M., the phone rang with the joyous news that Joan Moore O'Brien had been delivered of her first child, a baby girl. "Her name is Marianne," Gregg O'Brien reported happily, "she weighs six pounds, two ounces and she's gorgeous."

Joan Moore had lived next door to Alvirah and Willy in Queens, and they had watched her grow up, becoming close to her and her family over the years. As Alvirah put it, "A sweeter girl never walked the face of the earth."

She and Willy had maintained their contact with Joan even after their move to Central Park South in Manhattan and had been proud to be at her wedding to Gregg O'Brien, a handsome young engineer. They regularly visited the young couple in their apartment in Tribeca and joined in celebrating Gregg's rise up the corporate ladder and Joan's promotions at the bank. They also shared the O'Briens' terrible disappointment when Joan suffered three miscarriages.

"But now, finally, praise the Lord, they have their baby," Alvirah crowed to Willy as she heaped waffles on his plate. "You know I felt in my bones that this time it was going to work out. I'd even gone ahead and bought presents for the baby, although I really have to do serious shopping this morning before we go to the hospital. After all, we are the surrogate grandparents."

Willy smiled affectionately at Alvirah, looking with love at the woman with whom he had spent the best years of his life. Her blue eyes were bright with happiness, her complexion rosy. She'd just had her hair tinted yesterday, so now it was again a soft red, and all the gray had been firmly routed. She looked warm and comfortable in the chenille robe that followed the lines of her generous body. Willy smiled; he thought she was beautiful.

"We should have had six kids," he said, "and twenty grandchildren."

"Well, Willy, the good Lord didn't send them, but now we can have fun spoiling Joan and Gregg's little girl. I mean, it's practically an obligation since Joan's folks aren't around anymore."

At three that afternoon, they were entering the crowded lobby of Empire Hospital on West Twenty-third Street.

"I can't wait to see the baby, " Alvirah enthused, making her way past receptionists too busy to notice them.

"I can't wait to unload the presents," Willy commented as he strained to keep his fingers from slipping out of the handles of the heavy shopping bags he was carrying. "Why do they have to put little scraps of clothes in such big boxes anyhow?''

''Because they never heard the old saying that good things come in small packages. Oh, doesn't the lobby look cheerful? I love holiday decorations. They're so pretty.''

''I never thought of a life-sized balloon of Rudolph the Rednosed Reindeer as being pretty,'' Willy observed as they passed a cardboard sleigh, complete with balloon Santa Claus and reindeer.

''Gregg said Joan is in room 1121.'' Alvirah paused for a moment. ''There are the elevators.'' She hoisted one of the shopping bags she was clutching and pointed down the corridor.

''Shouldn't we get visitor's passes?'' Willy asked.

''Joan said to come right through. They really don't bother you if you look as though you know where you're going.''

They just missed an elevator and were the only people waiting when the doors of an adjacent one opened. In her haste, Alvirah almost ran into a woman who stepped out of the elevator carrying an infant. The heavy scarf that covered the woman's head fell forward, shielding her face. She was dressed in a ski jacket and slacks.

344

Ever maternal, Alvirah peeked down to admire the baby, who was nestled in a yellow bunting. Blue eyes opened wide, stared up at her, then closed again. A yawn enveloped the pink-and-white face, and small fists waved.

"Oh, she's gorgeous," Alvirah sighed as the woman hurried past them.

Willy was holding open the elevator door with his shoulder. "Honey, come on," he urged.

As the elevator lumbered up, stopping at every floor to take on passengers, Alvirah had the fleeting thought that in most hospitals, when a new mother and her baby were discharged, they were taken to the door in a wheelchair. Well, things change, she decided.

When they reached room 1121, Alvirah rushed in. Ignoring Joan, who was sitting up in bed, and Gregg, who was standing beside her, Alvirah hurried to the small crib against the wall. "Oh, she isn't here," she lamented.

Gregg laughed. "Marianne is having a hearing test. I can vouch that she'll pass with flying colors. When I scraped the chair against the floor this morning, she jumped in Joan's arms and started yelling."

"Well then, I guess I'd better pay some attention to the proud parents." Alvirah bent over Joan and hugged her fiercely. "I'm so happy for you," she said as tears ran down her full cheeks.

"Why do women always cry when they're happy?" Gregg asked Willy, who was trying to prop the shopping bags in the corner.

"Leaky tear ducts," Willy grunted as he grasped Gregg's hand and shook it vigorously. "I'm not going to cry, but I'm awfully happy for both of you too."

"Wait till you see her," Gregg boasted. "She's gorgeous, like her mama."

"She has your forehead and chin," Joan told him.

"And your blue eyes and porcelain complexion and—"

"Sorry folks," a voice interrupted. They all turned to see a smiling nurse standing in the door. "I've got to borrow your baby for a few minutes," she said.

"Oh, another nurse already took her. Just a few minutes ago," Gregg said.

When she saw the look of alarm on the nurse's face, Alvirah knew instantly that something was terribly wrong.

"What's the matter?" Joan asked, sitting up, leaning forward, her face turning ashen. "Where's my baby? Who has her? What's going on?"

The nurse raced out of the room, and moments later an alarm sounded throughout the hospital. An urgent voice over the loudspeaker announced, "Code Orange! Code Orange!"

Alvirah knew what the alarm meant, internal disaster. But she also knew it was too late. Her mind flashed back to the woman exiting the elevator just as they were coming up. She had been right—newborn babies and their mothers do not leave the hospital unescorted. Alvirah ran from the room to talk to security personnel, as Joan collapsed in Gregg's arms.

An hour later, at 4:00 P.M., in a small, cluttered apartment on West Ninetieth Street, seventy-eight-year-old Wanda Brown was comfortably propped up on a shabby couch and bestowing a moist-eyed smile on her granddaughter. "Such a happy surprise," she said, "a Christmas visit. You coming all the way from Pittsburgh with your new baby! You certainly have put your troubles behind you, Vonny."

"Guess I have, Grandma." The voice was monotone. Vonny's eyes, light brown and guileless, stared off into the distance.

"Such a beautiful baby. Is she good?"

"I hope so." Vonny jostled the baby in her arms.

"What's her name?"

"Vonny, just like mine."

"Oh, that's nice. When you wrote and told me you were expecting, I prayed that nothing would happen. No girl deserves to lose a baby that way, and to have it happen twice."

"I know, Grandma."

"It was better that you left the New York area, but I've missed you, Vonny. It's obvious that the stay in the hospital really helped you. Tell me about your new husband. Will he be joining you?"

"No, Grandma. He's too busy. I'll be here a few days, then go back to Pittsburgh. But please don't mention the hospital. I don't want to talk about the hospital. And don't ask questions. I hate questions."

"Vonny, I never, never said a word to anyone. You know me better than that. I've been here five years, and not a one of my neighbors knows anything about what happened. The nuns who visit me are wonderful, and I always tell them what a dear girl you are. I had mentioned that you were expecting a Christmas baby, and they've all been praying for you."

"That's nice, Grandma." Vonny smiled briefly. The baby in her arms began to wail. "Shut up!" she snapped as she shook it. "You *hear* me? Shut *up!*"

"Give the baby to me, Vonny," Wanda Brown pleaded. "And you go heat her bottle. Where are her clothes?"

"Somebody stole her suitcase on the bus," Vonny said sullenly. "On my way here I picked up some odds and ends at a thrift shop, but I have to get her some more stuff."

At eleven o'clock that night, sitting somberly side by side in the living room of their apartment overlooking Central Park, Willy and Alvirah watched the local CBS newscast.

The lead story was the bold kidnapping of eight-hour-old Marianne O'Brien from Empire Hospital.

Willy felt Alvirah tense as the anchorman said, "It is believed that the kidnapper was observed just prior to leaving the hospital by family friends, Willy and Alvirah Meehan, who had come to visit the proud and happy parents.

"Mrs. Meehan's description of the infant leaves little doubt that she had seen the

O'Brien baby. Unfortunately, neither she nor her husband could provide any significant details about the abductor, who apparently had disguised herself as a nurse. The O'Briens say she was about thirty years old, of medium height, with blond hair . . ."

"How come they don't talk about the yellow bunting?" Willy asked. "You noticed that especially."

"Probably because the police always hold something back so that they can tell real calls from quack calls."

Alvirah squeezed Willy's hand as she listened to the anchorman say that the heartbroken mother, Joan O'Brien, was under heavy sedation and that the hospital had announced a news conference, during which the father would broadcast a plea to the kidnapper.

Then the newsman interrupted himself in midsentence. "We're going live to Empire Hospital for a late-breaking bulletin," he said.

Alvirah leaned forward and squeezed Willy's hand again.

After a moment's pause, an on-the-scene reporter spoke from the lobby of the hospital. "Authorities here report that the uniform of a hospital attendant and a blond wig have just been found stuffed in the disposal container of a lavatory on the floor from which Baby Marianne was abducted. The lavatory is a facility reserved for hospital personnel and can be entered only by punching in a special code." The reporter paused for effect and looked intently into the camera. "Authorities now fear that this kidnapping may have been an inside job."

Or that the woman knew her way around the hospital, Alvirah thought. Maybe she had worked or was a patient there at some time. Or she could have just been visiting someone and gotten the lay of the land, watched what the nurses were doing. She was wearing a blond wig. That means we don't even know what color her hair really is. With that scarf so tight over her head, I didn't notice.

The news bite about the kidnapping ended with a doctor giving the baby's formula and the police commissioner promising compassion and help to the abductor if the baby was returned safely. Anyone with any information was asked to call a number that was flashed on the screen.

Willy pushed the remote control button and switched off the television; then he put his arm around Alvirah, who sat next to him, shaking her head. "You can't blame yourself, honey. Remember, if that woman was so desperate for a baby, she'll take care of Marianne until the police find her."

"Oh, Willy, I can't *not* blame myself. You know how my antenna just naturally goes up when something's out of whack. It's just that I was excited, so anxious to see the baby and to hug Joan and Gregg. I know there was something, something odd that registered in those seconds when I saw that woman." She shook her head again. "I just can't dig it up." Then she gasped, and her eyes brightened. "I've got it! I remember! Willy, it was the bunting, that yellow bunting. *I've seen it somewhere before!*"

Long after she and Willy went to bed, Alvirah lay awake trying to remember where she had seen the yellow bunting before yesterday and why it had made an impression on her, but for once her prodigious memory seemed to be failing her.

Ever since Joan had entered her eighth month and Alvirah had known that even if she delivered early, the baby would probably be all right, she had been shopping for it.

It was so much fun looking at everything and deciding on the kimonos and shirts and sacks and bonnets and receiving blankets. I don't think I've passed a display of baby things without window-shopping, Alvirah mused. But where did I see that bunting, or one just like it?

None of the gifts she and Willy had taken to the hospital had been opened; they had just stuck them in the closet of Joan's room. I've got to go through them and make a list of all the stores I was in, Alvirah decided.

Only after settling on this course of action was Alvirah able to relax enough to actually fall asleep. At breakfast she told Willy her plan. "The thing is, you don't see buntings the way you used to," she explained. "People just don't seem to use them much anymore. And that this one was yellow and folded back to show a deep, white satin border makes it especially unusual."

"White satin sounds expensive," Willy said. "I didn't get much of a look at that woman, but the outfit she was wearing certainly looked more thrift shop than custom made."

"You're right," Alvirah agreed. "It was a sort of run-of-the-mill dark blue nylon jacket and dark blue slacks, the kind you'd pick off a bargain rack. I just didn't pay attention to her. I was so busy trying to get a look at the baby. But you're right, a bunting with a satin border *would* be expensive."

Then her heart gave a sickening lurch. "Willy, do you think she stole the baby because she had arranged to sell it to someone else? If she did, there's no telling where they could be by now." She pushed back her chair and got up. "I can't waste time."

Despite the cardboard sleigh and the balloon figures of Santa Claus and his reindeer, the hospital lobby had lost whatever cheery atmosphere Willy and Alvirah had sensed there the day before. The corridor to the bank of elevators was now patrolled by a security guard, and no one without a visitor's pass was allowed down it.

When Alvirah gave Joan O'Brien's name, she was firmly told that no visitors would be allowed to see her. Finally she convinced the receptionist to call up to Gregg, and from him she learned that Joan had been moved from the maternity floor. "Yes, the presents are still in the closet of 1121," he said, when

Alvirah explained what she needed. "I'll meet you there."

Alvirah was stunned when she saw Gregg. He seemed to have aged ten years overnight. His eyes were bloodshot, and his face was etched with lines that creased his mouth and forehead. She was sure that any expression of sympathy would only make things worse; he knew how she felt.

"Help me open these packages," she ordered crisply. "Then I'll read the labels to see which stores the things came from, and you write the names down."

There were twelve stores in all, the gifts ranging from big items from Saks and Bloomingdale's, to hand-crocheted sweaters from a specialty shop on Madison Avenue, to small items like nightgowns and kimonos from obscure shops in Greenwich Village and the Upper West Side.

When the list was complete, Alvirah hastily stacked the purchases together and piled them into the biggest boxes. As she was closing the lid on the last one, a police officer came into the room, looking for Gregg. "There's a break in the case, Mr. O'Brien," he said. "A call came in to the hot line. Some guy claims his cousin's wife came home yesterday with a new baby she says is hers. Only thing is, she hadn't been pregnant."

A look of incredible hope came over Gregg's face. "Who is he? Where is he?"

"He said he's from Long Island and is going to call back. But there's one hitch. He thinks there ought to be a twenty-thousand-dollar reward."

"I'll guarantee it," Alvirah said flatly, even as a dark premonition told her that this was going to turn out to be a false lead.

"Vonny, the baby really needs some clothes," Wanda Brown said timidly. It was Wednesday afternoon. Vonny had been there a whole day and had only changed the baby's kimono once. "This place is drafty, and you only have one other kimono. For a baby that's two weeks old, this one is real little and mustn't get a chill."

"All my babies were small," Vonny told her as she examined the nursing bottle she was holding. "She drinks slow," she complained.

"She's falling asleep. You have to be patient. Why not let me finish feeding her and you go shopping? Where did you get the things you bought for her after her suitcase got lost?"

"The thrift shop was right down from the Port Authority. But there wasn't much left for infants, just the bunting and that." Vonny waved her hand at the kimono and shirt that were drying on the radiator. "They were getting more in. I guess I could try them again."

She got up and handed the sleeping infant to her grandmother. As an afterthought she gave her the bottle. "It's getting cold, but don't worry. And I don't want you walking around with her."

"I wouldn't try." Wanda Brown took the baby and tried not to show her shock at the icy feel of the bottle. Vonny didn't heat it at all, she thought. Then she shrank back as her granddaughter bent over her.

"Now remember, Grandma, I don't want people coming in here looking at my baby and handling it while I'm out."

"Vonny, no one ever comes here except the nuns who stop by once a week or so. You'd love them. Sister Cordelia and Sister Maeve Marie come most often. They're always making sure that people like me have enough food, and that we're not getting sick, and that the heat and the plumbing work. Only last month, Sister Cordelia sent her brother, Willy, who's a plumber, here because there was a leak under the kitchen sink that had the whole place musty. What a nice man! Sister Maeve Marie stopped in Monday, but none of them will be back again till Christmas Eve. They're bringing me a Christmas dinner basket. It's always nice, and I know there'll be enough for you too."

"The baby and I will be gone by then."

"Of course. You want to spend Christmas with your husband."

Vonny pulled on her blue ski jacket. Her dark hair was tangled on her shoulders. At the door she turned to her grandmother. "I'll pick out some nice things for her. I love my baby. I loved my other babies too." Her face twisted in pain. "It wasn't my fault."

"I know that, dear," Wanda said soothingly.

She waited a few minutes, until Vonny had been gone long enough to be out of the building, then Wanda laid the baby on the couch and tucked her frayed afghan around it. Reaching for her cane, she picked up the bottle and limped into the kitchen. A baby shouldn't drink such cold milk, she fretted.

She poured water into a small saucepan, set it on the stove, placed the bottle in it and turned on the gas. As she waited for the bottle to heat, she was troubled by the thought of Vonny and the baby on that long, cold bus ride to Pittsburgh. Then another thought struck her. On her last visit, Sister Maeve Marie had told her that the nuns were opening a thrift shop on Eighty-sixth Street. People could get clothes very cheap there, or even for nothing if they were broke. Maybe she should phone the sisters and tell them about Vonny losing the baby's suitcase. They might have some nice baby clothes on hand.

When the bottle was satisfactorily warmed, she limped back to the couch. As she fed the baby, gently rubbing her cheek to keep her from falling asleep again, Wanda pondered the pros and cons of calling Sister Maeve Marie. No, she decided, she'd wait. Maybe Vonny would have good luck and come home with some nice baby clothes. And, after all, Vonny had said she didn't want people looking at her baby. That probably even included nuns.

The baby finished four ounces of the bottle. That's not bad, Wanda thought. Then she listened intently. Was that a wheeze coming from the baby's chest? Oh, I hope she's not catching cold, she thought. She's so little, and it would break Vonny's heart if anything happened to her . . .

The television was on the blink, so Wanda turned on the radio to catch the noon news. The lead story was still about the missing O'Brien baby. The caller who claimed his cousin had the baby had phoned again and had been promised a twenty-thousand-dollar reward. Authorities were waiting for him to call back and make arrangements for the delivery of the money, at which point he would take the police to his cousin's home.

How awful, Wanda thought, as she cradled Vonny's sleeping infant. How could *anyone* steal someone else's baby?

Alvirah spent the rest of Wednesday and all of Thursday going down the list of stores where she had purchased baby clothes.

"Do you have, or did you carry a yellow bunting with a white satin border?"

The answer was always no.

Several clerks said that they didn't get many calls for buntings these days. Especially in yellow. And a white-satin border would be impractical. Wouldn't the bunting have to be cleaned?

I know it was yellow wool and white satin, Alvirah thought. It must have come from a specialty shop. Maybe I just saw it in a window? With that in mind, after she had inquired at a store where she had made a purchase, she walked around the immediate neighborhood in the hope that the window of another shop would trigger her memory.

In the late afternoon, it began to snow, light flurries accompanied by sharp, damp winds. Oh God, she thought as she headed for home, let whoever has the baby be keeping her warm and dry and fed.

The lobby of their building on Central Park South, so festively decorated for Christmas and Chanukah, seemed to mock her with its radiant warmth. When she got to the apartment, she made a cup of tea, phoned the hospital and was put through to Gregg.

"I'm with Joan," he said. "She won't let them give her any more sedation. She knows about the call and the reward. She wants to talk to you."

Alvirah thought her heart would break as she listened to Joan's whispered thanks for putting up the reward and her promise to pay back every cent.

"Forget the money," she said, trying to keep her tone light. "Just make sure Marianne's middle name is Alvirah."

"Of course. I promise," Joan said.

Alvirah added hastily, "I'm only joking, Joanie. It's no name for a baby, at least not in this day and age."

Willy came in just as she hung up the phone. "Good news?" he asked hopefully.

"I wish I thought so. Willy, if you knew your cousin's wife had someone's baby, and you'd been guaranteed the reward you asked for, why wouldn't you just say straight out where the baby is?"

"Maybe he's worried that the cousin's wife will go crazy if they take the baby from her."

"He ought to be more worried that something might happen to the baby. The reward is only if Marianne is returned safely. He knows that. Mark my words, Willy, that caller is pulling a hoax. He's trying to figure out how to get the reward and disappear."

Willy saw the misery in Alvirah's face and knew she was still blaming herself for what had happened. "I was just up with Cordelia," he said. "She phoned me right after you went out. She and the nuns are praying around the clock, and she's got all her people praying too."

Alvirah half smiled. "If I know her, she's probably saying, 'Now listen, God . . .' "

"Pretty close," Willy agreed. "Except now she's doing it while she works. Her idea of opening a thrift shop has really paid off. When I was by there yesterday, a bunch of people brought in good clothes in really nice condition."

"Well, Cordelia won't take any worn-out stuff," Alvirah said. "And she's right—just because you're down on your luck doesn't mean you have to be stuck with rags."

"And now Cordelia has a sign out asking for games and toys for kids. She's even lined up more volunteers to put Christmas wrappings on whatever people pick out for their children. She says kids should have packages to open come Christmas morning."

"Will of iron, heart of gold, that's our Cordelia," Alvirah said. Then she burst out, "Willy, I feel so helpless, so *damn* helpless. Praying is important, but I feel like I should be doing more. Doing something . . . more active. This waiting is driving me looney."

Willy put his arms around her. "Then keep busy. Go up to the thrift shop tomorrow and give Cordelia a hand. It was busy when you helped out there last week. And with only two days till Christmas, it's going to be a mob scene tomorrow."

• • •

On the morning of December 23rd, tension reached a fever pitch at One Police Plaza at the command center for the case that had become known among insiders as the Baby Bunting Kidnapping.

By then the entire team had come to seriously doubt the validity of the story told by the phone caller who claimed knowledge of the whereabouts of the O'Brien baby.

They had been able to keep the caller on the line long enough to trace the last two phone calls. Both of them came from the Bronx, not Long Island, and from phone booths within a few blocks of each other. Now undercover police were blanketing the vicinity of Fordham Road and the Grand Concourse, keeping the public phones under surveillance, prepared to close in on the mysterious caller.

Experts were studying December 20th security videotapes from Empire Hospital, particularly those from cameras in the lobby and the corridor to the elevators. The tape in which Alvirah and Willy could be vaguely made out revealed little of the woman carrying the infant. Only the bunting stood out, because of the wide satin border. There was still intense debate over releasing details about the yellow bunting. Of course, every police officer in New York had a description of it, but as one detective argued, "Let the kidnapper hear that bunting described, and it will show up in a trash can. At least this way there's a chance the abductor might put it on the baby when she takes her outdoors, and that one of us might spot her."

The informant had been due to call again at ten o'clock on the 23rd. As Joan and Gregg O'Brien clung to each other awaiting word, ten o'clock came and went. Eleven o'clock. Then twelve, and still no call.

At three the expected call finally came in. The caller had changed his mind. "I saw all those cops laying for me," he snarled. "You'll never see that kid again. Let my cousin's wife keep her."

He's lying. Everyone at the command post agreed on that. He was a phony right from the start.

Or was he? Had they botched the exchange? A few minutes later, the media were carrying frantic pleas. Call back. Reestablish contact. No questions asked. If you're wanted for a crime, you're promised leniency. Marianne's parents are on the verge of nervous breakdowns. Have pity on them.

The baby clothes Vonny had brought back from the thrift shop near the Port Authority were much too big for the tiny infant. "They were just about cleaned out," she had said angrily. It was after the noon feeding, and she was trying to pin an undershirt at the shoulders to keep it from sliding down the baby's arms. "Hold still!" she snapped at the infant.

"Here, let me do that," her grandmother said nervously. "Vonny, why don't you go down to the deli and pick up a nice hot coffee and a bagel. You didn't eat anything for breakfast, and you always love a toasted bagel."

"Maybe I will."

As soon as the door closed behind her granddaughter, Wanda limped to the phone and dialed the apartment ten blocks away where Sister Cordelia and Sister Maeve Marie lived with four other nuns. They jokingly called the apartment their miniconvent.

One of the elderly sisters answered. Cordelia and Maeve Marie were at the thrift shop, she told Wanda. They were getting some wonderful donations and sorting them as fast as possible. Oh, yes, Maeve Marie was saying they had a good supply of baby clothes. "You just send your granddaughter over and let her take what she needs."

But when Vonny came back with her coffee and bagel, Wanda could tell that her mood was even blacker than before, so she did not dare to talk about the thrift shop to her. She knew Vonny would guess that she had discussed her and the baby with someone.

Maybe tomorrow she'll be her sweet self again, Wanda thought, then sighed. She'd been sleeping on the couch since Vonny arrived, and the broken springs intensified the chronic arthritis pain that made getting around so hard. Nonetheless, she'd gladly given up her bed to Vonny, although she worried about her sleeping in the same bed as the baby. Suppose she rolled over on her the way she had with the first one six years ago, Wanda thought. Wanda would never forget that terrible night at Empire Hospital when they said the baby was gone. Or suppose she had one of her dizzy spells and fainted while she was bathing the baby, and the baby drowned. That had happened to the second one in Pittsburgh. It's a shame she had a third baby so soon after getting out of the psychiatric hospital there, Wanda thought. I just don't think she's ready to take care of an infant yet.

Alvirah found that in one way it helped to be busy, to be working with her hands and around people. In another way, though, it was incredibly hard to sort and fold baby and toddler snowsuits and overalls and T-shirts and sweaters, all of them gaily decorated with pictures of Mickey Mouse and Barney the Dinosaur and Cinderella and the Little Mermaid. It brought home with crushing, numbing pain the realization that Gregg and Joan might never see Marianne wear outfits like these.

"I'll work with the adult clothes," Alvirah told Cordelia after an hour of sorting baby items.

Sister Cordelia's steely gray eyes softened. "Alvirah, why don't you have a little trust in God and pray instead of blaming yourself all the time?"

"I'll try." Tears stung the back of her eyes

as Alvirah headed for the table where women's clothes had been stacked. Cordelia's right. Dear Lord, she thought, I'm no good as a detective this time. It's up to You now.

Alvirah usually enjoyed chatting with people. There was no one she did not find interesting in one way or another. But today she stayed at the sorting tables, efficiently matching skirts and jackets that had been separated, sorting items by size and placing them on the appropriate counters. Still, it gave her heart a lift to see people come in and hear them exclaim over the attractive clothing.

As she was putting teenage skirts and tops on a size 6 table, a woman exclaimed, "Everything looks so fresh. You'd think they were brand-new! My daughter will be thrilled. I didn't think I could afford to get her a pretty outfit for the holidays, but these are so reasonable. You'd think this one came right from Fifth Avenue!"

"Yes, you would."

Alvirah stayed until the shop closed at eight o'clock. Willy had been right—being at the shop, keeping busy, had helped. Yet she couldn't shake the feeling that she was missing something. And that "something" was nagging, nagging at her all the way home.

Willy had dinner waiting, but Alvirah found she had little appetite and could hardly swallow even a few bites of the stuffed pork chops that were his specialty.

"Honey, you're going to get sick," he fussed. "Maybe it wasn't a good idea for you to go to the shop today."

"No, it helped, it really did. And, Willy, you should have heard those people talk about the clothes they were selecting. One woman picked out an outfit for her daughter and said that it could have come right from Fifth Avenue, that it looked brand-new."

Alvirah laid down her fork. "Oh my God," she said. "That's it!"

"What do you mean?"

"Willy, I was in the thrift shop last week. *That's where I saw the bunting.* I'm sure of it. I was working with the men's clothes at the time, but one of the volunteers was matching baby clothes, and she held it up when she folded it." Alvirah jumped up, all trace of lethargy gone. "Willy, the kidnapper must have been in Cordelia's thrift shop. I've got to call the police hot line."

• • •

Christmas Eve dawned with heavy clouds gathering ominously overhead. Weather forecasters warned that by evening as many as six inches of snow would fall. A white Christmas was guaranteed.

For Alvirah it had been a long and intensely worrisome night. The Baby Bunting Kidnapping squad had agreed to meet her at the thrift shop at 8:00 A.M., when it was scheduled to open, but her call last night to Cordelia had brought disheartening news. Last week they'd sent some of their donated clothing, including baby apparel, to several other outlets sponsored by the convent. Two were in the Bronx. Another was near the Port Authority, in midtown Manhattan. Until they could round up all the volunteers and then get them to try and remember what had been shipped where, Alvirah couldn't be sure if the bunting had been sold at the Eighty-sixth Street shop or at one of the other locations.

"I'll have as many of my volunteers as I can reach at the shop in the morning," Cordelia had promised. "Let's hope that one of them remembers what happened to the bunting. And keep praying, Alvirah. You're already getting answers."

Alvirah had discussed the troublesome situation with Willy throughout the sleepless hours. "If we find out the bunting went to the Bronx, then there's a strong possibility that the caller was for real and does know where Marianne is being kept. On the other hand, if it went to the shop near the Port Authority, that woman may have just stolen the baby and gotten on a bus to God knows where."

By 6:00 A.M., Alvirah was certain she had put in the longest night of her life.

"I'm gonna go back today, Grandma," Vonny announced as she returned to the apartment at eight o'clock that morning, carrying a bag that contained two coffees and two bagels.

She was in a good mood. Wanda could see that. Just bringing the second coffee and bagel for her grandmother proved it. Vonny could be so sweet, Wanda thought. She had yelled at the baby once during the night but then had come out from the bedroom and heated a bottle for her. So she was settling down.

Wanda decided to take a chance on upsetting Vonny by protesting. "But the weather report isn't good, and on Christmas Eve, so many people are traveling."

Vonny smiled briefly. "I know they are, but I like that. I like to travel when there are a lot of people around."

Wanda took another chance. "Vonny, I didn't say anything before. You were so disappointed that the thrift shop downtown didn't have much baby stuff. But you know, there's a thrift shop right in the neighborhood that my friends the nuns run." She decided a small fib wouldn't hurt. "When Sister visited me the other day she said that they had wonderful clothes for children and babies. Why don't you just pick up some things before you leave? The baby has a little cold, and you've got to be sure she doesn't get a chill on the trip."

"Maybe I will. What time do you expect those nuns with the Christmas basket to come by?"

"Not before three."

"I'm getting a two o'clock bus."

She doesn't want to meet Sister, Wanda thought. Vonny always was a loner.

By 9:00 A.M., the investigators had interviewed all the volunteers Sister Cordelia had managed to gather at the thrift shop, and most important, they'd talked to one who distinctly remembered that the box with the yellow bunting had been sent to the outlet near the Port Authority.

"The worst possible luck," one of the detectives admitted to Alvirah. "If it had been sold here, we might be able to hope the abductor is in the neighborhood. If it had been sent to the Bronx, there'd still be hope that the caller was for real and not just an extortionist trying to latch on to reward money. We'll try to find out who sold the bunting, but even if we do succeed in getting a better description of the woman, my guess is that she and the baby aren't in New York anymore."

"I agree," Alvirah said quietly. "But I'm going to keep hoping anyway. And praying. Has anyone talked to Gregg this morning?"

"The inspector did. There was talk of O'Brien's wife going home today, but her doctor nixed it. She's so depressed, he's afraid of what might happen if she's not under observation at least until after tomorrow. Christmas is going to be one awful day for Joan O'Brien."

"But Gregg will be with her."

"That poor guy's so exhausted, the doctor said he could fall asleep standing up." The detective nodded as he received a signal from the lieutenant. "We're on our way downtown now. We'll keep you posted, Mrs. Meehan. And thank you."

I'm going to go too, Alvirah decided, then realized Cordelia was bearing down on her.

"Alvirah, I hate to do this to you, but won't you please stay until noon? I really need the help."

"Sure, Cordelia. What do you want me to do?"

"Sort the baby clothes. They're such a jumble again. A lot of the sizes got mixed up last night. Some people are just so inconsiderate."

Cordelia hesitated, then said, "Alvirah, after you called last night, we were talking about the missing baby and everything, and Sister Bernadette said something that I've been wondering about ever since. She said that someone called and asked if we had baby clothes in the thrift shop. The caller said her granddaughter was visiting with her new baby and that her suitcase with the baby's clothes had been stolen."

"Did the caller give her name?" Alvirah asked.

"No. Sister Bernadette is sure she recognized the voice but she can't put a face to it." Then Cordelia shrugged. "Are we all grasping at straws?"

Somehow for the next hour Alvirah managed to keep a smile on her face as she sorted and matched and stacked the baby apparel. The hardest moment came when at the bottom of the leftover pile she found a tiny yellow wool jacket with narrow white satin ruching on the hood. It reminded her of the bunting.

Then her eyes widened. Was it possible, she wondered? Could this jacket *belong* with the bunting? It must. In fact, she was sure of it! The same fine quality wool, the satin ruching. It must have been separated from the bunting and not been included in the shipment that went to the outlet near the Port Authority. She would turn it over to the police. At least that way they'd know the exact color and texture of the bunting.

"Can I see that, please?"

Alvirah turned. A woman of about thirty stood at her elbow. She was wearing a nondescript ski jacket and jeans. Her dark hair had a wide white streak down the center.

Alvirah felt a sickening lurch in her stomach. The woman was the right size, the right age. And no wonder she had worn a blond wig and a scarf. Anyone would notice that bizarre hair. She would be easy to spot and to remember.

The woman looked at her curiously. "You got a problem?"

Silently, Alvirah handed the jacket to the woman. She did not want to say anything. She didn't want the woman to pay attention to her, perhaps to recognize her. But then as suddenly as she had reached for it, the woman tossed the jacket down and hurried to the door.

Oh God, it *is* her, Alvirah thought. And she recognized me. Not waiting to get her coat, she rushed to the door, but in her haste she tripped over the pull-toy a toddler was dragging, and fell. "Wait!" she called.

Hands reached to pick her up. The mother of the toddler tried to apologize. Alvirah brushed past them and hurried onto the street. By the time she got to the sidewalk, the woman was halfway down the block.

"Wait!" Alvirah shouted again.

The woman glanced over her shoulder and began to run.

Passersby looked at Alvirah curiously as

she pushed her way through the crowded streets. Unheedful of the chill wind and the snow that was starting to fall, she ran, keeping the woman in sight, hoping to see a cop.

The woman abruptly turned left on Eighty-first Street. Alvirah caught up with her when she stopped at a car that was parked in front of the Museum of Natural History.

The driver of the car jumped out. "What's the matter, Dorine?"

"Eddie, this woman is crazy. She's following me."

The man hurried around the car and confronted Alvirah, who was panting for breath. "What's your problem?" he demanded.

Alvirah glanced into the backseat of the vehicle. A toddler and an infant were strapped in child seats. The infant had a mass of dark hair. "I *was* following you," she gasped to the young woman, "but I see I've made a mistake. I'm sorry. When you picked up that little jacket, I thought you might be someone else. Then when you threw it down, I was sure you'd recognized me."

"I put it down 'cause I could tell it's too small for my kid," she said, nodding toward the baby in the infant seat. "As for you, I never laid eyes on you, and the look you gave me, I thought you were nuts." Then she smiled broadly. "Hey, listen, it's okay. It's Christmas Eve. Everybody gets a little unstrung, right?"

Alvirah slowly retraced her steps to the thrift shop. I'm chilled to the bone, she thought. I'll phone the police and let them pick up the jacket and I'll go home.

When she reached the thrift shop, she fended off questions the other volunteers threw at her. "It was nothing. I thought I knew that woman." Then she headed for the table where she'd left the little yellow jacket. It was gone.

Oh no! she thought. Tara, a teenage volunteer, was working nearby. "Tara, did you notice someone pick up an infant-sized yellow wool hooded jacket?" Alvirah asked her.

"Yeah, just about three minutes ago. I'd helped her pick out some other stuff, clothes and blankets and sheets, then she spotted the jacket and was real pleased. She said that the other day she'd found the rest of the outfit in a different thrift shop. I guess it went with leggings or something. Wasn't that lucky?"

Alvirah thought her knees would buckle. "What did the woman look like?"

Tara shrugged. "Oh, I don't know. Dark

hair. About your height. Late twenties or so. She had on a dark gray, no a dark blue ski jacket. If you ask me, she should have looked at the racks of women's clothes while she was at it.''

But Alvirah was no longer listening. For an instant she thought about taking the time to call for help, but she knew that every second was vital. She grabbed the teenager by the hand. "Come with me."

"Hey, I'm supposed to—"

"I said, come!"

As they rushed out the door, Cordelia was emerging from the back room. "Alvirah!" she shouted. "What's wrong?"

Alvirah took an instant to reply. "Send for the police. The kidnapper was here a few minutes ago."

Columbus Avenue was crowded with shoppers. Alvirah looked around hopelessly and stopped. "You said the woman had taken other things. What did she carry them in?"

"Two of our big white shopping bags."

"If the bags are heavy, she won't be able to move too fast," Alvirah said, more to herself than to the girl.

Tara seemed to suddenly understand what had triggered Alvirah's reaction. "Mrs. Meehan, do you think the jacket went with the yellow bunting the cops were questioning us about? The bags were so heavy that I asked that woman how far she had to go and she said, not too far, just up to Ninetieth Street and over a few blocks."

Alvirah wanted to kiss Tara. Instead, she snapped, "Now listen hard. You go back inside and tell all this to Sister Cordelia. Tell her to have the cops blanket the area between here and Ninetieth Street. Tell her we're closing in on Baby Bunting!"

The early morning's pleasant mood that Wanda Brown had found so endearing in her granddaughter did not last. The baby had started fussing after her ten o'clock bottle and would not be soothed. Wanda didn't dare raise the subject of more baby clothes again.

Vonny grumbled and cursed and finally, to escape the infant's wails, headed for the thrift shop. Now, as she hauled the heavy shopping bags through the snowy streets back to her grandmother's apartment, the seven blocks from Eighty-sixth to Ninetieth and West End started to feel like miles.

As she trudged angrily along, her nerves

felt raw and stretched. "Damn kid," she said aloud. "Damn pest, just like the others."

The baby was still screaming when she got back. Wanda, looking frayed and weary, held it in her arms, rocking it gently.

"What's the matter with her now?" Vonny snapped.

"I don't think she feels well, Vonny," Wanda said apologetically. "I think she's a little feverish. I don't think you should take her out today. I think it would be a mistake."

Without acknowledging Wanda's remarks, Vonny crossed to her grandmother and looked at the baby. *"Shut up!"* she yelled.

Wanda felt her throat go dry. Vonny had that look, that angry scowl, that stubborn, blank expression in her eyes. Wanda had seen it before, knew how dangerous it could be. Still, she had to tell her. "Vonny, dear, Sister Maeve Marie phoned after you left. She's coming in a few minutes with the Christmas basket. They started delivering them early because the weather's turning bad."

Vonny's eyebrows molded together to form a single, angry black slash across her forehead. "Did you ask her to come early, Grandma?"

"No, dear." Wanda patted the baby's back. "Ssh . . . Oh, Vonny, her chest is getting raspy."

"She'll be fine when I get to Pittsburgh." Vonny stomped into the other room with the shopping bags, then returned immediately. "I don't want to talk to that nun, or to show my baby to her. Give her to me. I'll bring her into the bedroom until that nun is gone."

Alvirah hurried uptown, her eyes constantly roving back and forth as she passed the intersections. Along the way she stopped passersby to ask if they'd seen a woman in a dark blue ski jacket carrying two white shopping bags.

At Eighty-sixth and Broadway she lucked out. A news vendor said he had seen a woman of that description zigzag across the street. "She went toward West End," he said.

At Eighty-eighth and West End Avenue, an old man pulling a shopping cart claimed a woman with white shopping bags had passed him. He said he remembered because she had set her bags down for a minute. "She was mumbling to herself and swearing," he said disapprovingly. "Some holiday spirit."

The first squad cars arrived as Alvirah reached Eighty-ninth Street. Tara had obviously given an excellent account of what had happened. "We're going to canvas this whole area," a sergeant told her crisply. "If necessary, we'll make a house-to-house search. Why don't you go home, Mrs. Meehan?"

"I can't," Alvirah said.

The sergeant looked at her with compassion. "You're going to get pneumonia. At least sit in the squad car and stay warm. Let us take over from here."

It was at that moment that Sister Maeve Marie came up the block, carrying a heavy basket. Her short veil fluttered in the wind. Like Sister Cordelia, she chose to wear an ankle-length habit. When she saw Alvirah talking to the cop, her expression became startled. Moving as rapidly as she could, she hurried over. A former police officer herself, she knew the sergeant. "Hello, Tom," she said, then asked, "Alvirah, what's wrong?"

When she heard, she exclaimed, "The baby's kidnapper is in the neighborhood? God be praised!" Immediately the cop in her took over. "Tom, have you sealed off the neighborhood?"

"That's what we're doing just now, Maeve. We'll be going from door to door in every building, making inquiries. But please try to persuade Mrs. Meehan to wait in the car. She looks like she's going to keel over."

"Alvirah won't keel over," Maeve said briskly as other squad cars screeched into the block. "Alvirah, help me deliver the baskets. Two of us can move faster. Some of our people will be more likely to talk to us than to the cops. The van is parked at the corner." She looked at the sergeant. "Illegally parked."

It was something to do. It was action. And Alvirah knew that Maeve was right. For fear of repercussions, old and sick people often didn't want to get involved by cooperating with the police, even when they might know something critical. "Let's go," she said.

"I have four deliveries on this block," Maeve told her.

The first basket went to an elderly couple who had not been outdoors since Thanksgiving. Their neighbor did their shopping for them. Alvirah rang that neighbor's bell.

When she came to the door, she talked freely. "No," she said, "I'm in and out all the time and I'm one to gab with people, and nobody mentioned a new baby in this building." Nor had she seen anybody carrying a baby in a yellow bunting in the neighborhood.

The second delivery, three buildings away, was to a ninety-year-old woman and her seventy-year-old daughter. When Maeve introduced Alvirah, they knew all about her. Willy had replaced their toilet. "What a wonderful man," they told her. Unfortunately, they knew nothing about a baby.

At the third house, a woman with three small children had packages under the tree. "All of them from the thrift shop," she confided in a whisper. "The kids are dying to see what's in them."

But she too knew nothing about a woman with dark hair who had a new baby.

"This is it," Maeve told Alvirah as they shared carrying the last basket. "Wanda Brown is the nicest old woman. She's pretty crippled with arthritis and doesn't have any relatives except a granddaughter who lives somewhere in Pennsylvania. She doesn't talk about her much, but apparently the poor girl's experienced a lot of tragedy. She had two babies that died as infants."

They were about to enter the building at

the corner of West End and Ninetieth Street. Down the block they could see policemen going from house to house. Then Alvirah and Maeve stared at each other. "Maeve, are you thinking what I'm thinking?" Alvirah demanded.

"Sister Bernadette's call from someone asking about the thrift shop because her granddaughter had a new baby and no clothes for it. Oh, dear God, Alvirah, I'll get Tom."

Some raw instinct made Alvirah pull her back. "No! Let's get into that apartment now."

Vonny stood at the window watching the police activity below. The baby was lying on the bed, its cries reduced to tired whimpers. Then she saw a nun and another woman heading for the entrance ten floors below. Between them, they were carrying a basket.

Vonny went out to the living room. "I think your Christmas basket is coming, Grandma," she said flatly. "Remember, not one word about me and the baby."

Wanda smiled timidly. "Whatever you want, dear."

Vonny went back into the bedroom. The baby was asleep. Lucky for you, she thought.

"It's a three-room apartment," Maeve whispered as she rang the bell and called, "It's me, Wanda, Sister Maeve Marie."

Alvirah nodded. Every ounce of her being was vibrating. Please, dear Lord. *Please!*

The bell, a loud and raucous sound, echoed through the apartment. In the bedroom, the startled infant jumped and began to wail. An angry Vonny grabbed a sock, bent over the bed and scooped up the baby.

Wanda Brown made her painful way to the door. Smiling nervously, she greeted Sister Maeve. "Oh, you're too good," she sighed.

"Mrs. Meehan is helping me deliver the baskets," Maeve told her.

Alvirah brushed past the older woman, carrying the basket of food into the apartment. Her eyes raced over the small foyer and the cluttered living room. But there was no one else there. She could see into the kitchen. Pots were stacked on the stove, dishes piled on the table. But she could see nothing to indicate the presence of a baby.

The bedroom door was ajar, and through

the narrow crack she could make out the unmade bed and two sides of the narrow room. It had to be empty.

She scrutinized the living room. There was nothing here to indicate the presence of a baby, either.

"Wanda," Maeve was asking, "were you the one who called about your granddaughter needing clothes for her baby? Sister Bernadette thought she recognized your voice."

Wanda paled. Vonny was up to her old tricks, hiding behind half-opened doors and listening. She'd be furious. And Vonny in one of her rages . . .

"Oh, no," Wanda said, her voice quavering. "Why would I do that? I haven't seen Vonny in nearly five years. She lives in Pittsburgh."

Alvirah knew that the look of intense disappointment in Maeve's eyes was mirrored in her own.

"Well, enjoy Christmas," Maeve said. "We'll leave the basket on the kitchen table. The turkey is still warm, but be sure to refrigerate it after you've had dinner."

Alvirah's sense of urgency was overwhelming. Her premonition that the baby was in danger seemed stronger than ever. She wanted to get out of that apartment, to keep looking for her. She hurried across the room with the basket, carrying it into the kitchen. Then, as she turned, the sleeve of her sweater caught the door handle of the refrigerator, and the door swung open. She was about to close it when her eyes fastened on a half-empty baby bottle on the top shelf.

"You did make that call!" Alvirah yelled at Wanda as she burst back into the living room. "Your granddaughter is here. Where is she? What did she do with Marianne?"

Wanda's terrified glance at the bedroom was enough to give Alvirah the answer she needed. With Maeve on her heels, she charged toward the door.

Vonny stepped out from behind it. She was holding the baby at arm's length in front of her. The infant's mouth was gagged with an old sock and her eyes were bulging. "You want her," Vonny screamed. "Here, take her!"

Alvirah had just enough time in that split second to raise her arms, pluck the infant from midair and cradle it to her breast. An instant later, Maeve had yanked the gag from around Marianne's mouth, and the blessed wail of an angry infant filled the apartment.

The ambulance raced down Ninth Avenue, its siren blasting as it rushed toward Empire Hospital. The medic in charge was bending over Marianne, who, securely strapped on the stretcher, was staring up at him.

"She's a tough little bird," he said happily. "Other than a slight cold, I'd say she seems to be in remarkably good shape, considering the adventure she's been through."

Alvirah was sitting beside the stretcher, her eyes firmly fixed on the baby. Sister Maeve Marie was seated next to her, wreathed in smiles.

Alvirah still could not believe that it was over, that Marianne was safe. Her hands still tingled with the impact of catching the baby, of feeling that little heart fluttering beneath her fingertips.

Everything that had happened after that point was still something of a blur. She remembered snatches of things—Vonny running to her grandmother, crying that she didn't mean to hurt the baby, that she never meant to hurt any of her babies; Maeve hanging out the window and yelling to the cops below; the cops rushing into the apartment; the crowds of people and the cameras and reporters that materialized on the street in the few minutes it took the ambulance to appear. It was a jumble of images, like a crazy, dizzying, wonderful, happy dream.

The ambulance pulled into the driveway of the hospital, and as soon as it had stopped, the doors were thrown open by waiting attendants. As hands reached in to take the baby, Maeve stood and said firmly, "There's only one person who should hand that baby back to its mother, and that is Alvirah Meehan."

Less than a minute later, as cameras clicked and onlookers cheered, Alvirah strode triumphantly into the lobby of Empire Hospital, holding Marianne, now snugly wrapped in the yellow bunting. Minutes later she laid her small charge in the yearning arms of a radiantly happy Joan O'Brien.

"It certainly didn't take you long to bounce back," Willy observed as he and Alvirah walked home arm in arm along Fifth Avenue from St. Patrick's Cathedral. They had just attended Christmas morning Mass, which seemed especially joyous this year.

"Isn't that the truth," Alvirah responded, shaking her head. "Oh, Willy, I've never had a better Christmas. At Mass I prayed for that girl, Vonny. I know she's sick and needs help, and she deserves to get it. But let me tell you, my throat closed at the thought of putting in a good word for that skunk who called with all those false messages. But then I decided that since the cops had tracked him down, and I know he'll pay for what he did, I'd go ahead and mention him."

She looked around. "Isn't New York beautiful with the snow on the ground and the store windows all decorated? Tomorrow morning I'm going shopping again for Marianne—after, of course, I write a report on the Baby Bunting Case for the *Globe.* But today . . ." Alvirah smiled. "Today I just want to savor the miracle."

"That Marianne is okay?"

"That she's okay because of the way everything happened. I realized she was in that apartment only because my sleeve happened to catch on the handle of the refrigerator door, and that handle happened to be loose. That's the miracle, Willy. If that handle hadn't been so loose, if that door hadn't opened so easily, if I hadn't seen that baby bottle . . ."

Willy laughed. "Honey, be sure to mention that to Cordelia at dinner tonight. When I fixed the leak in Wanda Brown's kitchen last month, I noticed that handle was loose and promised to come back and fix it. And only last week Cordelia was bugging me about it, asking when I was going to get back there. But then you kept me so busy shopping and carrying packages, I just never got a chance." He paused. "I see what you mean. A miracle."

AUTHOR'S NOTE

MARY HIGGINS CLARK, born and raised in New York, is of Irish descent and constantly draws on her Irish background to create the characters in her books. "This was never more true than in the case of Alvirah and Willy," she says.

"Alvirah and Willy had worked all their lives—she as a cleaning woman and he as a plumber. Never having had children of their own, they lavished their affection on family members, friends and the needy. A couple who lived next door when I was growing up in the Bronx were my inspiration for Alvirah and Willy," she recalls.

"Their names were Annie and Charlie Potters. Charlie, whom Annie always referred to as 'my Charlie,' was a big, good-looking Irish cop. Annie had dyed red hair, a jutting jaw and a warm heart. What Annie couldn't wear she carried, and she'd sail out bedecked from head to toe in mismatched outfits, sure she was stepping out of the pages of *Vogue.* Annie and Charlie were wonderful neighbors, and I hope I have caught something of their essence in Alvirah and Willy.

"Winning the lottery changed the way Alvirah and Willy lived. But it never changed Alvirah and Willy's innate wisdom about what really matters in life."